W9-AFN-205

DRUMS FOR RANCAS

"Tout sera oublié et rien ne sera réparé"
(Everything will be forgotten, nothing
will ever be put to rights)

MILAN KUNDERA

DRUMS

FOR RANCAS

By MANUEL SCORZA

Translated from the Spanish by Edith Grossman

HARPER & ROW, PUBLISHERS

New York, Hagerstown, San Francisco, London

1817

To Cecilia, always

 For information address Harper & Row, Publishers, Inc., 10 East 53rd Street, New York, N.Y. 10022. Published simultaneously in Canada by Fitzhenry & Whiteside Limited, Toronto.

FIRST EDITION

Designed by Sidney Feinberg

Library of Congress Cataloging in Publication Data

Scorza, Manuel.
Drums for Rancas.
Translation of Redoble por Rancas.
I. Title.
PZ4.S422Dr3 [PQ8497.S36] 863'.6'4 72-9177
ISBN 0-06-013814-9

77 78 79 80 10 9 8 7 6 5 4 3 2 1

CONTENTS

Foreword

This book is the true account of a lonely battle: the battle fought in the Central Andes, between 1950 and 1962, by the men from certain villages found only on the military maps of the army detachments that wiped them out. The characters, the crimes, the betrayal, and the glory almost all are here called by their real names.

Héctor Chacón, Hawkeye, has been languishing for fifteen years in the military prison at Sepa in the Amazon jungle. The Guardia Civil is still hunting down the many-colored poncho of Agapito Robles. In Yanacocha one dull gray afternoon I looked in vain for Kid Remigio's grave. As for Fermín Espinoza, the bullet that sent him tumbling over the bridge into the Huallaga will tell the story better.

Dr. Montenegro, a magistrate for the last thirty years, still strolls around the square at Yanahuanca. Colonel Marruecos was given his general's stars. The Cerro de Pasco Corporation, for whose benefit three new cemeteries were opened, showed a profit of twenty-five million dollars in its financial report. The author is not a novelist so much as a witness. The photographs (which will be published separately) and the tapes which attest to the atrocities will show that the excesses narrated in this book are but pale reflections of reality.

Certain names, certain events, and the exact time of their occurrence have, in exceptional cases, been changed to protect just men from prosecution.

M. S.

> NEW YORK (UPI). The profits of the Cerro de Pasco Corporation will rise sharply during the first nine months of the year. Despite high production costs and an eight-week strike at one of its American subsidiaries, net profits for the nine-month period will total $31,173,912 or $5.32 per share, says Robert P. Koening, president.
>
> Sales in the first three quarters of 1966 totaled $296,538,020, compared to $242,603,019 last year. [*Expreso,* Lima, November 4, 1966]

CHAPTER ONE: *In Which the Observant Reader Will Hear of a Certain Very Famous Coin*

ONE damp September, from around the corner of the main square of Yanahuanca—the same corner from which the assault troops would one day emerge to open the second cemetery at Chinche—the late afternoon breathed forth a black suit. The suit boasted six buttons and a vest streaked with the gold chain of a genuine Longines pocket watch. Just as on every afternoon for the past thirty years, the black suit came down to the square and began its sixty-minute unperturbed stroll.

At about seven o'clock on that chilly twilit evening the black suit stopped, looked at the Longines, and headed for a large three-story house. As its left foot hung posed in the air and its right came down onto the second of the three steps leading down from the square to the sidewalk, a bronze coin slipped out of its left-hand trouser pocket, tinkled as it rolled, and finally came to rest on the first step. Don Herón de los Ríos, the Mayor, who had been waiting for a chance to tip his hat respectfully, called out, "Don Paco, you've dropped a sol!"

The black suit did not turn around.

The Mayor of Yanahuanca, the shopkeepers, the street urchins gathered around. The coin glowed in the last gold rays of sunset. The Mayor, his face sombered by severity, not nightfall, stared at the coin and raised his index finger: "No one must touch it!" The news spread at a dizzying pace. Every house in the province of Yanahuanca shivered at the news that Dr. Francisco Montenegro, the Magistrate, had lost a sol.

Thrill-seekers, lovers, and drunks came out of the shadows to stare at the coin. "It's the Judge's sol," they whispered excitedly. Early next day the shopkeepers on the square almost wore the coin away with their fearful glances. "It's the Judge's sol," they said in voices choked with emotion. At noon the school-children, gravely lectured by the Director—"Don't let your foolishness be the cause of your parents' going to jail"—gazed in wonder at the coin: it lay there sunbathing on the faded eucalyptus leaves. At four o'clock an eight-year-old boy was bold enough to poke at it with a stick: that was as far as the province's courage went.

No one touched it again for the next twelve months.

Once the excitement of the first few weeks had died down, the province became accustomed to living with the coin. The shopkeepers on the square, feeling themselves directly responsible, kept a keen eye on the curious. It was an unnecessary precaution: the most miserable wretch in the province knew that taking the coin, enough in theory to buy five soda crackers or a handful of peaches, would mean going to jail at the very least. The coin became an attraction. People got into the habit of taking walks to look at it. Lovers met by its light.

The only man blissfully unaware that a coin destined to test the honesty of the proud province was lying in Yanahuanca square was Dr. Montenegro.

Every afternoon at dusk he took his twenty turns around the dusty square. Every afternoon he counted off the 256 steps. At four o'clock the square is teeming with life, at five it is still a public place; at six it is deserted. There is no law against walking at that hour, but whether it be that fatigue overtakes the strollers, or that their stomachs call for supper, at six o'clock the square is empty. At five the half-body of a squat, pot-bellied man with little eyes set in a sallow face appears on the balcony of a large three-story house whose windows are always shrouded in a thick mist of curtains. For sixty minutes this gentleman with almost invisible lips stands quite still and contemplates the sun's demise. Where does his imagination wander? Is he listing his properties? Counting his livestock? Composing harsh sentences? Visiting his enemies? Who can tell? Fifty-nine minutes after beginning his solar communion, the Magistrate authorizes his right eye to consult the Longines, he goes down the stairs, crosses the blue threshold, and gravely marches toward the square. It is already empty. Even the dogs know that no barking is allowed between six and seven.

Ninety-seven days after the twilight in which the Judge's coin went spinning to the ground, Glicerio Cisneros' bar vomited up a motley band of drunks. On the ill-advice of a bellyful of rotgut, Encarnación López had decided to take possession of the legendary sol. They staggered into the square. It was ten P.M. Mumbling curses, Encarnación shined his flashlight on the sol. The drunks followed his movements as if magnetized. Encarnación picked up the coin, warmed it in his palm, put it in his pocket, and vanished into the moonlight.

The next day, when he recovered from his hangover, he learned from the gypsum lips of his wife exactly what his barbaric courage had brought him to. Passing by doors that closed on him hastily, he reeled toward the square, as pale as the fifty-cent candle his wife was lighting before Our Lord of Miracles. His color did not come back until he discovered that he had walked in his sleep and replaced the coin on the bottom step.

Winter, the heavy rains, spring, a tattered autumn, and once again the frosty season passed over the coin. And it turned out that a province whose main business was cattle-rustling found itself bathed in an aura of unexpected honesty. Everyone knew that a coin like any other lay in the square of Yanahuanca, a sol with the Seal of the Republic—chinchona tree, llama, and horn of plenty—on one side, and the solemn guarantee of the Bank of Peru on the other. But no one dared to touch it. This sudden flowering of propriety filled the old people with pride. Every afternoon they questioned the children coming home from school. "And the Judge's coin?" "It's where it belongs!" "No one has touched it." "Three mule-drivers from Pillao were staring at it." The old folks raised their index fingers with a mixture of severity and pride: "That's the way it should be. With honest people you don't need locks!"

On foot or on horseback, news of the coin traveled to every house for ten leagues around. Fearful that an imprudent act might provoke disasters worse than those caused by the evil eye, the Lieutenant Governors went from door to door with the warning that the coin was to grow old, untouched, in the square of Yanahuanca. How awful if some fool came to the province to buy matches and "found" the sol! The Feast of Saint Rosa, the anniversary of the Battle of Ayacucho, All Souls' Day, Christmas, Ash Wednesday, Holy Week, and once again National Independence Day: they all passed over the coin. No one touched it. As soon as a stranger appeared, the street urchins plagued him: "Be careful, sir, watch out for the Judge's coin." Outsiders smiled jokingly, but the stormy faces of the shopkeepers dampened their spirits. One traveling salesman, proud of his position with a wholesale house in Huancayo (it goes without saying he never received another purchase order in Yanahuanca), asked with a sly smile: "And is the coin in good health?" Consagración Mejorada answered him: "If you don't live here, you'd better keep your mouth shut." "I live anywhere I like," answered the rogue as he stepped forward defiantly. Consagración—who bore his destiny in his name—barred the way with his six-foot-tall body: "I dare you to touch it," he spat. The smile froze on the salesman's face. Consagración, who was really mild as a lamb, withdrew in confusion. On the corner the Mayor congratulated him: "That's the way, stand up for what's right!" That same night, at every fireside, it was learned that Consagración, whose only known achievement had been to drink a bottle of rum without stopping, had saved the village. He made his fortune on that corner. Because early the next morning the shopkeepers of the square, proud that a Yanahuancan had told a Huancayan bum where to get off, hired him for a hundred sols a month to unload their merchandise.

On the eve of the Feast of Saint Rosa, patron saint of the police, Solver of Mysteries, almost exactly a year to the hour since it had slipped from his pocket, the rat-like eyes of Dr. Montenegro spotted the coin. The black suit stopped in front of the famous step, picked up the sol, and then moved on. Pleased with his good fortune, he announced in the club that night: "Gentlemen, I found a sol in the square!"

The province sighed.

CHAPTER TWO: *Concerning the Universal Flight of the Animals from the Prairie of Junín*

THE old man Fortunato shuddered: the sky was the same raven-black as it had been on the morning all the animals took flight. One disjointed dawn the birds had flown away across that sky. Someone must have warned them. Sparrow hawks, kestrels, chingolo birds, thrushes, sparrows, hummingbirds all mumbled together in the same panic; forgetting that they were enemies, the hawks flew beside the sparrows. The sky became filled with terrified wings. Abdón Medrano found screech owls clustered all over the roofs. Worn out by the blinking of the horned owls, the people of Rancas saw scores upon scores of bats fleeing toward the open country. A great thickness of tired wings whispered on the roofs of the villages. Nobody could remember anything like it. Who could have remembered such an exodus? Someone must have passed on the word. The night creatures, wounded by the light, left the shadows and hurried away into the passes at Oroya. Rancas knelt down, murmuring prayers. His face covered with scratches, kneeling with arms outstretched, Don Teodoro Santiago called out: "It's the wrath of God, the wrath of God!" Surrounded by teeth that chattered as if suffering from malaria, he cried to heaven: "It's the wrath of God, the wrath of God!" Men and women embraced; children, hanging on their mothers' skirts, wept. And as if they had only been waiting for the migration of the night birds, waves of wild ducks, flocks of unfamiliar birds stained the air. The people knelt, pleaded, sobbed. To whom? God turned his scornful back. The sky creaked, as if about to cave in. A thunderstorm of dogs broke out from the eastern prairie: skinny sheepdogs fled from the villages with their tongues hanging out. Horses shivered with nausea; they no longer recognized the voice of the master who had raised them from birth, they stamped and kicked, green with sweat. Like the hares and the lizards, they fled from Rancas. And the sound and fear of the hooves had hardly died away when an avalanche of rats whipped through the village. Guinea pigs whose only memories were of comfortable firesides threw themselves pitifully and blindly into the hailstorm of hooves. And even the dogs, forgetting their names, moaned deafly among the dying sheep, whose heads were turned toward the fear that terrorized them. Rancas was one long sob. At noon it was the fish. Someone must have warned them. Rivers and brooks turned black. The trout abandoned the clean water of the mountains and swam downstream to suffocate in waters poisoned with mining wastes. They jumped through the muddied water. Someone must have told them about the water being shut off.

Fortunato trotted across the endless prairie of Junín. His face looked blue, but not from fatigue. He had been running for two hours with his mouth hanging open. His bruised feet slowed down to a walk and turned toward the highway. At any moment, perhaps right now, the fog would give birth to the heavy trucks, the leather faces that would overrun Rancas. Who would get there first? The convoy coming around the slow curve, or Fortunato, whose sweat dripped onto the rocks? Rancas, with the weight of thousands of dying animals around its neck, would sink slowly into drowsiness. Would he arrive in time? And even if he did warn them in time, how would they defend themselves? With clubs? With slingshots? The others would shout a warning just before they fired. He ran with his mouth open, swallowing up the sky filled with vultures. Evil omens galloped behind him. Dimly he made out the prairie. Every rock, every puddle, every bush, monotonous and identical to outsiders, for him were unforgettable. He ran, and ran, and ran. On that prairie cursed by strangers and hated by drivers, in that wasteland where the sun shines only two or three hours a day, Fortunato had been born, grown up, worked, wondered, conquered, and loved. Would he die there as well? His eyes took in the landscape of dead sheep—dozens, hundreds, thousands of skeletons picked clean by the vultures. He remembered the names of his animals: Cotton, Little Feather, Wild Flower, Prickly Pear, Streamer, Blacky, Flirty, Clover, Lazy, Pascal, and Fortunato, all jumbled together in the stink of the curse. "Prickly Pear, Prickly Pear, sweet little Prickly Pear." He threw himself down on the brittle grass. The trucks had not appeared yet. His eyes hurt against the iron lid of a sky unmoved by his outcry. Whom should he pray to? Father Chasán refused the hundred sols he usually received for interceding with God. He rejected the respectful entreaties of Representative Rivera. He did not want to deceive them. Father Chasán looked at the crucifix with a bowed head. Fortunato ran, and ran, and ran. Representative Rivera, Abdón Medrano, and Fortunato had gone down to Huariaca to ask the good Father to interrupt his novena. They had pleaded and pleaded. The priest had come to the filthy little church packed with sinners. Rancas still dreamed that holy water would save her. Who would arrive first? Guillermo the Butcher or Fortunato the Slow? Someone must have told the animals that the Fence would close off the world. Humans knew it already. The Fence had been born weeks ago in the hayfields of Rancas. He ran, afraid of being overtaken by the Fence, this Snake which had such an advantage over living creatures: it did not eat, it did not sleep, it did not even get tired. The Rancasans, the Yanacochans, the Villapascans, the Yarusyacans found out before the owls or the trout that the sky was about to cave in. But they could not run away. The Fence had barred the roads. They could only pray, terrified, in the square. It was too late. And even if the barbed wire had not kept them from leaving, where could they have gone? The people from the lowlands could go down to the forest or climb the mountains. But they lived on the top of the world. A sky too proud to listen to prayers hung over their heads. There was no longer escape, or pardon, or going back.

CHAPTER THREE: *Concerning an Illegal Meeting Which the Gentlemen of the Civil Guard Would Have Liked to Know About in Good Time*

"EVERYBODY is here now," said Rustler.

"How many have come?" asked Hawkeye Chacón, just for the sake of asking: his eyes, able to see a lizard's track at night, made out the faces from the boulders of Quencash as they waited on the rocks, on the grass, under the oilcloth of darkness.

"Seven men and nine women, Héctor."

"We women are tougher," boasted Sulpicia in her heavy, ragged skirt.

"Have you posted guards?" worried Horse Thief.

"Tell us what's on your mind, Héctor," said the man with the scar.

"Got a drink?"

Horse Thief pulled out the corn liquor and passed the bottle. Héctor Chacón, Hawkeye, reviewed the line of tense faces and exhaled smoke from his cigarette. For ten years he had dreamed of these cigarettes, these voices, these hatreds.

You could barely hear his resentment. "In this province there is a man who walks all over us. I've seen prisoners pray in jail to Christ the King: the murdering sons-of-bitches kneel down and cry the prayer to Christ, the Merciful Judge. The Lord Jesus relents and pardons them, but we have a Judge that words and prayers can't soften. He's more powerful than God."

"Jesus, Mary!" Sulpicia crossed herself.

"As long as he lives, none of us will be able to pull his head out of the shit. It's useless to ask for our land back. The community Representative makes appeals for the fun of it. The authorities are only lackeys for the big guys."

"The Representatives," said Horse Thief, "are the Judge's friends. Bustillos and Valle take turns. One is Representative one year while the other takes a rest. The next year they change places: the other one becomes Representative."

"They're strong because they're buddies," said Sulpicia.

"And who's going to stop them?"

"When I went to jail," continued Chacón, "we had twice as much land as we have now. In five years Huarautambo has gobbled it all up."

"The Representative has filed a complaint," said Rustler. "They'll issue the summons on the thirteenth."

"You'll see," laughed Chacón. "Dr. Montenegro will wipe his ass with the summons. That man runs two prisons for his enemies: one on his ranch, the other in the province."

"There's no way out for us," said Rustler bitterly.

"What's on your mind, Héctor?"

"They'll issue the summons on the thirteenth. On that day I'll kill him."

The owls screeched.

After a deep silence, Rustler shivered. "The day that man is killed, the police will burn Yanacocha and kill everyone in it."

"That depends."

"How come?"

"You have to be smart."

"What do you mean?"

"You have to fake a fight; if two or three of our people die too, the police will say it was just a quarrel."

"If that man dies"—Sulpicia's voice was hard—"no one will be able to say, 'I own Yanacocha.' "

Rustler scratched his head. "What will happen to the killers?"

"They'll get out of jail in five years."

"If you know how to play it right," said Chacón, "you can come out of jail a better man. I know lots of guys who learned how to read in jail."

"I learned in jail," said Horse Thief modestly.

Sulpicia thought of her husband, dead in the Yanahuanca prison; she got up and kissed Héctor Chacón's hand passionately. "God bless your hand, Héctor! I'm ready to spend ten years in jail just to protect you."

"Which of us are going to die?" asked Horse Thief, sucking at his gums.

Only Hawkeye, able to pick out the gray presence of the vizcachas, could see Rustler's clenched jaws.

"There's no hope for Kid Remigio," said Rustler. "He gets worse and worse. Every day he falls down foaming at the mouth. I've seen him cry when he comes out of one of his attacks. He throws himself down on the ground and tears out handfuls of grass. 'What am I living for? What am I living for? Why doesn't God take me?' That's how he talks."

"What do the rest of you think?"

"It would be good if the poor man could rest."

"If he dies," said Horse Thief, "we'll give him a good funeral."

"We'll buy him a nice coffin," added Rustler, "and every year on All Souls' Day we'll bring him flowers."

"Let's vote."

In the darkness Hawkeye looked at all the raised hands.

"And what about the others?" asked the one with the scar.

Rustler spat angrily. "Isaías Roque is a traitor to the people. From him Montenegro knows everything we're thinking. He brings him all the news, all the gossip. I think he should die."

"Roque brags about being the Judge's godson. It's only right they die together," said Sulpicia.

"What do the rest of you think?"

Horse Thief finally managed to dislodge the strand of coca leaf.

"Let's vote," said Hawkeye.

Everyone raised his hand.

"Tomás Sacramento," said Horse Thief, "is another one who should die. He informs on anyone who talks against Montenegro. A lot of people have been sentenced because of that man."

"What do you think, Héctor?"

"One time the hands from Huarautambo overturned a sower that belonged to the communities. The Representative told me to complain to the police. Sergeant Cabrera said: 'Get me some horses and fix me some good barbecue. I'll go up and investigate tomorrow.' I got everything ready, but was stupid enough to give Sacramento the job of bringing the horses. I know that Sacramento talked to the Judge and that Montenegro told him to play dumb. He took the horses to pasture. He didn't do his job. When the Representative came down to find out what had happened, they arrested him."

"We're all in danger. He'll turn us in any day now."

"We have to get rid of the weeds once and for all."

Everyone raised his hand.

"It would be better if we expelled them from the community," said Rustler. "The ones who don't cooperate should not be allowed to go on living. Let them die like stray dogs!"

"No!" said Chacón. "If we throw them out, the law will get suspicious."

"And who will kill the Judge?"

The night curdled like an old maid's disposition.

"I'll do it. From the front, from behind, whatever you want. And if you like, I'll kill the others too."

"You're not the only man in the province, Héctor," said Rustler resentfully.

"We'll stone the Judge to death," Sulpicia said expectantly.

"No," said Chacón, "that would be too messy."

"And how much will we have to give lawyers?"

"We don't need money."

"And our families?"

"The community will take care of our families."

"The community," said Rustler, "will work the land for the prisoners and send them food."

"The prisoners can take care of themselves: they can weave baskets or chairs, they can make combs."

"I'm ready," said Rustler solemnly.

"A year in jail," said Chacón, "is a mouthful of smoke. Five years is five mouthfuls of smoke."

CHAPTER FOUR: *In Which the Idle Reader Will Take a Tour of the Insignificant Village of Rancas*

THEY don't like strangers in Rancas. As soon as one comes into the village, a long line of kids shouts, "Stranger, stranger!" Suspicious doors open a crack. The ragged chorus of children warns the authorities. Inevitably, the traveler meets someone from the Representative's office in the main square.

There was a time when no one paid them any attention. "But that was then," says Remigio, "and now it's a different story." There is no way to explain the hostility. Who the hell would want to visit Rancas? Sergeant Cabrera, who had been stationed there, says that "Rancas is the asshole of the world." There are fewer than two hundred houses in Rancas. The only two public buildings, the Municipal Building and the District School, sit in boredom on the main square, a rectangle of earth covered with patches of icchu grass. A hundred yards away, near the hills that turn gold in the light of dust, leans a church, a church where the candles are lit only on holy days. In the old days Father Chasán visited Rancas. The Rancasans collected one hundred sols to pay for the masses. Father Chasán is very well liked around the villages. He gets drunk with the men from the community and sleeps between the legs of the women parishioners. At the time of the Terror, Father Chasán said mass every Sunday. Rancas proved its piety. The confessional was swarming with sinners during the Great Terror. Today the good Father could not even get holy water. It is true most of the water comes down to the village poisoned with mining wastes.

Nothing ever happened in Rancas.

One muddy morning a hundred years ago, more than a hundred years ago, weary bands of soldiers rode out of the fog. They were an army in retreat, but a proud army, because the officers ordered the dusty horsemen to form ranks just to ride through a miserable little village where only scrawny dogs waited to welcome them. The troops stopped to water their horses, worn out by the ten-hour march. Three days later, on a morning bathed in a glaring light, another army occupied Rancas. Filthy soldiers made camp, bought potatoes and cheese from astonished shepherds: six hundred men jammed together in the square. A general pirouetted on his horse and spoke some words into the sunshine. The soldiers roared their answer and marched off into the endless prairie. They never returned.

Every year, on the anniversary of the independence of the Republic of Peru, founded by the force of arms on that prairie, the students of the Daniel A. Carrión Secondary School organize an excursion. The shopkeepers look forward to the day. Bands of students dirty the town, urinate in the square, and wipe out supplies of crackers, soda, and Ambina Cola. In the afternoon the teachers recite for them the proclamation engraved in bronze letters on the mildewed wall of the Municipal Building: the speech that the Liberator Bolívar proclaimed in that square just before the Battle of Junín on August 2, 1824. Groups of pale and badly dressed students listen to the proclamation in deadly boredom, and then they leave. Rancas huddles back into its solitude for another year.

Nothing ever happened in Rancas. That is, nothing ever happened until a train arrived.

CHAPTER FIVE: *Concerning the Visits that Dr. Montenegro's Hands Paid to Certain Cheeks*

WHOEVER offends Dr. Montenegro with a malicious word, with a crooked smile, with a yellowish gesture, can rest easy: he will be slapped publicly. In the thirty years that he has favored the courtroom with his talents, his hand has visited many an arrogant cheek. Didn't he slap the Education Inspector? Didn't he slap the Health Officer? Didn't he slap almost every Director of the School? Didn't he slap Sergeant Cabrera? Didn't he slap the manager of the State Bank? All of them accepted the insult, and all of them begged his pardon. For Dr. Montenegro resents any person who forces him to take punitive action. From the moment his hands have made their choice, the chosen one can tip his hat as often as he likes: he is invisible to the Judge. And the Judge's forgiveness is more to be feared than his censure. To win his pardon, one has to depend on the intercession of friends or relatives. Those who have been punished give parties; only in the warmth of liquor does the black suit deign to give his pardon. Both the punishment and the pardon are public. The province realizes that the Judge's hands are longing for a face, that's all. No one knows when the insolent offender will receive the resounding caress. Will it happen when he is leaving mass? In the club? On the square? In the middle of the street? At the door of his house?

The man chosen by the black suit's hands stews in his own anxiety. Once the leading citizens were playing poker in the Social Club. The Director of the School was dealing. They were on their second hand when the Devil spoke with the voice of the Sub-prefect: "Don Paco," said Don Arquímedes Valerio (this was his first mistake: in public the Judge likes to be called by his title), "one of your field hands has filed a complaint at my office." The cards froze in the Director's hands. The other players hid behind their hands. The Sub-prefect bit off a smile. Too late. The Judge stood up, politely moved a chair out of the way, and his hands paid a visit to the fat cheeks of the leading authority in the province. The Sub-prefect's double chin trembled in an earthquake of jelly. The frightened cardplayers were absorbed in imaginary royal flushes. The Sub-prefect—a shrewd fellow—pretended to be drunk. "I never could take beer," he stammered, and smoothing back his hair, he staggered out.

At eleven the next morning the bleary-eyed Sub-prefect, having pondered the enormity of what he had done, carefully washed his hands, elbows, and even his neck, put on his formal blue suit and a red-striped tie, and went to seek forgiveness. The Judge would not see him. "The Judge doesn't feel well," mumbled his servants with downcast eyes. The Sub-prefect asked permission to wait. At five in the afternoon, not daring to look up at the balcony where the injured party was recuperating in the sun, the mortified official finally left. He returned the next day. "The Judge's liver is still acting up," Señora Pepita told him in a voice that left no room for doubt that he, Valerio, was responsible for this attack of jaundice. Despair ravaged the Sub-prefect's flabby face. He returned on the third day: the Judge was "still not feeling well." Crushed by the burden of his guilt, the Sub-prefect crossed the square thirty times; thirty times he returned to his office with shoulders bowed.

The terrified town shared his misfortune. Deprived of its highest officials, Yanahuanca was paralyzed. All administrative business suffered from rheumatism. In his office the demoralized official burst into tigerlike rages at the slightest provocation. Prompted by their own bad luck, three unhappy wretches filed an insignificant petition: they left the Sub-prefecture in handcuffs. The leading political authority grew fond of exploding into unheard-of fits of anger. Even Santiago Pasión did not dare submit documents to him. Only once did he insist on showing him a thick folder of telegrams from the Prefecture: "It's urgent, sir." "To hell with that urgent shit!" roared the leading authority, and he tore up the papers, ripped up a calendar on which brazen geishas were smiling, threw an inkwell at the picture of the President of the Republic, and kicked the secretary out of the office. "Help, murder, help!" yelled Pasión in terror. The uproar woke the guards, but there was nothing they could do; the guards looked at the enraged Sub-prefect and clicked their heels in military fashion as they raised five fingers to their greasy visors in salute. Nobody dared go back to the Sub-prefecture. The school charity bazaar was postponed because they had no permit. All parties were postponed so that the Sub-prefect, in no condition to stand the noise of an orchestra, would not be annoyed.

The Sub-prefect let himself go. One day he crossed the square unshaven and with his fly open, a situation which was simply not in keeping with his position as representative of the President of the Republic. That morning the miracle occurred: Dr. Montenegro received him. When Don Arquímedes Valerio heard from Señora Pepita's own mouth that the Judge had said, "Have him come in," he almost collapsed. He burst into tears. The Judge was waiting for him with bowed head and open arms. Overcome with emotion, Don Arquímedes, who only minutes before had sentenced two men to thirty days in jail for some petty misdemeanor, threw himself against the bosom of his friend, who, with a half-pitying, half-disillusioned smile, said, like the good Christian he was, that he forgave him his trespasses.

"Don Paco," blubbered the Sub-prefect, "forgive me if I offended you in my drunkenness."

"Between friends there can be no offense," said the black suit.

"We're the same friends we always were, Valerio," and he embraced him.

It was six in the afternoon; the Sub-prefect asked permission to send for some punch. The black suit agreed. At nine Don Arquímedes asked the Judge to be best man at his wedding. Three months ago Doña Enriqueta de los Ríos' brother had fallen off a cliff on the road to Chinche, leaving a sizable estate. The temptation of becoming a landowner and the desire to show off with a really imposing best man moved Don Arquímedes to cross the wide Rubicon of his fiancee's forty-eight years. "I don't know if I'm going too far, Judge," he coughed timidly, "but I'd like you to be my best man." Incapable of harboring a grudge, the Judge sent for a bottle of La Fourie, the local champagne. Tongues wagged faster than the speed of light; when the province learned that the Sub-prefect had not only been forgiven—that afternoon he accompanied the Judge on his walk—but that the Judge had even agreed to be best man at his wedding, the envious turned so green they could not show themselves on the streets. They bit their tongues: nobody wanted to miss the wedding party. Proud of a friendship that had been darkened by a little cloud that the evil-minded had confused with the darkness of night but which in fact had been the prelude to a dazzling noontime, the Sub-prefect made preparations for the most magnificent party ever held in the province. One month before the celebration the Guardia Civil received final instructions: the most minor traffic violation, the slightest disturbance was to be rigorously prosecuted. The Mayor, Don Herón de los Ríos, admonished the police officers so vigorously that a dram's short weight or some mules going the wrong way down a one-way street were transformed into heavy fines in either money or goods: goats, chickens, guinea pigs were stuffed into the tiny barnyard behind the barracks of the most noble and loyal Guardia Civil. One week before Father Lovatón was to give his blessing at the ceremony, Sergeant Cabrera asked permission to call off the hunting party: there was no room to squeeze in any more animals. There was no space left in the storerooms of the Sub-prefecture either; they were packed solid with delicacies sent in from Lima: Tacama red wine, Ocucaje white wine, Poblete champagne, canned tuna, enormous fruit cakes, biscuits, and crystallized fruit.

On the first Sunday in September, Father Lovatón blessed the mature bride and the groom (between them the couple was almost one hundred years old). The crowd cheered itself hoarse as the bridegroom left the church with a blushing half-century on his arm. The guests, with the best man leading the way, in accordance with the text of the invitations—printed in Cerro de Pasco in red ink on heavy blue stock—entered the "banquet rooms"—that is, the dining room of the Sub-prefecture. They were thunderstruck: the tables—reinforced by the prisoners with wooden supports—groaned under mountains of full-grown and suckling pigs, chickens, and baby goats. If the Sub-prefect, undoubtedly possessed by the demon of vanity, had looked at his best man's face, perhaps he would have tempered his blunder, but the gods always blind those they wish to destroy. Warmed by flattery, which does more harm than drink, Sub-prefect Valerio went to his downfall. He failed to notice that Dr. Montenegro did not deign even to try a mouthful of the meats so pompously offered him. At about six in the evening the Sub-prefect raised his glass and proposed the fatal toast: "To my best man. You have afforded me the pleasure of giving you the best party ever held in the province." The black suit grew pale. What did that greasy drunk mean? Weren't the Magistrate's parties just as good? Didn't his house overflow with delicacies infinitely superior to that roasted thieves' loot? Was there any human being in the province who could provide his guests with better food? Was that chubby man the bridegroom? And even if you could conceive of anything so absurd, did he have to announce it on the day when absolutely every leading citizen in Yanahuanca could hear him? The Judge's face was ashen; he threw his glass down on the whitewashed cement floor. He adjusted his bowler hat. The people who had been talking to him blanched. The Sub-prefect turned into a statue with a glass in its hand. The pale bride guessed at the abyss about to swallow up the man who had been her lord and master for the past six hours, and came toward the Judge with open arms. Judge Montenegro moved her away delicately, pushed aside two chairs, a Mayor, and two schoolteachers, and slowly remembered what to do. His left hand supported his heart while his right hand took flight. He slapped him three times.

CHAPTER SIX: *Concerning the Time and Place of the Fence's Birth*

WHEN was it born? On a Monday or a Tuesday? Fortunato did not witness the birth. Neither Representative Rivera nor the authorities nor the men in the pastures saw the train arrive. The children found two cars resting at the crossing when they left school. The older people saw them at nightfall. It was a small train, only a locomotive and two cars. For some time the authorities had been asking the Company to have a stop at Rancas, if only for courtesy's sake. They had asked in vain. The trains from Goyllarizquizga, proud of their minerals, passed through the village without so much as a glance. Finally, now, a train had stopped. If they had known about it, the Representative's office would have organized a welcome. Hiring trumpets and drums is not difficult. There are plenty of devil masks, plenty of fancy gear for the horses out on the prairie; unfortunately, the Rancasans were watching their sheep when the train began to disgorge the strangers. The people of Ondores, Junín, Huayllay, Villa de Pasco are well known, but nobody in Rancas knew who these men in black leather jackets were. They unloaded bales of wire. They finished at one o'clock, had lunch, and then began to dig postholes. They put in a post every ten meters.

That's how the Fence was born.

The Rancasans come back from the cattle ranches at five. It is the best time to close livestock deals or to gossip about baptisms and weddings. They returned from their pastures that evening as they did on all other days. They found Huiska fenced in! Huiska is a barren hill. It hides no minerals. It has no water. It refuses to grow the most miserable grass. Why would anyone want to fence it in?

With its barbed-wire necklace Huiska looked like a cow stuck in a corral.

They almost died laughing.

"What kind of idiot would fence in Huiska?"

"They must be geologists."

"They must be from the telegraph company."

"Which telegraph company?"

"As long as they don't bother us, what difference does it make?" said Representative Alfonso Rivera.

That night the Fence slept on the hill called Huiska. The shepherds went out the next day still shaking with laughter. When they came home, the Fence had crawled another seven kilometers. Not only was Huiska chewing its cud inside the corral: Huancacala Hill was now there too, an immense black jaw strewn by the grace of God with holy images: the Mother of Sorrows, the Holy Crucifix, and the Twelve Apostles, all carved in stone. The barbed wire had the saints. The Rancasans are men of few words. They said nothing, but their faces showed the marks of the blow. In the square they heard more news: the crews of workmen were not from the government. That afternoon in Cerro, Abdón Medrano had met the manager of the Telegraph Office. The manager, a sour man, had lost patience: "What kind of nonsense are they gossiping about now? Those men in jackets don't work for the Telegraph. I know the men in Public Works. Those guys aren't with the government. I've never heard of them."

"What do they want Huiska for? That rockpile isn't worth anything," laughed Representative Rivera.

"As long as they don't bother us, what difference does it make?

If they want to take over the rocks, it's their problem."

"That fence is the work of the Devil. You'll see. Someone is doing the work of Satan." Don Teodoro Santiago kept raising and lowering his eyebrows.

They laughed. Don Santiago was always prophesying some catastrophe. He had said the bell tower would collapse. Had it fallen down? He had predicted a plague. Had one broken out? Don Santiago always looked on the black side of things. What was the good of arguing with him?

We shouldn't have laughed. Instead of filling our mouths with foolish talk, we should have attacked the Fence, killed it, trampled on it while it was still in the cradle. Weeks later, when the Great Panic gripped us in its jaws, Don Alfonso realized we had all been asleep. Don Santiago had been right, but by that time the Fence had infected the whole Department.

Fortunato stopped and slumped down weakly on the grass. His heart was jumping like a frog. He raised himself slightly and peered at the fog-covered curve; any minute now, perhaps while he was catching his breath there, the trucks would appear, but his eyes could not make out any lights; curled up like a cat, the road to Rancas was dozing.

CHAPTER SEVEN: *Concerning the Amount of Ammunition Required to Stop a Man Breathing*

AN early winter splashed over the roads. Footsteps were lost in the mud. December thundered in the mountains. Huddled in their cabins, the people watched the horses' hooves sink. One rainy Wednesday a Civil Guard appeared on the road to Yanahuanca. Civil Guardsman Paz's doglike face headed for the house of Representative Agapito Robles. A crowd gathered. They were mistaken: the guard brought no warrants for arrest. It was Sub-prefect Valerio's confirmation that the summons for the dispute between Huarautambo Ranch and the Yanacocha Community would be served on December 13. Guardsman Paz thanked him for the glass of rum and disappeared into the fog.

"It's very strange," said Melecio de la Vega, "very strange that the authorities are paying so much attention to us."

"Don't be suspicious," said the Representative. "The Judge must be tired of so many warnings. Perhaps he wants to work something out." He scratched his calf and laughed. "Perhaps violence won't be necessary."

"We have to make plans for the welcome," said Horse Thief.

"A decent welcome," advised Rustler. "We can't let what happened to the Chinchinians happen to us."

Horse Thief burst out laughing. The authorities crossed themselves. For months the Chinchinians, pushed back by the ranch's assaults, had requested that a summons be issued. Worn out by yards of petitions, the authorities agreed to a trip by Inspector Galarza. Chinche, still new to the twistings of the law, was in an uproar. Representative Amador Cayetano hired all the drums and bugles for five leagues around, and had a triumphal arch erected. He even went down to the provincial capital to buy a new shirt and to ask Clerk Lorenzana to write a speech for him. The famous orator composed a dithyramb worthy of the Prefect. On the eve of the great day Cayetano traveled to Tambopampa with the community's best horses. Tambopampa is a handful of huts scattered around the beginning of the Chinche road. Cayetano arranged for everything except the winter. The trip between Cerro and Tambopampa normally takes five hours; but the rains were brutal and washed out the highway. The Inspector, expected at eleven in the morning, showed up at eight that night. Filthy with mud and fatigue, his face sour, he got down from the truck blanched by the storm.

"How is Your Excellency?" asked Cayetano.

The Inspector looked at the huts swept by the hailstorm.

"Your Excellency's horses are ready."

"Damn it, do you want to kill me?" shouted the Inspector. "You can't see your hand in front of your face. We can't possibly travel in this weather. We'll stay here. Get me something to eat and then I'm going to sleep."

Cayetano was in a state of confusion.

"There's nothing to eat?"

"We have some barbecue in Chinche, Excellency."

"Cut out that 'Excellency' shit."

"Very well, Excellency."

It took them an hour to light a fire. In one of the huts Cayetano found a bottle of coffee essence. The Inspector waited, more dead than alive; he hadn't eaten anything since seven that morning. Cayetano finally appeared with a pitcher. Galarza blew on the boiling coffee and sipped it; he made a face and spat.

"What is this stuff?"

"Coffee, Excellency."

"Show me the coffee!"

They brought him the turbid bottle. The Inspector uncorked it and turned his nose away in disgust.

"Where in hell did you get that from?"

"It's pure essence, Excellency, bought in Huancayo."

"When did you buy it, you imbecile?"

"A year ago, Excellency."

The Inspector threw up his arms. "My God, will these savages never change? Will they ever become civilized? Can you at least give me a bed?"

They offered him a sheepskin. Inspector Galarza fell into a despairing sleep. The authorities from Chinche went out blaming each other. The Inspector, in his fury, would decide against them! The Representative asserted his authority and stopped the confusion of blows. "Whatever happens," said Cayetano, "we have to give him a good breakfast." It was a noble thought. The storm had washed the roads away; they scavenged through the houses. They couldn't even find a crust of bread. At midnight they decided to reconnoiter the area. The storm had not let up. Fermín Espinoza—an ex-sergeant, a tenant farmer from Chinche who had been evicted and taken refuge in a cave—found a chicken. He confiscated it. It was almost dawn.

"Do you know how to cook?" asked Cayetano.

"In the barracks you learn how to do everything."

"Then fix a nice stew."

When hunger woke the Inspector, a glorious sun was forgiving all sins and a stew was steaming on a wooden case decently covered with a yellowed page from the *Commercial News.*

"Your breakfast, Señor Inspector," announced Cayetano.

Inspector Galarza realized the enormous effort they had made, and smiled. He almost pounced on the stew; but barely had he put the spoon to his mouth when he looked up.

"What the hell is this?"

"Chicken, Excellency," Cayetano informed him. "I plucked it myself."

"This is shit," choked the Inspector.

Cayetano smelled the stew and doubled up with laughter. It was shit, exactly what the Inspector said.

"Listen, Espinoza. Did you cover the pot?"

"What pot?"

"You stupid son-of-a-bitch!" roared Cayetano. "Don't you know that when you cook over dung you have to cover the pot so that the whole thing doesn't stink of shit?"

The tragedy that had befallen the Chinchinians sent a shiver down the spines of the Yanacochans.

"We have to make plans," worried Agapito Robles fearfully.

"It would be a good idea to hire a band," advised Rustler.

"That would cost three hundred sols."

"It's worth it."

On the morning of December 12 the Representative and sixty men on horseback rode down to Yanahuanca. The square had never seen such a cavalcade. Astonishment shook the guardsmen out of their siestas. Sergeant Cabrera adjusted his cartridge belt and crossed the square frowning. He did not dare do anything else. A waspish buzzing preceded Héctor Chacón, Horse Thief, and Rustler as they entered the square. The men waited, smoking, talking, or drinking. The fog presided over an early nightfall. At seven o'clock two lights trembled on the high curves of the road to Chipipata.

"There they are!" shouted the Representative.

Thirty minutes later a truck spattered with mud drove into the square. The band broke into the first notes of "March of the Flags." The Inspector took off his hat.

"The authorities of Yanacocha," said the Representative in a dignified voice, "welcome you, illustrious Inspector."

Rustler and Horse Thief were busy with the luggage. The band and a cheering crowd accompanied the Inspector to the Hotel

International. The Inspector walked toward the hotel dizzy with the altitude and the applause.

"I'm very tired," he said as he went up to the door.

"Not through there, Señor Inspector," said the Representative.

"What?"

"You have to go up through the patio," Rustler informed him.

The Hotel International was one of the beneficiaries of the talents of Simeón the Forgetful, the only practicing architect in the province. Simeón forgot everything, whether it be insults or plans. While building, he always forgot a door, a window, a hallway. Thanks to his genius, many Yanahuancans slept in the dining room and ate in the attic. In the Hotel International he had mislaid the stairs. Faced with the choice of tearing down the building or putting up a ladder made of eucalyptus, the owners opted for mountain-climbing, a solution that had one advantage: it kept the drunks away.

"I'm going to sleep," said the Inspector with resignation.

"What time do you want the horses?"

"At nine o'clock."

Representative Agapito Robles bowed.

The band again exploded into "March of the Flags." The Inspector climbed amid cheers and applause.

"Tomorrow, everyone in the square!" shouted the Representative.

"The bells will let you know when," added Felicio de la Vega.

The riders vanished in the darkness. The hoof-beats of the horses faded away. An hour later they were splashing through the mud of Yanacocha.

"See you tomorrow," yawned the Representative.

"Wait a minute," ordered Chacón.

"What is it?"

Hawkeye showed him a little bag.

"What's that?"

"Forty-five rounds."

The Representative leaped back in his saddle. "Héctor," he

said, clearing his throat, "I've had a bad dream."

Hawkeye amused himself watching a spider trying to climb to Minaya's roof.

"I dreamed that the prairie was swarming with Guards."

Hawkeye cracked his knuckles.

"Héctor, maybe the Judge will give in."

"The Judge will give in the day pigs fly."

"We authorities haven't approved the death you're planning. You can't risk the whole village, Héctor."

"Did you dream that too?"

The Representative was pleading. "Nobody can do anything without authorization."

The revolver burned in Hawkeye's hand. "Then what have I been getting ready for?"

"What have you lost by getting ready?"

"All right," shouted Hawkeye, and spurred his crossbreed horse. The horse dashed away.

"Héctor, Héctor!"

Hawkeye was already galloping across the endless prairie. He didn't take pity on the horse until dawn. Tiger came out to rub against his legs, wagging his tail.

"This way, Papá, this way," the voice of his son guided him.

"He thinks I'm drunk," he said to himself.

The boy's face, grimy with sleep, peered out the door.

"Get a candle, Fidel."

The boy kissed his hand and lit a candle end. The flickering light scattered along the wall. Potato sacks, saddlebags, saddles, riding gear, and boxes were piled up in the room; his daughter snored rhythmically. Suddenly an old fatigue pulled at his legs. He unbuckled his belt and put the revolver and the bag on the table. The bullets spilled out.

Fidel's eyes shone as he looked at the gun.

"Tomorrow I am going to die," thought Hawkeye. "The Guardia Civil will riddle me with bullets, they'll tie me to a horse and drag me through the streets. No one will be able to recognize me. Neither my wife, nor Juana, nor Fidel, nor Hipólito."

"I'm going to kill Montenegro," said Hawkeye. "Tomorrow I'll finish the bastard off. If we're going to keep any pastureland, he has to die."

The boy stroked the revolver as if it were the back of a cat. "Do you need so many bullets to kill one man, Papá?"

"Just one is enough."

"Will the Guards kill you?"

"I have a lot of bullets."

"Will they shoot you?"

"They can't even hit a deer, let alone me. That's enough, Fidel. It's late, go to sleep."

The boy's eyes burned. "Get rid of all the ranch-owners, Papá. I'll help you. Tomorrow I'll carry your guns, under my poncho, so they won't suspect anything."

Chacón fell into a dreamless sleep.

The voices of Fidel and Juana awakened him.

"Hurry up, sister," shouted the boy in the kitchen, "today's the big day. Buy bread and cheese."

"You wipe the snot off your nose and shut up."

"Don't you know what we're doing today?" He picked up the revolver. "Today we're killing Montenegro."

"Put that down!"

"No, sister, women mustn't touch things like that. This is no joking matter. Be quiet and make a good breakfast for Héctor."

Stretched out on the sheepskin, Hawkeye counted the bells. He got up and dressed: he went out to the patio and wet his head, feeling no anger. An oilcloth sprinkled with flowers and fruit covered the table where a pitcher of goat's milk, two loaves of bread, and some cheese were waiting for him. Fidel came up and kissed his hand.

"Lazy bum," he scolded him, "you just got up."

"I've been up since four," protested the boy. "I've fixed your breakfast. Don't worry, Héctor, drink your milk! I'm going to the corral to get a good horse ready for you." He went out with a rope in his hand.

Hawkeye calmly chewed the bread soaked in milk.

Juana came over, crying. "Is it true you're going to kill Montenegro, Papá?"

"Who told you that?"

"Fidel has a pistol and a cartridge belt."

"I have to do it so we have pasture for the animals," said Chacón softly.

"It will make things worse, Papá. The police will come after us." Tears streaked her narrow eyes.

"No matter what, I'm killing Montenegro," he thought, and in a flash he pardoned the other condemned men. Kid Remigio, Roque, Sacramento would not die. Only one of them was guilty. "I'll kill his face, I'll kill his body, I'll kill his shadow, I'll kill his voice."

A heavily built young man with square shoulders blocked the doorway.

"What's the news, son?"

Rigoberto took off his hat and kissed his hand. "The square's crawling with people. Much gossip, Papá."

"They're issuing the summons today."

"People say you're going to kill Montenegro. There's trouble in the streets."

"What?"

"You shouldn't have told anyone, Héctor."

"There were very few of us, Rigoberto."

"Very few? Everybody knows you met at Quencash. The people are scared, Papá."

"Let them talk."

"You'll go ahead with it, Papá?"

"I'll finish it, one way or the other."

Desperately Rigoberto tried to learn his father's face by heart.

CHAPTER EIGHT: *Concerning the Mysterious Workmen and Their Even Stranger Occupations*

DON Alfonso, I am not accusing you. We elected you Representative for Rancas because you know about sheep-raising. You know how to take care of them. You can tell the difference between indigestion and worms from leagues away. Rancas had great plans: setting up a ranch of fine breeding animals to improve the stock. Junín had done it. Why not Rancas? We knew that the Senator, interested in re-election, would provide facilities to villages that could demonstrate their ability to breed fine animals. That's what Rancas wanted: the opportunity. With a little effort, in a few seasons we could have sold sheep crossed with breeders from the Farming Office. We elected you to run the ranch, Don Alfonso. I am not accusing you. I would never have allowed them to stone your house. I understand your good faith. You thought that the work crews were fencing in the hill to test the wire. What else was there to think? How could you suspect? I am not accusing you, Don Alfonso. The truth is that only Don Teodoro Santiago suspected their real plan, but how can you believe a man whose lips are perpetually stained with prophecies of disasters that never take place? It is true that once the Fence had enclosed Huiska, it rushed on to Huancacala Hill. Even so, I can still understand your calm, Don Alfonso. On the way down from Huancacala there is the uncrossable current of the Yuracancha. I understand how you must have said: "The current of the Yuracancha is too strong. The Fence will have to stop there."

That is what you said at nine o'clock. At ten you went to the Simón Bolívar Municipal Building to file a petition. It was laughable—perhaps we should not even think of it at a serious time like this. One of your sons had been recorded as a girl at the Civil Registry in Rancas. You filed your petition. The recorder insisted on proof. You had to ask permission to take your son out of school. Your poor little boy had to pee to convince the Registrar that he was not Josefa but José del Carmen. You returned at eleven and your mouth fell open in astonishment: the Fence had jumped the Yuracancha.

Dusk, that hypocritical dusk, showed that words were not enough. For the first time the Fence barred the way to the returning shepherds. The flocks had to go a league out of the way to reach Rancas. Rancas began whispering. What was the Fence up to? What were its secret plans? Who had ordered the partitioning? Who owned the barbed wire? Where did it come from? A shadow that was not nightfall darkened the bewildered faces. The prairie belongs to all travelers. There have never been fences on the prairie. That night we talked ourselves hoarse. You did not say anything. You, Don Alfonso, had already made your plans: you would demand an explanation from the work crews. And that is what you did. You got up early and put on your black suit. You walked fifteen kilometers to find the Fence's head. You approached with your hat in your hand. Men with rifles stopped you.

"No admittance."

"Gentlemen, I am the Duly Elected Representative for Rancas. Whom do I have the pleasure of addressing?"

"No admittance."

"Permit me to inform you, gentlemen, that you are on lands that belong to the Community of Rancas. We should like—"

"We have orders not to talk. Get out!"

Such a strict prohibition gave rise to speculation that the workmen were serving a prison sentence. That night the old men remembered that in the days of Don Augusto B. the government ordered political prisoners to build a railroad to Tambo del Sol. In Lima they cherished the idea of running a railroad right up to the forest. The railroad would begin in the prairie. It was a marvelous idea. Instead of doing nothing and learning more mischief in jail, the political prisoners would lay rail. They brought them in by the hundreds. There was no lack of will: what they did lack was air. People from the coast suffocate in the highlands. We ourselves know that at five thousand meters it is foolhardy to use a shovel. They died like flies. That was the difficulty, they all died off. The old men do not lie; here and there among the abandoned crossties their bones are bleaching. So, when Don Mateo Gallo said that the workmen were political prisoners, we calmed down. There are plenty of rebels in the jails. The Civil Guard is never short of workers.

Señora Tufina reassured us all: "I'll ask my nephew next Sunday when I go to the prison."

"Yes, good, ask Fats."

"Fats should know what jail the prisoners come from."

Señora Tufina could not hide her pride. Now nobody thought of the things that Fats had done: sleeping with married women and stealing cattle from sleeping men. That bastard Fats had been transformed into the savior of the village!

But Abdón Medrano threw cold water on all of us: "I don't think those leather jackets are prisoners."

"How do you know?" shouted an aggressive Don Mateo.

"Prisoners are always guarded by government men. There are no government men out there."

Forgetting that Don Abdón, a former Representative, is a sensible man, we flew into a rage. More than anything we wanted to believe that the Fence was a mirage, a nightmare. Because even while we were talking, the Fence was on the move. Not even Cecilio Cóndor, who can spot a vizcacha hidden in the depths of Stone Forest, could see where it ended.

That was Saturday. On Sunday, Doña Tufina traveled to Cerro with a basket of biscuits and cheese for Fats. She was upset when she returned at six o'clock.

"Fats says that no prisoners have gone out to work from the Cerro jail."

Maybe they're prisoners from Huánuco," tried Don Mateo, without conviction. No one answered.

You could not see the end of the barbed wire even if you stood on the hilltops. It never stopped moving. Hills, pastures, waterholes, caves, lakes, it swallowed up everything. By Monday at four o'clock it had devoured Chuco Hill. The prairie was partitioned. The Fence cut the prairie in two. Now it was a five-hour trip to villages that had been an hour away. The hour's journey to Huayllay took a day. The merchants from Ondores who used to come to the Sunday market were furious. "Those pricks in Rancas are trying to ruin us!" That is how they talked in their anger. Wrong: we could not even get to the waterholes ourselves; it became harder and harder to get any water at all.

No one laughed at the Fence any more. Fear wheeled round us like coal-black ravens flying out of the dust. Even so, people had one glimmer of hope: beyond Chuco Hill there is only Gaviota Pond, a foul swamp haunted by evil spirits, and beyond that, just water poisoned by mining wastes. To go out there is like looking for the mouth of hell.

At noon on Tuesday the Fence encircled Gaviota Pond and disappeared over the horizon.

CHAPTER NINE: *Concerning the Fortunes and Misfortunes of a Ball of Rags*

EVERY week a procession of men on horseback files through the streets of Yanahuanca: the foremen from the Huarautambo Ranch come down to escort Dr. Montenegro. At their head is a thin man, with a rotting smile and eyes set deep in mistrustful cheeks, who enjoys running down dogs: it is Chuto Ildefonso. Showing his teeth aged in nicotine, Fat Ermigio Arutingo is invariably waiting for them on the threshold of the big pink-walled house with blue doors and red balconies. Chuto, oblivious to any sense of delicacy, comes up to the house to smoke a cigarette while Judge Montenegro, his hat pulled down over his eyebrows, is in the dining room finishing his plate of ram's testicles with onion and slowly drinking his coffee.

At nine o'clock the patio paved in stone carves out the figure of Dr. Montenegro. Together the twenty horsemen remove their hats and salute the black suit. A straw brim shades him from the sun: a hat from Catacaos, so fine that you can fold it into a matchbox. Fat Arutingo sidles up with his slimy jokes. Chuto Ildefonso leads a magnificent chestnut by the reins: Triumphant, the Judge's pride, is the only horse in the province that forages for food wherever it wants to. No one dares sue for damages. Last July 28, National Independence Day, Triumphant ran in a race.

The Mayor, Don Herón de los Ríos, came back from a trip to Huánuco determined to organize a horse race in Yanahuanca. He stirred up a wasps' nest. Excited by an event that would draw the crowd, the shopkeepers offered a silver cup as a prize. The municipality unanimously approved a thousand sols for the winner besides offering all the registration fees as prize money: fifty sols for each horse, an enormous sum. On July 1 the Municipal Secretary posted the registration notices around the square. It was all anyone talked about. There are plenty of proud horses in this province. On the day they posted the public notices Apolonio Guzmán entered Dumb Bird, an albino that was stupid only in name. Ponciano Mayta also scraped up fifty sols. He hadn't bought his Morning Star, he had raised him from birth, with love and affection. Pedro Andrade pirouetted right through the door of the Municipal Building on the back of Boob, an ugly, insolent horse with a white forehead. When he came out he ran into the threatening spurs of a legendary pair. Melecio Cuéllar and his Bobtail, whose missing tail gave him an advantage when he raced. All this equestrian splendor did not discourage Tomás Curi, who put all his trust in his white-footed Lightning (he had paid fifteen hundred sols plus a bull for him). Boastful riders excited Yanahuanca. The province was in an uproar. The old women who keep the world turning with the energy of their tongues forgot all about the adulterers and put their attention to the carryings-on of the men on horseback.

No one knows whether the idea was a child of Arutingo's paltry brain or whether Dr. Montenegro felt stirred by a noble impulse of the competitive spirit. One morning a blue fifty-sol note from the Doctor put the fear of God into the Municipal Secretary. Triumphant would run. When the other competitors found out that they would be racing against a horse suspiciously named Triumphant, they tried to withdraw. Too many drinks made Amador Cayetano foolish enough to mourn his fifty sols out loud. César Morales went even further; he went to the Municipal Building and asked for his fifty sols back.

"What did you say?" roared Don Herón, turning purple. "Have you come here to make a fool of me?"

"I don't think Dr. Montenegro will ever let another horse win."

Don Herón choked. "What did you say? Are you trying to insult the Judge publicly? Have you had enough of being a free man? What's happened to your sportsmanship? Damn it! I'll throw the first man who withdraws into jail."

It was this timely reminder of the Olympian spirit that kept the others in the race.

A patriotic reveille, courtesy of the barracks of the Guardia Civil, awakened Yanahuanca on the twenty-eighth of July. Eight Guards presented arms at the Pavilion. Forgetting that Father Lovatón was celebrating a mass in memory of General San Martín, the curious swarmed over the track. Three days earlier the Guardia Civil, anxious to celebrate the anniversary of the Fatherland, had ordered the prisoners to build a reviewing stand that was now decorated with two-colored streamers, a gift from the schoolteachers. At eleven o'clock Sub-prefect Valerio, the Mayor, the Director of the School, the lieutenant who was Platoon Officer, the manager of the State Bank, and the teachers took their places on the straw chairs arranged around the place of honor reserved for Dr. Montenegro. Radiant in a new flannel shirt, Fat Arutingo was taking all bets and swearing that Triumphant would break the two-toned ribbon to win the race.

The idlers had invaded the track. Sergeant Cabrera ordered them to disperse. At twelve o'clock Don Herón de los Ríos, sweating in a blue serge suit, stood up. At the far end of the track nineteen riders were lined up. But Don Herón wanted no clouds to darken the brilliant day: "Gentlemen" (the word was a clever piece of diplomacy when spoken to farmhands unused to such polite treatment from the authorities), "this race is not meant to gratify anyone's vanity. This competition celebrates the sacred anniversary of our country." The riders removed their hats. Under the beating sun, the Mayor scratched his head. "What does it matter," sighed Don Herón, "who wins? Perhaps the best thing for everyone would be for the Judge to have his way!" and he cast his gaze over the competitors. "What the hell ever made me enter?" sighed Alfonso Jiménez, picking his nose. He was being openly disrespectful to the office of Mayor, but rather than punishment for his insolence, Don Herón shrewdly chose philosophy: "A courtroom, gentlemen, is like a soapmaker's shop: if you don't walk in, you slip in. No one is completely innocent, no one should boast and say, 'That's a thing I'd never do' "—and he ended with this paradox: "Gentlemen, by losing, you will win." The consoled riders lined up. The eyes of the province followed them. From the place of honor, Dr. Montenegro watched the track through long-range binoculars, an attraction that rivaled even the race itself in the interest it provoked. The Mayor announced: "Ladies and gentlemen, the municipality of Yanahuanca wishes to celebrate this joyous patriotic occasion of our country's anniversary with an unprecedented event. The best riders will compete for a cup donated by our worthy businessmen. May God be with them, and may the best man win!"

Applause broke out. Corporal Minches shot the regulation pistol into the air. The horses leaped forward together. Whether it was because the timely reminders of the Mayor had dampened everyone's spirits, or because he was indeed the best horse, Triumphant took the lead. Thanks to his spectacular binoculars, the black suit followed the race with a smile on his lips. But man proposes and the horse disposes. Hummingbird, César Morales' chestnut, was deaf to the wisdom of Don Herón's arguments and defeated Triumphant. Morales swears he did everything he could to prevent the outrage: he sat down hard in the saddle, he dug in with his calves, he pulled on the right rein and cut into Hummingbird's lips. It was all to no avail: the damned horse just wouldn't stop until he reached the finishing post.

Dr. Montenegro, responsible for awarding the cup donated by the honorable Council to the winner, suffered the humiliation of witnessing the catastrophic defeat of a horse ironically named Triumphant. He cut the Mayor dead with an ominous look. Don

Herón immediately grasped the sense. He got up and stumbled toward the confused group of riders. No one ever found out what César Morales and Don Herón said to one another. The Mayor returned to the judges on the stand. Arutingo's wooden face was resigned to paying out the winnings. "Gentlemen," announced Don Herón, sweating, "the other riders have made serious accusations against Morales. Morales lashed the other riders during the race. Our respect for a patriotic occasion does not permit us to tolerate such irregularities." The leading citizens smiled, relieved. How could one allow such an action on the anniversary of National Independence? A moment later the panel of judges nullified Hummingbird's victory and announced through the mouth of Don Herón that first place belonged to Triumphant. This led to another problem: it was obvious that Dr. Montenegro, whose duty it was to present the cup, could not very well receive it from his own hands. But it was Don Herón's day: he asked Doña Pepita de Montenegro to condescend to honor the winner on behalf of the distinguished city of Yanahuanca. Blushing with emotion, the ranch-owner handed the cup and the 1950 sols to the Judge. There was another crackle of applause.

A crowd of hangers-on sees Triumphant pirouetting, and they run off through the streets. "The Judge is coming! There they come! Here they come!" they shout. Triumphant, saddled with a Huancayan harness engraved with a silver monogram of F and M, impatiently chews on the silver-plated bit. Comforted by his second cup of coffee, the black suit moves through the passageway of doffed hats and crosses the stone-paved patio. Arutingo comes up to tell him what happened when "Iron Drawers" enrolled her daughter in a nuns' school. Chuto Ildefonso holds the reins while the Judge climbs into the saddle. By this time the streets that the horsemen will ride through are empty. Only the shopkeepers, unable to leave their businesses, come to the doors to greet the leading citizen. He comes down Huallaga Way, a little street where the Chinaman's Restaurant and a water fountain humbly beg everyone's pardon. Fifty yards farther on it slopes down to the bridge. Twenty riders follow a capering Triumphant, who trots along amid the retailers' salutations. Reveling in Triumphant's pranks, the equestrian statue does not respond to their bows. The cavalcade crosses the bridge and sets out along the road to Huarautambo Ranch. They pass through Racre. For an hour the riders, excited by stories of the wild things that happened on the day "Cot-breaker" found a turtle in her bed, travel along the banks to the source of Huallaga River. After a league they begin the hard climb to Huarautambo: a rough, winding track also a league long. Fortunately, the men in the saddle know the tortuous path. Comforted by tales of the awful things that happened the day "Bronze Ass" asked "Cot-breaker" how many leaves a clover has (an innocent question that provoked a charge with fixed bayonets by the regiment stationed at Huancayo), they finally see the boulders where the hard road softens into a beautiful flat meadow. Accustomed to the roughness of the stones, their eyes are shocked by the light rushing of the Huarautambo River as it plunges headlong over seven foaming rapids lit by brilliant flames of yellow broom. Deceived by a stone splashed by the spray, Triumphant slipped just as he was climbing past the third set of rapids, then recovered his balance. Not deigning to cast a single glance on the brave efforts of the waterfalls, the Judge rode on indifferently. After a mile they could see the willows growing on the ranch. They approached the bridge, barred by a huge colonial gate of carved wood which artists had scarecely dared to tamper with except by adding the F and the M which the saddlemaker had the honor of engraving on the harness. Dr. Montenegro stopped five yards from the gate. The Magistrate put his hand in his pocket and took out an enormous, heavy key. The bridge is the only way of reaching the ranch. Except for ants and lizards, no one crosses it without a permit bearing the signature and seal of the Judge. Years ago the black suit had traveled to Lima to deposit three hundred thousand sols in the bank. In the last-minute rush—biscuits and cheese for all the relatives—he had forgotten to leave the key to the bridge. Dr. Montenegro had planned to spend a week in Lima, but the strutting of a female who gave everyone at Five Corners plenty to look at kept him there the whole summer. Every soul on the ranch had to wait for the brunette to reject him before they could leave the property. The teacher of Huarautambo bit his nails for three months. "Rules are rules," was Chuto's judgment. Nobody crosses the bridge without permission, not even—that is, least of all—Don Sebastián Barda, Doña Pepita's brother, owner of the other bank and the poorer part of the ranch. When Don Sebastián gets drunk, he makes no secret of the fact that he got the shitty end of his father's inheritance. "It's my fault, I'm such a blockhead," he proclaims in a rummy voice. And it's the truth. When Don Alejandro Barda died, Doña Pepita proposed: "Brother dear, we'll take turns at drawing from the estate: you manage the property one year, and I'll run it the next." Don Sebastián, who had recently come into some money, accepted the proposal, and spent the year in the brothels of Huánuco. It wasn't a bad idea. In Huánuco, a hot country, there are women who can get milk from a stone. Worn out by the hundred days of debauchery, Don Sebastián bought a magnificent horse and returned to Huarautambo: he found the bridge gate locked. He kicked, he demanded, he insulted, he complained. All he got for his insolence was that Dr. Montenegro, the new "owner" of Huarautambo, refused to let him use the waterholes. "If he wants water," said the happy newlywed, "let him look for it in the mountains." Without so much as a glance at the broken-down shack where Sebastián chews on his resentment, the Judge crossed the bridge and rode on between mud walls topped with manes of cactus.

Triumphant splashed through the puddles on the path as misfortune pointed its finger at Juan Chacón, the Deaf One. Busy playing with a ball of rags sewn together with threads from a worn-out sack, he did not hear the thundering of the horsemen. He had lost his hearing dynamiting rocks on orders from the Judge. The Deaf One did not hear the noise of the horseshoes; his back was turned to the road where the property-owner who permits such pleasant games on his land was riding. The Deaf One jumped to catch the ball, but missed it. Carried by the Devil's hand, the ball flew into the face of the Judge. Triumphant stopped short. The Judge could not believe the outrage of which his senses told him; but surprise, close relative of knowledge, gave way to anger, first cousin to violence. The Deaf One turned, his face smeared with a stupid smile; he found his world closed off by a monument of fury.

"Who is this damned moron?" roared the Judge.

"He's one of your hands," stammered Chuto.

"Follow me, you idiots," fumed the Judge, already galloping away. The sun beat down. Triumphant, dripping with sweat, stopped in Moyopampa field. Out of the whirling dust of his hooves there emerged the grass-colored face of the Deaf One and the shit-colored face of Chuto. "Have this flea-bitten slob build a wall around the field. That will teach him what to do with his hands," shouted Dr. Montenegro, lashing him in the face with his whip. And he turned, very, very slightly, to Chuto, who was trembling. "Today you'll padlock this imbecile's house," and he flailed him with the whip again. "Until the wall is finished, these shits can sleep outside. If anyone dares to help them, you let me know!"

Overwhelmed by a misfortune worse than his deafness, Juan hit on the only words possible: "Thank you, Judge."

Chuto Ildefonso, who took payment for his humiliations in cash, kicked the Deaf One's family out of their hut and padlocked it. The skins they slept on, a pot, a bucket, and a sack of potatoes were all the family could manage to bring with them to help them face the elements. Building a wall around a field three hundred yards long on each side is a terrible sentence, but, however excessive the punishment might be, the Deaf One was right to express his gratitude: it was lucky for him that even in his anger the Judge had been guided by his own judgment. What would have happened if Fat Arutingo—delighted to tell what happened the day that "Electric Cunt" met a deaf-mute in the middle of a bridge—had added his own fury to that of the Judge? Besides the wall, he would have gotten something extra: running around the master's house all night, dancing until he fainted, or eating a sack of potatoes as the late Odonicio Castro had to do.

The Deaf One began to build the wall. He had to carry stones from the river. Five days later his son—winner of the game of rag ball—risked missing school to help him. The disconcerted teacher wavered between anger and compassion. "It's hard to build that wall alone," said the boy in a tone that already suggested a man's voice. "All right," said the teacher, backing down, "I'll go over your lessons with you." They lugged stones, piled them up, and packed them together with mud. At nightfall they would stop almost too exhausted to throw themselves down on their sheepskins over the meager heat of the rocks. It seemed impossible, but sixty days after that noon when misfortune had winked at Juan, the Deaf One, they had built a wall along one whole side of Moyopampa. One hundred ninety-three days later—one hundred ninety-three mornings, one hundred ninety-three middays, one hundred ninety-three afternoons, one hundred ninety-three dusks, one hundred ninety-three nights—a skeleton asked permission to show his work.

"Let's hope the Judge likes it," grumbled Chuto.

The black suit came out of the house and looked the wall over, biting into a peach as he did so.

"It'll do," he admitted. "Give them back their house and let them have a bottle of rum."

Filled with gratitude, the Deaf One repeated the only words he had said in one hundred ninety-three days:

"Thank you, Boss."

The sun of an early twilight bore down on the grass. The befuddled farmhand took off his hat. In the hatband, hidden beneath a scab of mud, shone the remains of a quail feather. On the day the Deaf One had taught his son to fish for trout with his hands, the boy had put it in his hat. A cold breeze blew; the little boy looked at the clouded eyes of his father, then at a lizard sunning himself, proud of his new tail, then at the scornful rider disappearing into the first shadows of dusk.

It was the first time—he was then nine—that the hand of Héctor Chacón, Hawkeye, had longed for the throat of Dr. Montenegro.

Years later, after serving his second jail sentence, a thin man with flashing eyes left the prison at Huánuco, climbed onto a truck, and returned to Yanahuanca. Winter was furiously attacking the last leaves. The man, who wore stained pants and a thin shirt, slowly walked into the main square. At one of the corners he put down a green cardboard suitcase, squatted, and took out a small box. Dr. Montenegro appeared at the opposite corner. It was time for his stroll. The main square in Yanahuanca is an irregular rectangle. The north side is fifty-two paces long, the south fifty-five, the east side seventy-five, and the west side seventy-four: 256 paces that the judge repeated twenty times every afternoon at six. The stranger began to smoke. Dr. Montenegro, nearsighted when it came to field hands, continued walking. Héctor Chacón, Hawkeye, began to laugh: his laughter grew into a shout, a rallying signal for conspiring animals, a secret learned from owls, a foam forced out by the explosions of dry guffaws like the shots of the Civil Guards that fell to the ground whipped by spasms of a fearful glee. People came to their doors. In the barracks, the Civil Guards cocked their rifles. Children and dogs stopped chasing each other. The old women crossed themselves.

CHAPTER TEN: *Concerning the Place and Time When the Wire Worm Appeared in Yanacancha*

I DIDN'T know about the Fence yet. Since raising cattle doesn't give me enough to live on, I opened a bar on the outskirts of Yanacancha, twenty miles from Rancas. Sergeant Cabrera, who had made many enemies during his time there as a guard, says that Yanacancha doesn't even have a square. It's true. I collected old pieces of corrugated metal and built a cabin. I got hold of a table, a flowery piece of oilcloth, and some benches, and to cheer up the customers I painted a sign: "You're better off here than over there." "There" is the cemetery across the way. The miners liked my watery coffee. What does Yanacancha need a square for? Its hotels are scattered haphazardly along the road down to Huariaca. Winter or summer, the people walk around with their hands in their pockets and their faces hidden in their scarves. Only the noon sun gives a little warmth. Dogs wait anxiously for that warmth, and follow it until it is lost on the plain. Night falls all at once. The wind comes out of the caves and angrily licks at the naked earth. Yanacancha being where Cerro de Pasco ends: in the cemetery. Travelers are surprised when they see that graveyard, too big for the village. The fact is that before the man with the red beard came, Cerro de Pasco had twelve vice-consuls. Prospectors from all over the world climbed up to the snow-covered peaks, looking for the fabulous mother lode. They came for treasure and left their bones. They wasted away their young years wandering around the mountain ranges. One day the fever surprised them, and between fits of delirium they begged that someone would use their gold to buy a good coffin at least. There they are, in their coffins, cursing the snowstorms.

One Thursday, behind one of the cemetery walls, the night gave birth to the Fence.

I crossed myself over and over again. A crowd of men in jackets watched it creep along; before my eyes the Fence crawled around the cemetery and came down the highway. It's the time when the trucks pant toward Huánuco, happy to come down into tree country. At the edge of the highway the Fence stopped, thought for an hour or so, and then split into two. The road to Huánuco began to run between two barbed-wire fences. The Fence crawled along for two miles and headed toward the dark countryside of Cafepampa. Something bad is going on here, I thought. Paying no attention to the hailstorm, I ran to tell Don Marcelino Gora. But Don Marcelino was in no mood for news. That morning a pair of cattle-rustlers—damn them!—had made off with two of his bulls. It was the third time that year that the thieves had shown him their affection. Sitting in the door of his cabin, glaring at the ground, Don Marcelino was brooding over what part he would tear off the thieves' bodies when he put his hands on them. I came up to him in the rain, holding a jute sack over my head.

"Listen, Don Marcelino, a very strange Fence has just been born on the road to Huánuco."

"If I catch those bastards, I'll cut off their balls."

"Don Marcelino, the highway is running between two suspicious-looking barbed-wire fences."

"Someone's cast the evil eye on me, Fortunato. I found crosses drawn with ash on my door."

"A 'strange one' lives in Yanahuanca who solves all the robberies in his dreams, but even he is called Rustler. What do you think of the Fence, Don Marcelino? Wouldn't it be a good idea to ring the bells and call all the people together?"

"They must be engineers, Fortunato."

"When did the roads ever have fences? A fence is a fence; and behind a fence there's always an owner, Don Marcelino."

Don Gora counted the raindrops in a fury.

I went back to the bar. My throat was begging for a drink. The snow was letting up. I went up the hill, and my mouth fell open in surprise: the Fence was swallowing up Cafepampa. That's how the bastard was born, one rainy day, at seven in the morning. At six in the evening it was three miles old. It spent the night at the Trinity watering hole. The next day it ran all the way to Piscapuquio: there it celebrated its six-mile-long birthday. Do you know the five springs at Piscapuquio? It's a treat to drink from them for anyone who comes there. It's a pleasure to remember them when you leave. Now no one will ever love those springs again. The third day the Fence had another three-mile-long birthday. On the fourth it crossed the gold-washings. On these stone skeletons built by the old ones long ago, the Spaniards had washed their gold. I don't advise crossing those wastelands at night: a headless man begs for alms holding his head in his hand. The Fence spent the night there: at dawn it crawled toward the canyon where the highway hurries off to Huánuco. Two uncrossable mountains guard the pass: reddish Pucamina and Yantacaca, always in mourning; even the birds can't fly over them.

On the fifth day the Fence outdid the birds.

CHAPTER ELEVEN: *Concerning the Good Friends and Acquaintances that Héctor Chacón, the Denied, Met as He Left the Huánuco Prison*

IF through sheer stupidity one of the traveling salesmen who come down to Yanahuanca every month selling those samples of flowered fabrics whose splendors cause so many headaches for men bold enough to sleep with two different women—if one of them asks for Héctor Chacón in an offhand way, the permanent guests at the Hotel International stare intently into their greasy stew; and if, obviously bent on driving away customers, the representative of the wholesale firm persists, the guests lose their appetites and leave; and if this hypothetical investigator, carried away by his ill-fated curiosity, goes to the little settlement of Yanacocha that hangs on the side of the mountains a thousand meters farther up, this inquisitive nature will run into a solid wall of negatives: no one knows the man with the strange-looking eyes etched into his face; and if he visits the houses where Héctor Chacón once ate and laughed and got drunk, he will hear the same thing: We don't know the man who came down to the fountain in Yanacocha's main square one muddy afternoon wearing a shirt that mocked at winter; and if the pigheaded traveler directs his steps to the houses of Héctor Chacón's own friends—Agapito Robles', for example, or Isaac Carbajal's—the owners will look him up and down with distrustful eyes and say, "Just a minute." In a little while that inquisitive soul will realize how useless it is to wait: the men he was questioning have jumped over the fences around their patios and vanished into the eucalyptus trees; and if, to have done once and for all with the unfortunate hypothesis, the traveler knocks at the door of Héctor Chacón's own house, his wife will give him the same answer: "I don't know him." For dozens of leagues around, only one person will admit to knowing him.

"I know where Héctor is," says Kid Remigio, the man with the mutilated smile.

"Where is he?"

Kid Remigio bursts into laughter. "He turned into a firefly!"

Nevertheless, on a rainy afternoon Héctor Chacón, the Denied, slowly crossed the square in the direction of the dusty fountain where a peeling angel can no longer shoot his arrow because some son-of-a-bitch broke off one of his arms. He was wearing the same clothes he'd had on when he walked out of the Huánuco jail. Five years earlier he had turned that same corner with his hands tied to a rope pulled by the horses of the Civil Guards. He lit a cigarette. His glance lingered on forgotten objects. He exhaled his second mouthful of smoke. A thin man in a garish plaid shirt, with a yellowish face, slanted eyes, and disheveled hair, embraced him with a look.

"Don Héctor, Don Héctor!" he shouted.

It was Agapito Robles, the new Representative for the community. Héctor Chacón, who could see a spider in the dark, did not recognize him.

"I'm Agapito Robles, Don Héctor," said the Representative while a noisy crowd of children crossed the square, their faces hidden beneath a crust of hardened snot.

Chacón smiled: his unfailing memory did not betray him. The last time he had crossed the square, tied to the twin ropes of the Civil Guard and public disgrace, Agapito had been a boy playing marbles.

"How glad I am to see you, Don Héctor!" he said with emotion.

"Thank you, Don Agapito."

Two other men, a giant almost six feet tall and a stubby man with powerful jaws and square shoulders, shouted as they ran up: "Héctor, Héctor!"

Hawkeye slapped his thighs with joy. "Hey, brother! Hey, pal!"

"I knew you were coming," said the giant with a smile that revealed no teeth.

"How did you find out, comrade?"

The toothless man smiled. "From the animals."

The animals always brought him advance notice of everything. His father, a hunchback skilled in dealing with those who lived on the Other Side, had abandoned him when he was five years old, leaving him the language of the animals as his only inheritance. At seven he talked to the colts; when he was eight, no animal could resist him; and his mother had to use a whip to keep him from spending his whole childhood in conversation with the only teachers who ever taught him anything worthwhile. Every three months necessity, which is even uglier than hitting one's own father, compelled him to go up into the mountains. He did not steal the horses: he wooed them away. With a handful of crisp new bills, he pretended to be interested in buying horses and, taking advantage of careless foremen who were in any case helpless in the face of such skill, he gained the confidence of whole teams of horses, telling them of places where the grass grew taller than a bull and the galloping mares had colossal hindquarters: the animals listened to him with glistening eyes. Horse Thief arranged to meet them in the wilds, and they, more faithful than women, always kept the appointment, and they would go away together through the rough, winding mountain passes. Weeks later he would show up in Canta, in La Unión, or in Yauyos with horses for sale. But he would sell them only after checking the corrals to see that the buyers kept their animals well.

Rustler too, every three months, wrapped himself in a filthy poncho, pulled a wild-colored snow mask down over his face, and took off for the barrens: for weeks he raided the ranches, then crossed the rough Oyón Mountains with his herds. He would reappear, drunk, at rowdy barbecues.

"I've been pardoned," he would laugh.

"Who pardoned you?"

"I've been stealing from the ranches. A thief who robs another thief is forgiven a hundred years of grief."

The ranch-owners, infuriated by the epidemic of rustling, would order the roads to be patrolled, but it was wasted effort. Rustler had the power to foretell the future in his dreams: days before the patrols even thought of searching a particular trail, he knew exactly where they would post the useless snipers.

"Thirty days ago," said Rustler, "I dreamed you came back wearing these same clothes, just like you are now."

And, indeed, he was clairvoyant. People who lost things would pay him a bottle of rum and a sum of money, which he accepted only to prove that he earned a living somehow. He always found the lost articles. Rustler had discovered where the late Matías Zelaya had hidden the deeds to his farm without ever thinking that Death may take a man by surprise. He learned that one of the guests at the Hotel International had been falsely accused of stealing twelve silver teaspoons. The Widow Lovatón herself had accidentally dropped them into a sack of grinding corn. But as the years went by he tried to curtail his power: too frequently the authorities asked him to track down fugitives. Only once did he fail outright: the blacksmith from Yanacocha—a gigantic bull of a man with a tool so inhumanly large that his wife refused to go to bed with him—had forced him to accept a cask of rum: he wanted to learn the identity of the man who was making love to his wife.

At dawn the brute appeared in Rustler's doorway. "What did you dream?"

"I dreamed about fish. I can only see water. The wind keeps me from seeing into my dream," answered a disheartened Rustler.

"What the hell happened to your power?" roared the blacksmith.

People began to laugh. "Rustler is using tricks to get his liquor free." But Rustler knew perfectly well who was sleeping with the blacksmith's wife: *he* was. And he also learned who was warming the pants of the Governor's daughter. In his dream he saw her lying beside the man who would marry her, a teacher from a distant settlement, but he saw so much sadness in his eyes that Rustler preferred to suffer the embarrassment of returning the ten-sol fee.

They embraced and went for a drink.

"This deserves a dozen beers," said Horse Thief.

"Why so stingy, friend?" Rustler asked him.

They entered Don Carmelo's shop, a poorly furnished little room where twenty-four bottles of beer, eight cans of Gloria milk, half a dozen tins of sardines, and a small sack of salt were growing weary on the shelves.

"What'll you have?" asked Don Carmelo, annoyed at the prospect of an afternoon's work. He was a dedicated follower of Saint Tippler's advice: "If alcohol interferes with your work, then stop working."

"Take down a dozen bottles," ordered Agapito Robles.

"Take them all down," Chacón corrected him.

They drank the whole afternoon.

"How are things at home?" Rustler asked him when it was dark.

"I haven't been home," said Chacón, and he turned to Robles. "So you're the new Representative?"

"At your service."

"I suppose you have enough butter."

They all laughed. The former Representatives of the Judge had kept quiet about his land grabs. They had plenty of cheese and butter in their houses: the farmhands brought it down from Huarautambo every week.

"At your service," repeated Robles.

Chacón summed him up shrewdly with eyes that could see toads under rocks. "I want only one thing. That's what I came back for."

"I want it too."

"Are you sure?"

"There are men made of straw and men made of bone, Don Héctor," and courage and fear formed deep pools in his eyes.

Thirty days later Héctor Chacón dreamed that he was riding down a snowy path which was, absurdly, overgrown with flowers. The sound of a lonely song—he could not understand the words—was calling men together: ten, a hundred, two hundred, five hundred, a thousand, four thousand men came down the same road singing the same extraordinary song. For months they rode through different regions of the country, feeling neither thirst nor fatigue, until they found a trail that led to the capital of the province. They went down, they crossed the bridge, they flooded into the square. On seeing this crowd, the Civil Guards fled in terror. The multitude crossed the square and battered down the blue doors of Dr. Montenegro's house. The pale foremen fled, the Judge himself ran from room to room, they chased him through a labyrinth of enormous rooms, some covered with snow, others filled with dense undergrowth, and, still singing, they captured him and took him out to the square. It was three in the morning, but the sun, a sun bright as a diamond, was shining. With their bugles the police officers called together all the men and animals of the province to pass judgment on Dr. Montenegro. The chief of the Guardia Civil was dressed in white and asked: "Is there anyone who has not been hurt by this man?" No one stood up. "Forgive me, I won't do it again," the black suit sobbed. The chief asked the dogs for a statement. "Is there any dog who has not been kicked by this man?" The dogs' tails were still. The chief persisted. "Is there any cat who has not been burned by this man?" The swift birds, the carefree butterflies, the lively chingolo birds, and the sleepy guinea pigs all gave testimony. Not one forgave the Judge. They put him on a burro and expelled him from the province to the sound of music and firecrackers.

Chacón awoke with a dry mouth, got up and went out to the patio, looked for a jug, and took a long drink. It was still dark. He wet his head. He sat on the stone bench to wait for dawn. A week ago, on this same stone, he had been pierced for a second time by the overwhelming urge to kill Dr. Montenegro.

As the dawn broke, the longing to kill him grew stronger and stronger.

He squatted and picked a blade of grass; he chewed on it. It grew lighter. He returned to the room where his wife, eased by his lovemaking, was rearranging his clothes. He took out the new shirt bought in Huánuco with the money from the sale of the last twelve straw chairs he had woven in jail, put it on, and went out to the street. Five minutes later he walked into Rustler's patio.

Squatting on his heels, Rustler was getting ready to slaughter a sheep. "What's the matter with you, Héctor?"

Hawkeye knelt down and helped to tie the animal's legs to the stakes. The sheep bleated feebly. He tied the hind legs. Rustler took out his knife and slit the animal's throat in a single stroke. The blood spurted out into the black cooking pots. A yard away the dogs smelled it and trembled.

"Are there people in this village who can be trusted?"

"To do what?"

"To cut an arrogant man down to size."

Rustler scratched his head. "There might be," and he threw the offal to the dogs.

"Can you get them together?"

Rustler cleaned the blood-stained knife on the grass. "Where?"

"Anywhere, as long as it's at night."

Rustler looked deep into the other man's serious thoughts. "I'll see."

CHAPTER TWELVE: *Concerning the Route Taken by the Worm*

NINE hills, fifty pastures, five ponds, fourteen waterholes, eleven caves, three rivers so deep they don't freeze even in winter, five villages, five graveyards—the Fence devoured them all in two weeks.

Before the Representatives could meet to decide exactly what the Fence was up to, the barbed wire had swallowed up the prairie. Ashen rumors laid waste the plain. Travelers, forced to spend the night in Rancas, whispered that the Fence was not the work of men's hands, that it was springing up in dozens of hamlets all at once, that soon the Fence would come into the villages and even into the houses. Suddenly the Fence raised its head twelve miles away in Villa de Pasco. Fortunato ran, and ran, and ran. Through the red fog of his weariness, Fortunato caught glimpses of the frightened face of Adán Ponce, the frowning faces of the notable citizens of Villa de Pasco. The Fence had infected that area too. Near Villa de Pasco lie two sleepy ponds: Big Yanamate and Little Yanamate, two lonely stretches of water visited only by wild ducks. The Fence appeared between the two ponds. The poor shepherds, who had known for weeks about its outrageous doings, ran to warn Adán Ponce, the leading citizen at Villa de Pasco. Adán stopped fixing a pair of rusty scissors and rode out with twenty men. The Fence was already in the process of swallowing up the Buenos Aires prairie. It spent the night there. The next day it crept on to Buenavista and cut off forty families. The men and women who could not leave their houses began to weep and wail. Their only way out was a treacherous road through the snow-covered mountains. On the third day the Fence climbed the Pumpos Slope and cut off another eighteen families. That afternoon it stopped, ten miles away from its birthplace, on the slippery banks of the San Juan River. It encircled another thirty families. The San Juan River is born in the Chauca Mountains, and is fat with beautiful trout; unfortunately, we never see them here: the water poisoned by mining waste kills them. Down here the San Juan is a river of dead water. But its foul waters did not stop the Fence. The Fence jumped the San Juan and advanced toward Yuracancha, the most miserable village on the prairie. When God Almighty visited the villages around here, he refused to enter Yuracancha. That, at least, is what the inhabitants say, resentful of the barren wasteland that the Lord Jesus Christ conferred on them. Yuracanchans travel many a weary league in search of grassland. That afternoon the Fence appeared. The trembling Yuracanchans came out to fight it, armed with sticks and stones.

But when it was two hundred yards from the village the Fence turned its back, changed direction, and disappeared scornfully into the prairie.

But it did come into Yarusyacán. The unsuspecting men were out watching their sheep. Only the women and the old men were left in the village. The Yarusyacánans are brave men. They would never have allowed the Fence to come into the village. There are a few hunting rifles in Yarusyacán. They would have defended themselves. But until that time the Fence had not violated any village. It devoured land, drank up ponds, swallowed hills, but it had not dared to penetrate the villages. But three hours after it had rejected poor Yuracancha the Fence came down the main street of Yarusyacán without any warning. The women, the only ones there during working hours, ran out screaming, their eyes bulging with fright. The bravest grabbed their slings and attacked the work crews from a distance. The schoolchildren stoned them as well, but one charge on horseback was enough to beat off the ineffectual attack. The Fence divided the village in two: there was no longer any way to go from one side of the street to the other. It passed through Yarusyacán and disappeared into the prairie. Enormous vultures circled around in the ash-colored afternoon.

No one slept in the villages any more. That same evening the last mule-driver came to Rancas: a dealer in prickly pears who had been held up on the roads for three days. He told them: "Gentlemen, this Fence is not only attacking the prairie. The barbed wire is spreading its tentacles over the whole world. It is gulping down whole districts. In some places the people who have been encircled are dying of hunger and thirst. I saw the highway to Huánuco cut off. Another mule-driver, to whom I gave my pears, which were rotting, told me that on the other side of Huariaca there are hundreds of trucks marooned. The passengers are dying and the merchandise is rotting."

The Great Panic came three days later.

All week there had been signs. Don Teodoro Santiago found that the watering places in Yanamate were full of holes. In Junín a cow gave birth to a pig with nine legs. In Villa de Pasco a mouse jumped out when they cut open a sheep. The signs were there for all to see. Even the night before it happened, someone should have been suspicious because the dogs were so nervous. Someone must have told them that the world was being fenced off. Run before it's too late. Someone must have warned them. And the trees were also seized with panic. I did not see it myself, because no trees grow here. But in Huariaca, three thousand feet below, the eucalyptus trees went mad. There was no wind: that is why everyone noticed it. The breeze was sleeping peacefully when the willows and the molle trees were suddenly struck with epilepsy: they twisted, they shivered, they shook, poor things, as if they wished they had feet to run away with. Someone must have whispered to them that the earth was being cut off. They twisted, they wrenched themselves: they drove their thorns into their own bodies. They suffered for half the afternoon and the rest of the night. Some trees managed to drag themselves a few yards. Dawn found them covered with a strange, milky sap. But then nobody felt sorry for the trees: the animals were running away. The foxes, because they were smart, had been escaping since four in the morning. Without a word, without talking to anyone, they went down the highway to La Oroya: thousands and thousands of muzzles cut through the darkness. At seven o'clock people found owls blinded by the light. Someone must have told them. The people knelt down with faces the color of the wall in front of you. Christ, have mercy on us! Blessed Virgin, for the love of Your Son's wounds. And Don Santiago on his knees, whipping the panic into a frenzy: "Confess, sinners, confess before it's too late." And they confessed. Mayta began to bite his nails. Filthy nails, damned nails! "I stole your chickens, Don Jerónimo, I'm a poor thief, forgive me." Don Jerónimo answered with a sob. They embraced, weeping. Clodomiro also confessed: it was he, not Fats, who was guilty of stealing Don Jerónimo's flour. And Odonicio's wife scratched her face as birds and fish fought for the paths in the sky. Black sky, green sky, blue sky, earth-colored sky. Oh, Good God, may my womb be purified in the fire! I fornicated with my brother-in-law! Bring me burning coals to swallow. That's how it happened: taking advantage of Odonicio's sickness, they had wallowed on the floor only a yard away from the paralytic. Crimes were exposed. Rancas, on its knees, raised its helpless hands toward the sealed lips of God.

CHAPTER THIRTEEN: *Concerning the Incredible Good Fortune of Dr. Montenegro*

RUSTLER could not fathom Chacón's thoughts. He plunged into the jet-black pools of his dreams without success. Chacón defied the night. The teller of dreams is powerless against the man who does not sleep. For three nights Rustler wandered through the thickets of his dreams: for three nights Chacón refused to unlock the doors of his waking mind to him. Rustler grew weary and left for the settlements. There are four hundred men in the province who boast of being the Judge's friends, eight hundred eyes more slippery than the icy roads in January. On the pretext of buying animals, Rustler made his way through rundown little villages and arranged to meet those who could be trusted. It was not easy to get them together without arousing suspicion.

Luck was with him. One morning, Doña Josefina de la Torre, Director of the Educational Center for Girls, awoke to the inspired idea of acquiring a globe for the school. "The girls must travel," said the dean of all the gossips in the province. She surprised everyone with her idea of organizing a bazaar. Because they were sympathetic to the idea of their daughters traveling to strange lands, and especially because they wanted Doña Josefina —Fina to her friends—to give her evil tongue a rest, the town supported the project. After two weeks of secret meetings—a real boon to all the sinners—Doña Josefina announced her sensational program. The people were overwhelmed. A yellow poster proclaimed the astounding festivities. Doña Josefina's enemies spread word that half of the events existed only in her imagination, and indeed some of the attractions were symbolic: (1) The Visit of Dawn, (2) Patriotic Reveille by the Most Worthy Civil Guard, (3) General Happiness, (4) The Decoration of the Town with Flags, (5) Firecrackers, (6) Gala Breakfast. But there is no denying that the program also offered attractions known only to the most adventurous travelers: for who else in Yanahuanca had ever heard of sack races, greased poles, and a torchlight parade? And there was more: proving that her talents were wasted on gossip, Doña Josefina devised the two crowning events: the Food Fair and the Raffle of Breeder Sheep. The Director of the Center got every mother to donate her specialty. That is saying a lot. It is easy to deduce from the respectable size of the leading citizens' bellies—stomachs with more than enough room to paint any number of globes on them—that in Yanahuanca cooking is no minor art. There are hands in Yanahuanca that can make a stew out of stones. The women divided up the work: Doña Magda de los Ríos, the Mayor's wife, contributed her celebrated chicken in chili sauce; Doña Queta de Valerio, the Sub-prefect's wife, offered her famous dried-potato stew; Doña Queta de Cisneros promised her tamales, so well known that the Prefect of Cerro de Pasco himself once requested them. A Babylonian feast was organized: roast suckling pig stuffed with nuts and apples, mutton-head broth country style, sweet corn cakes, sensual rice with duck Chiclayan style, roguish baby goat northern style, pompous potatoes Huancayan style, and potatoes Arequipan style, good enough for a gluttonous bishop. The magnum opus would be a huge barbecue. The most worthy Guardia Civil had promised that every animal it confiscated would be buried beneath the spiced volcano of hot stones decorated with the Peruvian flag. The main attraction however was the Raffle of Breeder Sheep. Señor Cisneros, Director of the Boys' School, thought of asking the ranch-owners to donate animals; but Doña

Josefina, in an ecstasy of inspiration, outdid him. Why not ask the Farming Office in Junín for thoroughbreds?

"It's madness," objected Señor Cisneros. "I say this with all due respect, my dear Doña Josefina, but who would ever think of asking a government office for help in a matter concerning the people?"

"All we have to lose is the postage," answered Doña Fina, and she wrote to the Office, which, astonishingly, replied by return mail: it offered to provide twelve Australian sheep "with the sole purpose of fostering the production of fine animals in this worthy province." The election campaigns were approaching. The Senator from Pasco, up for re-election, had instructed the Office to offer "maximum aid to the local communities." But despite the official letter signed and sealed, the people had their doubts. Hadn't the authorities promised to repair the bridge, build the public health center, provide desks for the schools in the outlying settlements, construct the electric power station? Even Doña Josefina continued her negotiations with the ranch-owners, who were apparently indifferent to the girls' desire to see the world. But one muddy Saturday a yellow truck surfaced from the sharp curves of Chipipata: twelve enormous sheep baaed through the grating of the heavy Ford cattle truck. Everyone was in an uproar. The drunks and even the shopkeepers came out of the stores to stare at the magnificent animals.

Rustler did not tell Horse Thief, or Hawkeye, or the Representative that he was dreaming about them. For the first time in his life Rustler was puzzled by a tangle of strange dreams. He dreamed that he went to Tambopampa. For reasons that none of the inhabitants could explain satisfactorily, the sun had stopped at some indeterminate hour and hung motionless in a pallid sky. Night did not approach, the day did not pass. After a few weeks the sun began to rot. Little by little the sunlight turned into tumefaction: on the day he arrived the sky was an open wound, its light draining away drop by drop. With great difficulty Rustler made his way through bloated shreds of sunlight. He went down to the huts. He found Horse Thief sitting on a stone. He was happy to see another human being among all the livid swelling. "Where are you heading for, compadre?" Horse Thief had not noticed the awful transformation of the sky. "Don't you know, compadre? It's nine o'clock! Don't you know?" He laughed and shouted: "Let's go to Murmunia Peak!" "Let's go," agreed Rustler and then he stopped, dumbfounded: Horse Thief stood up on enormous feet. Horse Thief, the most fearless man in any of the communities, was standing on terrifyingly big feet—feet higher than Rustler's waist, toes thicker than his trunklike arms. Rustler was speechless. "Hurry up, compadre," said Horse Thief, "don't waste any time!" Rustler managed to squeeze out a few small drops of voice: "What disease is this, compadre?" Horse Thief uncorked the bottle of his foaming laughter. "Ah, my compadre, this is no disease, this is a precaution!" And he explained that a long, exhausting race had been announced and that he, Horse Thief, was to be the winner. His friends the horses, his hooved cronies the colts, had told him about it. The horses had advised him to let his feet grow. It was easy: all he had to do was to soak them in a pond for seven nights. And yes, each night he had to paint his feet a different color: red, blue, yellow, green. Horse Thief had done what they advised. His laughter shattered the rocks. "I want to see them! I want to see the Sub-prefect's face, the authorities' faces the day they present me with the winner's cup. Who can stop me with feet like these?" And he doubled over, laughing. Rustler awoke trembling. He went out to the patio and put his head down into a bucket of freezing water; while it was still dark he saddled his horse and went up to Pillao to look for Polonio Cruz.

When the onlookers saw the disgust with which the recently arrived sheep refused to eat the humble grass on the main square, it was clear to them that such aristocrats could only come from blond-haired Australia. Even Doña Fina's enemies—those who claimed that if Doña Josefina were to bite her tongue she would drop dead, struck down by poison—acknowledged her accomplishment. A crowd followed the aristocrats to the modest municipal corral. A fierce ambition shone like gold nuggets in everyone's eyes. Imagine what the haughty Australians were worth if even Dr. Montenegro himself interrupted his solar meditation—something which he had done only once before, on the day a certain individual crossed the square with his hands tied to the horses of the Civil Guards—to look at them. He came through his patio door and mingled with the crowd like any ordinary citizen. The people applauded. With his thumbs hooked in his vest and his other fingers stretched across his chest, the Judge headed for the cattle enclosure. The sons-of-bitches made way for him, the dumb animals bleated.

"Who is selling the raffle tickets?" asked the Judge.

Doña Josefina de la Torre, notified by crowds of excited children, ran up breathlessly.

"Oh, how nice!" said the good lady. "How many tickets would you like, my dear Judge?"

"Give me ten, Finita." The Magistrate smiled, and he gave her a new hundred-sol bill.

On Friday afternoon the prisoners, gallantly provided for the occasion by the most worthy Guardia Civil, finished the booths. On Saturday the schoolteachers decorated the posts with charming chains and flowers made of tissue paper.

"I want you to come down to Yanahuanca for some important business," said Rustler.

Polonio Cruz bent his leg and rested it on a stone so that he could scratch it more easily. "What's it about?"

"It's men's business."

"Can't you tell me anything more?"

"No."

Polonio spat out a green glob of coca leaves. "Talk, that's all you can do. I've been in jail three times for meeting behind the backs of the authorities. Nobody even brought me water. What are you? You're all nothing but mouth. You'll run away when the going gets rough."

Rustler was annoyed. "Are you coming or not?"

"Where?"

"To the Quencash ravine at the new moon."

"I'll come," said Polonio.

That's how lightly he decided his fate.

Every young fop in Yanahuanca searched through his trunks for clothes. On Saturday the shopkeepers sold their last bottles of Agua Florida toilet water. By nine o'clock on Sunday every mother in town had her place in the square. Doña Josefina spent an hour trying to stuff her body into a corset she had bought in Huancayo in a fit of wild optimism. At ten the square was packed with people. The authorities—Dr. Montenegro, Sub-prefect Valerio, Don Félix Cisneros, Director of the Boys' school, Doña Josefina de la Torre, the manager of the State Bank, Lieutenant Peralta, the Platoon Officer, Sergeant Cabrera, Corporal Minches—arrived at eleven. They sat down on the platform graciously constructed by the prisoners of the most worthy Guardia Civil. The sun joined the party. A p.a. system rented in Cerro de Pasco played records lent by one of the traveling salesmen.

"I loved her, my brother,
She was the best-looking girl on the block,"

lamented the phonograph as it burst into a flood of tumultuous feeling. The singer proclaimed his misfortune for all the world to hear.

"Today they told me the news,
Her boyfriend has left her."

Sergeant Cabrera interrupted the creole waltz and told the band to play "The Uchumayo Attack." The master of ceremonies shouted at the top of his lungs: "Ladies and gentlemen, the moment this august assembly has been waiting for has finally arrived. Only a few moments to go before the sensational drawing begins! Five seconds, four, three, two! Come and admire them. Animals like these have never been seen before in this province—in this Department. They are the cream of the world's livestock!"

"Three cheers for Doña Josefina!" shouted a student anxious to earn the lady's good graces. "Hip! Hip! Hip!"

"Hurrah!"

Doña Josefina could not control a sob. The master of ceremonies asked permission to begin the drawing. Sub-prefect Valerio removed his hat. A boy dressed in a sailor suit walked up to a small tin barrel painted in the colors of the flag, thanks to the most worthy Guardia Civil. The audience held its breath. A fetid breeze was blowing from armpits inimical to soap and water.

The boy put his hand into the barrel, fished out a number, and handed it to the master of ceremonies.

"Number forty-eight," called out the announcer.

Everyone looked around to see who the lucky person was.

"Here," shouted the choked voice of a man with an unattractive face; it was Egmidio Loro.

"Come up to the platform," ordered Doña Josefina de la Torre.

The man with the pockmarks and blemishes approached the platform with sweating palms.

"Congratulations!" Doña Fina smiled. "Choose any one you like."

"Any one, any one I like!" sighed Loro.

They presented him with a sheep of mythical proportions.

Rustler let Springtime's reins go slack, trusting to the horse's knowledge of the road. He was thinking. For the first time in his life he could not make out the words that the Old Ones were saying to him in his dreams. The Old Man of the Water, the Old Man of the Fire, and the Old Man of the Wind were mouthing sentences made of wool. He could not decipher the message. He tried to purify himself, he fasted for several days, and even ab-

stained from visiting his women. He could hear them no better than before. The Old Ones were showing him a faceless stranger, a man with a wall of smooth flesh for a face crossed by six black lines. The Old Ones led him along the Chinche road and then disappeared among the rocks. The faceless Man with the Six Lines continued walking along the road followed by a crowd of equally faceless men. They were walking toward Murmunia. The faceless men were gasping for breath, and Rustler realized that they were strangers to the mountains. He melted into the ranks. Near Murmunia they saw a man on horseback. Even from a league away the tangled reins revealed the rider's drunkenness. Rustler approached and suddenly paled—the rider was himself. He could not keep from staring at his own face sprinkled with flour, his bull neck wrapped in streamers. What party was he coming from? The other Rustler brushed past Rustler without recognizing him. And even worse: as if the dreamer were invisible, Rustler stopped beside Rustler and urinated streamers. The Other One was not alarmed: he was not so much interested in the ominous stream as in reading the message spelled out in streamers. He could not, and was annoyed. Rustler approached and he tried to read: he could only make out confused words: ". . . carnival . . . pond . . . run, run . . . the baker of dead men."

Rustler pushed his forebodings to one side and saw Sulpicia's hut. The old woman was digging at one end of her small field. He tied up the horse and went toward the perspiring woman.

"Working on Sunday, Mamá?"

"Don't my children eat on Sunday?" Sulpicia smiled gently with only one side of her toothless mouth.

"Can you come down to a secret meeting, Mamá?"

"I can come down, but I'm not sure of coming back up again." She wiped her sweaty brow. "There are lots of people who talk too much."

"Chacón wants to talk to you."

The woman's eyes burned like two flames brighter than the noonday sun. "So Héctor's come back to settle his debts!"

"I don't know, Mamá."

"But you know everything. I wouldn't come down for any of the rest of you. You're nothing but mouth, but I'll go for Héctor's sake. He's one man who has it in for the ones in power." And she knelt down to take a drink of cool water from the jug.

And at this point the histories grow confused. Certain chroniclers claim that as soon as the Judge heard the winning number he tore up his tickets and banged on the table shouting: "This is a swindle!" Other historians object, stating that he did not bang on the table, but all agree on what he said next. "This man," said the Judge, pointing at Loro with his index finger, "is related to the people who organized the raffle." The onlookers shuddered: the Magistrate's accusation was true. Loro with the blemished face really was the brother-in-law of Doña Josefina de la Torre's niece three times removed. Not even the winner had known that his wife—who apparently had left him three years before because he beat her—enjoyed this slenderest of family connections with a lady so distinguished as Doña Josefina, whose threshold, it must be noted, he had never crossed. The Judge's implacable memory had uncovered the deception. One cannot march in the procession and ring the bells at the same time. The feet of the organizers turned to ice. On less evidence than this there were people rotting in the Yanahuanca prison. The Judge's stormy face showed his inflexible determination to prevent the exploitation of an honest and simple people's faith. In the silence following that moment when justice let one of her heavy scales fall, only Don Herón, the Mayor, a man who displayed savage courage on such occasions, could manage to whisper: "Put on the music!"

"Loving is no sin,
Even God has loved.

"My blood may not be noble,
But it's as red as any other,"

lamented the phonograph. The waltz insisted on the misfortune that besets the poor man who dares raise his eyes toward a decent woman. All the fires of Purgatory will not wipe out the unforgivable original sin: poverty. Again the waltz laid bare the centuries of prejudice, the universal hatred of love, while Don Herón engaged Doña Josefina in conversation behind the platform. What did they say to each other? Did Don Herón confess his love to Doña Fina? Did they agree to meet at some isolated spot along the river? No one knows. That moment is in shadow. With faces that revealed nothing about the historic enigma, Don Herón and Doña Fina returned to the stands.

"Which numbers do you have, Judge?" asked an agitated Don Herón.

Dr. Montenegro proffered his raffle tickets at the end of a scornfully extended arm, while Doña Josefina, with blushing cheeks—had Don Herón told her he loved her?—was getting things back to normal.

"Go on," she ordered.

"They drawing a winner, they're drawing a winner!" barked the master of ceremonies. The little sailor turned the tin barrel. Lovers took advantage of the suspense to hold hands. Destiny's messenger took out a ticket and handed it to Doña Josefina.

"Thirteen," sang out the Director of the Center.

"Who has number thirteen?" asked Don Herón.

"I do," answered Dr. Montenegro modestly.

The Judge had not flinched before the ghastly reputation of the number repudiated by all superstition: a grateful thirteen changed his luck for the better. And seven, admired by the cabalists, rewarded him with the second sheep; thirty-four—a fat, respectable number—presented him with the only black-spotted animal; zero, the height of Hindu wisdom, gave him the fourth, a splendid stud which was, unfortunately, to die that same week; seventy-six brought the fifth sheep to his corral. The people were struck dumb with joy at such good fortune. It is unusual for a crowd to be silent, but that is what happened in Yanahuanca. Drawn by the magnet of his awesome good luck, the people left the booths. These simple folk did not know what to make of it.

"It's incredible!"

"What luck!"

"When God gives, He gives with both hands!"

"Such luck with such unlucky numbers!"

"Sixty," Señora Josefina called out.

"Here!" answered a radiant Doña Pepita.

"I'll sit in for you, my friend," joked the Sub-prefect.

"Your turn will come," the Magistrate consoled him, and to Señora Josefina: "It's too much, Doña Fina, I'll withdraw, Finita!"

"No, no, no," said Doña Fina self-righteously. "Do you want to insult us? Will any of us allow the dear Judge to withdraw?"

"If that's the case, I'll stay the rest of the afternoon, Finita."

Ninety, a dark number with no ancestors, made him owner of the ninth sheep, and sixty-nine, a number that always provokes scoundrels to laughter, sent the tenth sheep into his corral. The people could not shake off their fascinated silence. The loud-speaker played a tango which proclaimed the futility of fighting against destiny: "You never win when you play with fate," lamented the unforgettable Carlitos Gardel.

CHAPTER FOURTEEN: *Concerning the Mysterious Disease Which Ravaged the Rancas Flocks*

THE highway to Cerro de Pasco was a sixty-mile-long necklace strung with dying sheep. Starving herds chewed the last blades of grass growing on the narrow strips of land tolerated by the Fence on either side of the highway. That grass lasted two weeks. The third week the livestock began to die. By the fourth week one hundred eighty sheep had died; by the fifth, three hundred twenty; by the sixth, three thousand.

They thought it was an epidemic. Señora Tufina bought an ointment for the treatment of worms. Her daughter brought some holy water besides. Neither the ointment nor the holy water could stop the sheep dying. They died by the thousands. The highway ran between a set of gums covered with flecks of white spittle.

"It's the wrath of God, the wrath of God!" bellowed Don Teodoro Santiago as he drew crosses on the houses of the slanderers and the adulterers. "You are to blame! Because of your rotten tongues and your filthy desires, the good God has spat on Rancas!"

The sinners knelt down. "Forgive us, Don Santiago."

"Don't ask me for forgiveness, you sacrilegious fools! Pray to God!"

That night the old men stoned the house of Mardoqueo Silvestre. Mardoqueo has the tongue of a viper. And not only that:

Mardoqueo knows about herbs. On certain moonlit nights he has been seen wandering through Stone Forest. The old men got together and stoned his house.

Mardoqueo came out with the picture of Our Lord of Miracles and knelt down in the mud. "I swear my thoughts are clean! I swear by my soul that I have nothing to do with those on the Other Side!"

"What do you do in Stone Forest?"

"I hunt for vizcachas, neighbors."

"Do you swear you'll never slander again, Mardoqueo?"

"Good neighbors, I swear on my soul," answered Mardoqueo, kissing the holy card.

The old men sprinkled Mardoqueo's door with holy water. It did no good. The sheep continued dying. The old men were desperate. Not even in the hidden corners of their memories could they find anything like this.

"Our hour has come," said Valentín Robles. "Soon they'll fence in the village. We'll turn into cannibals. The father will eat his own child; the child will eat his own mother."

"If we could, we would go to other villages to beg, but what's the use? There is nothing but wind on the prairie."

"It would be better for us to die. I hope the Fence does come into the village. I hope we all die. Once we're dead we won't have to ask anyone for anything."

"The Day of Judgment is approaching! The Fence is only a sign. You'll see: not only will the animals run away, soon the dead will rise!"

"In Yurahuanca they found graves without corpses."

A fat, pale man, splattered with mud, spoke from the doorway. "It is not God, neighbors, it's the Cerro de Pasco Corporation!"

It was Pisser, a Huanacayan who came to Rancas every year selling odd merchandise: magnetic belts, ointments to combat witchcraft, syrup of jimson weed for attracting men, salves to prevent nightmares. That year he was selling guitar strings. In every village there is a guitar that cannot be played for lack of an

E string. The owner is ready to pay any price for what he needs. The result: Pisser always had plenty of beer.

"The Fence," said Pisser, "is over sixty miles long."

"How do you know?"

"Who has a match?"

Representative Rivera handed him one.

"And now, who has a cigarette to go with this match?"

Without a cigarette he would not talk. They passed him an Inca. He inhaled the smoke greedily.

"The Fence is more than sixty miles long," he repeated. "The barbed wire begins in San Mateo."

The people despaired.

"The Fence begins at milestone one hundred on the road to Lima."

"Who is the owner?" asked Representative Rivera.

"The Cerro de Pasco Corporation."

"How do you know?"

"I have friends who are drivers," said Pisser, gulping down a glass of rum.

"And where does it end?" asked Rivera in a choked voice.

"It doesn't end," said Pisser, knocking back his second drink. "It's going to fence in the whole world."

CHAPTER FIFTEEN: *The Most Curious History of Aching Hearts Not Born of Sadness*

ONLY Don Medardo de la Torre, Don Migdonio's father, did not mind spending his life on horseback in an effort to measure with his own eyes the endless boundaries of El Estribo Ranch. Don Migdonio de la Torre, a haughty tower of muscle topped by a Spanish head warmed by imperial whiskers, preferred to find consolation in reading through his title deeds. But the boundaries of his estate, which ranged over three different climates, the size of the harvests, the fattening of the livestock were not what interested him. The only things that lit up his blue eyes were his "goddaughters." He had hundreds of them. All of his farmhands' daughters belonged to him. Rather than the dubious honors of the Senatorship that was repeatedly offered to him, he preferred the feathery fields of his enormous bed that rested on four solid eagles' talons. A stuffed condor spread immense wings over his wakeful bed. Nothing—not the ledger of the Ranch Store, or the Livestock Register, the wholesale and retail accounts which bore witness to his wealth—nothing absorbed him like the Register of Births. Greedily he turned the pages of the book where they entered the date of birth of every girl born on El Estribo Ranch. On her fifteenth birthday each was brought to his bed to improve the breed. This was not unusual on the ranches. What was astonishing was the legendary appetite of his third leg. It was insatiable.

Five girls a day were not enough for him, and once, after breaking the back of every whore in a Huánuco brothel, he went outside to water the flowers with his own snow-white dew. It was colossal. His own field hands were proud of the vigor of his tool, and they often took bets on how many goddaughters he would wear out on the nights when sleep eluded him. Besides his nocturnal exercise, his only other interest was testing his strength. From time to time he would leave his bedroom to show the strength of his oaken arms. None of the men who tamed horses could withstand the pressure of his grip. Only Espíritu Félix, a boy who could throw a young bull by the horns, was able to match but not surpass Don Migdonio's strength.

But fame called him away from his perpetual orgasm.

What motivated the Platoon Officer to look for conscripts at El Estribo? A mystery. One Friday the Lieutenant appeared at El Estribo, wearing his uniform and his regulation pistol and looking for men eligible for service. Don Migdonio greeted him with a smile tinged with mockery and good breeding, but the Lieutenant was unmoved. Not even the goddaughters that Don Migdonio sent along to his room changed his mind. The orders from headquarters were final. None of the ranches was to be exempted. The next morning Don Migdonio capitulated as he stood before a steaming barbecue.

"At least," he sighed, "let me choose the conscripts."

"No problem there, Don Migdonio," conceded the Platoon Officer.

Don Migdonio ordered the field hands to line up in the great stone patio. He told them to open their mouths: he chose the five best sets of teeth to serve their country: Encarnación Madera, Ponciano Santiago, Carmen Rico, Urbano Jaramillo, and Espíritu Félix. The boys shed enormous tears. The Lieutenant took them away immediately. Don Migdonio, who had dressed only to receive the Lieutenant, returned to the giant bed on the eagle talons: that day two of the goddaughters he desired most were having birthdays.

The incident was forgotten until thirty months later when the recruits came back to the ranch from military service with the dazzling spectacle of their new boots. They all left Cerro de Pasco proudly because of their new boots, but Madera, Santiago, Rico, and Jaramillo lost their courage as they approached El Estribo. When they were a league away they prudently took off their boots. Only Espíritu Félix came into the patio of the ranch house tapping his heels. The barracks had transformed him. In the solitude of the watchtowers, other soldiers had shown him how big the world was. In the cold of the outposts he had learned that there was something called a Bill of Rights, a Constitution, that protected even pig farmers and uneducated country boys. And he learned more: that a mysterious piece of writing proclaimed that the powerful and the humble were equal. And something else: one night when they were celebrating Santiago's birthday in a back alley in Vitarte, a party to which they dared to invite their corporal, the noncommissioned officer from Cuzco astounded them with the news that a man named Blanco was organizing a farmers' union in the ranches of the south.

"What does that mean, Corporal?"

"It's something like a brotherhood to fight the exploiters."

He did not really understand, but five weeks later, not to celebrate a birthday but to console themselves at being snubbed by some maids who were proud of working in Miraflores, they found refuge in a miserable little bar in Chorrillos. That Saturday a sergeant from Chinche named Fermín Espinoza explained it all to him.

"It would be a good idea to organize that brotherhood on El Estribo," said Espíritu, his eyes shining.

"Nobody is man enough to do that to Don Migdonio," sniffed Jaramillo, who was drunk.

Espíritu made a cross with his fingers. "I am," he swore, and kissed the cross.

When Don Migdonio saw Espíritu's marvelously polished boots from the window, he ran down the wide stone stairs three at a time.

"Good morning, Boss," Espíritu managed to say with an uneasy smile inspired by memories of their tests of strength.

"Damn it, you're taking those boots off right now, you shit!" roared Don Migdonio. "Who do you think you are, Mr. High-and-Mighty? I'm the only one who wears shoes on this ranch. Do you hear me, you miserable son-of-a-bitch?" He was frothing at the mouth, on the verge of apoplexy.

Espíritu's eyes filled with tears, but he did not dare reply or even look at the fire where his kerosene-soaked boots were burning. For Madera, Santiago, Jaramillo, and Rico, prudence paid off. Their bags were not searched, and they kept their boots. Just to recall their days in the barracks, a time which was disappearing down into the ragged seas of habit, they would take out their rough boots every once in a while and admire them privately. Thirty years later, on his deathbed, Santiago would beg to be allowed to see his boots.

But Espíritu did not give up. His sorrow over the burning shoes was combined with the fervor of that distant oath. Delicately, like someone feeling a broken ankle, he continued to caress the farmhands' courage. Santiago was the only one of the five who had shared blows and sorrows in Lima who failed to join in. After twenty-two months of meeting secretly in caves and lonely mountain passes, Espíritu suddenly confronted a dozen hands with his dream of the great brotherhood. Incredibly, they accepted.

"They'll hang us upside down," shuddered Jaramillo.

"Nobody ever died of that," Espíritu Félix retorted.

That winter he dared the impossible: he asked to speak to Don Migdonio. The servants listened to the request and slammed the door in his face. He persevered for three days. On the fourth day they let him in. Don Migdonio, who perhaps remembered the old challenges, agreed to go out to the patio. There under one of the stone arches was the unbelievable sight of Espíritu dressed in his corporal's uniform. But the anger that consumed Don Migdonio did not burn in his blue eyes.

"So you want to form a union?"

"With your permission, Boss."

"Aha!"

"We'll be happier in our work."

"Aha! How many of you are there?"

"There are a few, Boss."

"How many?"

"Twelve, Boss."

"It's not a bad idea. Get them together and come to see me. I want to talk to all of you."

They could not believe it. Not only had Espíritu walked out of the ranch house a free man, but Don Migdonio, in a polite voice heard by all the house servants, had invited him to come back. They were enraptured. Félix held a meeting with the other conspirators. There were now fifteen instead of twelve. A week later they appeared before the imperial whiskers of Don Migdonio. Perhaps it was that he had found a gold nugget between the legs of one of his goddaughters, perhaps the brilliant morning stirred his benevolence; at any rate, Don Migdonio asked them to come in. They felt they were going too far: from time immemorial nobody could remember any field hand ever having been inside the ranch house. To try to organize a brotherhood is one thing, to fraternize with the bosses is another. Whether it was a mere whim, or the fulfillment of a vow he had made to the memory of his dear mother, Don Migdonio repeated the invitation. There was nothing they could do but go inside. Their throats were dry. Félix could not help remembering the afternoon when, standing to attention at six paces, he had spoken to a colonel, which is almost the same thing as talking to a ranch-owner.

"Come in, boys, sit down," said Don Migdonio from the doorway as if he were under the spell of a love potion.

Almost as if in a dream they saw the red leather armchairs and the sofas flecked with yellow flowers, the furniture snowy with lace antimacassars crocheted by the marble-white hand of the mother of the man they were trying to harm. "This is enough, Boss," they answered. The brine of betrayal burned in their mouths.

"What is it you want, boys?" asked Don Migdonio affably.

Espíritu felt his knees tremble. "Boss, I . . ."

"Look, Félix, you can stop worrying. I'll tell you once and for all that I'm not opposed to the union. It's all right with me," he said as simply as if he were telling them "Just drink from the river" or "You can urinate out of doors." "No, I have nothing against it; on the contrary, I congratulate you. I want the ranch to progress and to change. Let's have a drink on it!"

And he turned to a servant.

"Bring me the decanter of rum from the dining room."

The servant—it was he who had closed Don Medardo's eyes!—went out not bothering to hide the disgust which this apotheosis of ingratitude aroused in him. He returned with the decanter and served the drinks.

"I'll toast with an empty glass. I had too much last night," said Don Migdonio jovially. "Okay, boys, cheers!"

To escape the whirling dizziness, they downed their drinks in one gulp. Don Migdonio ordered that the glasses be refilled.

They emptied their glasses again.

"What's wrong?" said Jaramillo, raising his hands to his throat. "I can't breathe."

"Something doesn't agree with me," whispered a livid Madera, clutching at his stomach.

He was the first to fall. Three others fell to the floor as if struck by lightning, and the bodies of the others writhed with agonizing stomach cramps. Don Migdonio stared at them all with a stony look. Too late Rico understood everything. He knocked over the portrait of Don Migdonio's mother in his dying spasm, but he was too far gone to spit on it.

"Son-of-a-bitch . . . !" Espíritu Félix managed to say before he spat out his poisoned guts.

Fifteen minutes later, work crews with bulging eyes pulled them out feet first, the contorted faces barely hidden in their ponchos. The patio was pierced by mourners' cries, but the relatives had no time for weeping. The mules were ready. For the one thing that Don Migdonio feared most was the Evil Eye. That giant who bowed before no human trembled in his bed whenever the dogs howled at a passing spirit. He allowed no burials on his ranch. As soon as a dying man had given up the ghost, his relatives rushed to wrap him in a sheet filled with aromatic herbs.

On a donkey or on a mule, the dead began what was really their last journey to distant graves dug beyond the boundary lines of El Estribo where the bitter gall of the dead could not kill the flowers or poison the water. There was no time for weeping. The wake was a long walk. But since El Estribo extended almost indefinitely, one had to travel for days to dispose of the corpses. At first the freezing mountain weather preserved them, but later the heat of the passes overcame the desperate efforts of nostrils stuffed with rue. Even the mules suffered because of the dead, angry at having no candles, no prayers.

They took them out at twelve o'clock. At twelve thirty one of the servants galloped in the other direction. Five days later he sent the following telegram: "Dr. Montenegro, Judge of the Lower Court, Yanahuanca: Respectfully inform you death fifteen hands El Estribo Ranch due mass thrombosis. Migdonio de la Torre."

"What the hell!" said Dr. Montenegro.

CHAPTER SIXTEEN: *Concerning the Changing Colors of the Cerronians' Faces and Bodies*

SIX minutes before noon on March 14, 1903, the color of the Cerronians' faces changed for the first time. Until then the happy citizens of rainy Cerro de Pasco had had copper-colored faces. But on that day their faces changed: a man came out of a bar where he had been drinking a poisonous rum and his face and body were blue; the next day another man who had got drunk in the same bar turned green; three days later a man with orange face and hands walked through Carrión Square. It was only a few days before Carnival: everyone thought they were practicing to be devils. But Carnival came and went and people kept on changing color.

Cerro de Pasco is the highest city in the world. Its narrow streets twist and turn at an altitude greater than that of the highest mountains in Europe. It is a city where it rains two hundred days a year. Day breaks on a perpetual snowfall. Cerro de Pasco crouches at the end of the Junín prairie. Even for the drivers, wrapped in scarves up to their eyes, the prairie is a difficult journey. All the truck-drivers paste pictures of the Blessed Virgin of Humay on their windshields; they commend their trucks to Her care. Don't let any breakdown happen on this endless plain gleaming perpetually with ice, on this prairie where soroche, the mountain sickness, strikes so many lowlanders! Travelers who know that desolate wasteland guarded by the jealous eye of Junín Lake cross themselves as soon as they enter the rocky passes of La Oroya. Virgin Mary, Guardian of Travelers, help us! Saint Tecla, Protectress of Pilgrims, pray for us! they plead, green through lack of oxygen, biting down on the lemons that do no good against the nausea that comes from too little oxygen. The strings of lemons and the prayers are useless in the treeless wasteland. Those who don't go down to Huánuco see neither trees nor flowers: they have never seen them; they don't grow here. Only the dwarf grass defies the anger of the winds. Without that grass, without the icchu, no one would survive. That coarse stubble feeds the flocks of sheep, their only wealth. Thousands of sheep browse on the prairie until three in the afternoon. At four the guillotine of darkness falls. Sunset is not the end of the day; it is the end of the world.

What was it that brought men to this province of hell? Mineral ore. For four hundred years Cerro de Pasco has hidden the most fantastic deposits in Peru. There, on a naked hill, brushing almost against the testicles of the sky, the battered graves of the prospectors are lined up in rows. They came for fortune and left their bones: Three hundred years after the pigheaded Galicians, came the hard Germans, the suspicious Frenchmen, the rigid Serbians, the dangerous Greeks; all of them sleep in their graves cursing the snow.

The deposits gave out in 1900. Cerro de Pasco, proud of her twelve vice-consuls, died. Miners, shopkeepers, restaurant-owners, and whores all left. Nobody stayed in Cerro. The district census of 1895 lists 3,222 houses. In the next five years the wind blew down 2,832 of them. Cerro gradually reverted to wasteland. In 1900 there were only a few houses huddled around Carrión Square when a blond giant arrived one evening during Holy Week. He had laughing blue eyes, a flaming red beard, and an enormous capacity for feasts and drunken orgies. He was an engineer and a phenomenal fornicator who mixed with the people right from the beginning and got along well with them. At first everyone distrusted the Yankee, but they saw that the redbeard was more interested in looking for the Indian girls than in surveying mine galleries with instruments, and they became more friendly. The gringo spent several months collecting samples and improving the breed. People took a liking to him. Unfortunately, the redbeard went off his head. One afternoon at about three o'clock he went into the Brave Man of Huandoy, a rundown little bar where a case of whiskey from the good old days still survived. He drank one bottle, then two, then three. At dusk he went out into the street to pass the whiskey around. At seven he went berserk. Perhaps he had had too much to drink; perhaps the altitude had finally got hold of him: he began to laugh as if he had been bewitched. The people kept on drinking—they were getting drunk at the laughing man's expense—but little by little, when his laughter turned into a waterfall of guffaws, into a foaming sea, into a surging tide of merriment, they grew afraid and left. They had no reason to. An hour later the man with the unforgettable beard the color of the setting sun dried his tears, put down a little pile of gold coins, and walked out of the Brave Man of Huandoy. He never returned.

The owner of that laughter had had the last laugh on the miners and prospectors of the past four hundred years, the last laugh on Cerro de Pasco, on the wind that carries away houses, on the three-foot-deep snowfalls, on the ceaseless rain, on the dead who shiver with cold, on the loneliness. He had discovered the most fabulous mother lode in the history of American mining right underneath the exhausted veins. After four hundred years of enriching kings and viceroys, Cerro de Pasco was still virgin. The city itself, the dying town, had built its hovels over the most incredible deposits in Peru. The rundown, unpainted houses, the bare, treeless squares, the muddy streets, the Prefecture on the verge of collapse, the one school—all were nothing more than the crust that covered massive wealth.

The Cerro de Pasco Corporation was established in 1903. But that's another story. The Cerro de Pasco Corporation, Inc., of

Delaware, known here simply as the Cerro or the Company, showed that the creator of the unforgettable laughter, the legendary goatbeard, knew what he was laughing about. The Company built a railroad, brought in unheard-of machinery, and built a foundry three thousand feet below in La Oroya, where the single smokestack asphyxiated all the birds for thirty miles around. Attracted by the pay, a crowd of ragged men climbed up to the mines. Soon thirty thousand men had dug mine galleries deep into the earth. In Cerro de Pasco the Company built itself a monument to architectural ugliness, a squat three-story building, the Stone House, center of the greatest mining empire known in Peru since the days of Philip II. The ledgers of the Cerro de Pasco Corporation show that in fact the man with the beard the color of the setting sun had permitted himself only the smallest of chuckles. In a little more than fifty years, Fortunato's age, the Cerro de Pasco Corporation had excavated more than five hundred million dollars' worth of net profits.

In 1900 no one would have dreamed it possible. The Company, which paid the extraordinary wages of two sols, was joyfully welcomed by everyone. A crowd of beggars, of fugitives from the ranches, of reformed cattle-rustlers, streamed into Cerro de Pasco. Only months afterward did they discover that the smoke from the foundry was killing the birds. One day they learned that it could also discolor human beings: the miners began to change color; the smoke produced a variety of hues: red faces, green faces, yellow faces. And better still, if a blue face married a yellow face, they produced a green face. At a time when Europe had not yet discovered the ecstatic pleasures of Impressionism, Cerro de Pasco was enjoying a permanent carnival. Of course, many were frightened and returned to their villages. The rumors spread. The Cerro de Pasco Corporation posted a bulletin on every streetcorner: the smoke was harmless. And as for the colors, the change was a unique tourist attraction. The Bishop of Huánuco gave sermons saying that the change in color was a protection against adultery. If an orange face went to bed with a red face, they could not possibly produce a green face: it was a kind of guarantee. The city calmed down. One July 28 the Prefect declared from the speaker's podium that at this rate the Indians would soon be blond, and this hope of turning into white men ended all their doubts. But the farmers did not stop complaining: seed was not growing anywhere, neither in the blue earth nor in the yellow earth. A few months later—1904—the Cerro announced that, despite the notorious lie that the smoke was poisoning the land, the Company would buy all of it in good faith. And in fact it bought the Nazarene Ranch of forty thousand acres from the Convent of the Nazarenes. That is how the Livestock Division of the Cerro de Pasco Corporation was born. But the barbed-wire fence of the Nazarene Ranch did not rest: it soon enclosed the Pachayacu Ranch, and then the Cochas Ranch, and then the Puñascochas Ranch, and then the Consac Ranch, and then the Jatunhuasi Ranch, and then the Paria Ranch, and then the Atocsaico Ranch, and then the Puñabamba Ranch, and then the Casaracra Ranch, and then the Quilla Ranch. The Livestock Division kept growing and growing.

By 1960 the Cerro de Pasco Corporation owned more than 1,250,000 acres. Half of all the land in the district. In August 1960, maddened perhaps by the passage of half a century, perhaps because it suffered an attack of soroche, the mountain sickness, the Fence could no longer contain itself. In its delirium it longed for the whole world. And it began to travel.

One day an unscheduled train stopped at the railroad crossing in Rancas.

CHAPTER SEVENTEEN: *The Sufferings of Kid Remigio*

IT was Rustler in person who crossed the Yanahuanca square at six in the morning leading a magnificent chestnut horse to the bakery where Kid Remigio was sleeping. But Kid Remigio was not sleeping: he was waiting, fully dressed. Rustler arrived leading Dapple by the reins, and then he crossed the square again with Remigio. The Kid was wearing a red flannel shirt, an orange neckerchief, and one of Rustler's hats. The early risers rubbed their eyes. That a man as haughty as Rustler should ride down from Yanacocha with a horse—the best saddle horse after the winged Triumphant, which at that moment was being saddled for Hawkeye!—for an insignificant creature like Kid Remigio seemed like witchcraft. They rode across the square arrogantly.

Baby Consuelo was coming out of mass. The maiden could not believe the splendid sight, and her mouth fell open in wonder. The disdainful hunchback did not even look at her. Baby Consuelo had been rejecting Kid Remigio for ten years. The object of the passion that filled the bow-legged lover's soul was a dwarf with red bulging eyes, a body overwhelmed by an enormous belly, and a head of hair flaked with dandruff. Her only beauty lay in the burning brands of her eyes, bright with hatred for cats and contempt for Kid Remigio. She doused the cats with boiling water, and she insulted Kid Remigio in public. Why did Remigio adore her so? If Baby Consuelo were made up by the angels and had her hair combed by the Hand of God Himself, and if she were to appear before all creation and God were to ask "Who wants to marry this girl?" even the damned would look away. But fate, which takes pleasure in ridiculing man, decreed that the only human being capable of loving Baby Consuelo should live in the same century, the same country, and even the same town as she did. Baby Consuelo showed no gratitude. If someone, just to annoy her, would say "Your boyfriend is waiting for you on the corner," this Dulcinea would spit with leaden anger, "Someday I'll get my hands on that cripple and drown him in the river!" and bitterly predict that Remigio's hump would "one day rot." The Kid did not even dare to climb the belltower to spy on her. The gossips whispered that once some people from Tusi had found them all tangled up together among the weeds along the river. Did that explain the morbid hatred of Baby Consuelo and the doglike devotion of Kid Remigio?

Step by step, taking pleasure in the silver riding gear, the hunchback rode into the last morning of his life on a horse meant only for sub-prefects. On that same corner, thirty-nine hours earlier, Kid Remigio had dared to offer a bouquet of bellflowers to Baby Consuelo. Remigio had approached her with the gentle smile that won over even the greediest of shopkeepers—they gave him broken crackers—and offered her, tried to offer her, the innocent flowers. Baby Consuelo spat in his face.

"You llama, you vicuña!" responded the pale, insulted lover.

In his despair Kid Remigio had resorted to slander. Vicuñas, those mysterious animals swift as a shooting star, did indeed spit, but they walked with an elegance that this virgin would never equal.

Baby Consuelo drooled with amazement. Not deigning to look at her, the rider wheeled Dapple in every direction. Rustler stopped and stared in surprise. Baby Consuelo had turned her eyes too late toward the unyielding horseman.

In Yanacocha, the Representative went into the house of Héctor Chacón, the Denied. Either the night or his wife had calmed him.

"Are you ready, Héctor?"

Chacón raised his arms. "Today I will stain my hands with the blood of an abusive man."

The Representative scratched his head; slowly his fingers searched out the louse bites. "Héctor, the Inspector suspects something."

They turned their heads at the same time.

"How do you know?"

"This morning I went to greet him in his room. He saw me while he was eating breakfast. 'Listen,' he warned me very seriously, 'I'm letting you know that only the authorities will go to the hearing.' 'But, sir, the community has made plans.' 'Nothing doing. If you insist, I won't go.' "

"Is that what he said?"

The Representative was embarrassed. "He said something else."

"What?"

" 'Under no circumstances will Héctor Chacón be one of the five who accompany me.' "

"But the Inspector doesn't even know me!"

"He knows you."

"Some son-of-a-bitch must have talked to him."

"Nobody talked to him."

"You're all so scared, it's written all over you."

The Representative was sweating. "Héctor, Bustillos advises us not to commit the crime. He's been an authority for a long time. He knows the law. We're in no position, Héctor."

While the Representative was not looking, Rustler winked at Hawkeye.

"Don't do it," pleaded the Representative. "Don't dirty yourself with this crime."

"Why have I made my plans? Am I some kind of puppet?"

"Don't murder that man."

"It's not murder. It's justice."

"You can't do anything by yourself."

"All right," said Chacón with resignation, more determined than ever.

"Do you have a gun?"

"You can arrest me if you want."

They heard the bells ring for the third time.

"Let's go," said Rustler. "It's late."

They mounted the horses. The square in Yanacocha was filled with men on horseback. The Rabi district and the Tambo district were lined up behind their flags. The women were herded around Sulpicia: the married women waited behind a red flag, the single ones behind a yellow flag, the widows behind a black flag.

Sulpicia saw Chacón and came up to Triumphant. The men in charge of the corrals, who, like all the Yanacochans, knew that Chacón's soul was on fire, had given him Triumphant, the best horse in the community.

"May Christ the Kind be with you!" said the old woman. "May Christ the Protector watch over you! May God guide your hand, my friend!"

Chacón's stormy face did not soften. "Do you know that the Inspector has said that the community can't go?"

Sulpicia's face turned pale. "Who says so?"

"The Representative himself says so."

"Only the authorities will go," said the Representative awkwardly. Fear and confusion flooded his eyes.

"The land doesn't belong to one man," said Sulpicia. "It belongs to everybody, and everybody will go. The reason Montenegro doesn't want a lot of people around is so that he can take advantage of us."

Ignoring the Representative, she turned around. "What will we do, Héctor?"

"We'll go, Mamá. The authorities will go with the Inspector, but you'll follow and keep out of sight."

"Take clubs and slings with you," advised Rustler.

"Rustler and Horse Thief will ride with me. You, Sulpicia, stay at the head of the community. You'll follow us by the shortcut. We'll meet at Parnamachay. I'll go with the authorities, but I'll turn back to warn you. If I raise my hand and shake a handkerchief, you come running."

They left. The hired trumpets and drums were mute; they marched in silence toward Huarautambo. The authorities waited until the community had rounded the bend and then they headed for Inspector Galarza's room. The Inspector, rested after a good night's sleep, was sitting in the warm sun on the patio.

"Good morning, Señor Inspector," said the Representative. "Did you sleep well?"

"Very well, very well," answered the red-faced man.

"Did you enjoy your breakfast?"

Melecio de la Vega rode up leading a splendid chestnut horse saddled with Huancayan gear.

"A very fine horse," complimented the Inspector, and he turned to the Representative. "You know what I said. If the people insist on being there, I'm not going."

"Why, Señor Inspector?" asked Chacón in a voice so respectful that Galarza could not help answering.

"I've had many years of experience. I've attended many hearings. If there's a crowd, you can't do anything."

"But the land," insisted Chacón's velvety voice, "belongs to everybody."

They rode past the last houses. The morning shone silver through the eucalyptus trees.

CHAPTER EIGHTEEN: *Concerning Fortunato's Anonymous Battles*

BY September more than thirty thousand sheep were dead. Deafened by the thunder of their misfortune, the villagers could only weep. Sitting in the woolly sea of their dying sheep, they sobbed without moving, their eyes fixed on the highway.

On the third Friday in September, Representative Rivera sent for Father Chasán. The good Father came to say mass. All the sinners, all the Rancasans, filled the church. The priest gave a sermon while they listened on their knees.

"Father," asked the Representative when mass was over, "why has God sent us this punishment?"

The priest answered: "The Fence is not the work of God, my children. It is the work of the Americans. It is not enough to pray. You must fight."

Rivera's face turned blue with surprise. "But, Father, how can we fight the Company? They own everything: the police, the judges, the guns, everything."

"With God's help you can do anything."

Representative Rivera knelt down. "Bless me, Father."

Father Chasán made the sign of the cross.

And they began to fight back. At four in the morning Rivera

knocked at every man's door. They met in the square. It was very cold. They jumped up and down on the stones to keep from freezing. They armed themselves with clubs and slings. They passed around three bottles of brandy. They hid while it was still dark, in wait for the Company's night patrol. The sun had not yet freed itself from the cobweb of the pink fog. Shadowy figures on horseback emerged from the mist. They attacked the riders. Fear hardened their angry fists. Shining with excitement and dew, the dogs shared their fury. The surprised patrol, covered with bruises, their faces cut by stones from the slingshots, disappeared into the fog.

"Break down the Fence!" ordered Representative Rivera, spitting out a tooth.

"What did you say, Don Alfonso?"

"Break down the Fence and let the sheep in!" repeated the Representative, wiping the blood from his nose with a filthy handkerchief.

They obeyed. They went back to Rancas for the sheep: they had to drag them. But grass can work miracles; an hour later the lambs were eating and jumping again among the dogs, mad with joy. That night, for the first time in weeks, there was laughter in Rancas. Everyone boasted of real or imaginary deeds. Even the shopkeepers gave credit with a smile. Don Eudocio treated everyone with a bruised face or cut lips to drinks on the house.

They continued fighting. Every dawn they faced the patrols of the Cerro de Pasco Corporation. Once they had gone out with the sheep to pasture; now they went out to participate in the most ancient of male rituals. They came back bloody. Egoavil, the head patrolman, a hulking man almost six feet tall, brought in reinforcements. There were no more five-man patrols; now the horsemen from the Cerro rode out twenty at a time. Even so, they kept on fighting. And the most fearless were the old men. "We don't have any teeth anyway," they would say. "What do we care if they hit us in the mouth? You young ones should take care of your teeth so the girls will like you. What else are we good for?"

But Egoavil was not stymied. One morning the herdsmen from La Florida came into Rancas weeping behind a herd of cattle that bellowed pitifully. The cows looked like guinea pigs: they had no tails. That's how the violence began. Any sheep found by the work crews was a trampled sheep. And things got even worse: early one morning three shepherds were warming themselves in front of a dung fire. The fog was thick. They were sitting at the foot of a hill when they heard someone burst out laughing. They stood up, alarmed; something round rolled down to their feet. They walked up to it: it was the head of Mardoqueo Silvestre.

The people slipped back into their old ways. The last man who dared to fight came crawling back. The Representative knocked on stubborn doors in vain. Toward the end of September not even the bravest dared resist. One day the patrolmen brought men in uniform with them. From then on a detachment of the Federal Guard escorted the patrols. Attacking them meant attacking the Armed Forces. Egoavil rode into Rancas accompanied by three Federal Guards, made a great display of riding up and down the street, clattered through the square, and went into Don Eudocio's tavern.

"A dozen beers for these gentlemen guards," he snarled, leaning on the bar.

There was nothing else to do but serve him.

Fortunato was the only one left in all the vastness of the fenced-in fields.

The Federal Guard stationed sentinels every two miles in little wooden booths hurriedly constructed by the carpenters of the Cerro de Pasco Corporation. No one dared attack.

No one except Fortunato.

When Egoavil, the gigantic head patrolman, looked at the Company's only adversary, his laughter almost knocked him out of his saddle. He laughed until he cried, and then he rode off. But the next day the patrol met the old man again. Two flames were burning in his flat face. The old man saw the riders and showered them with stones from his slingshot.

They dismounted and beat him with their fists. Fortunato dragged himself home. The next morning he was back. Egoavil ordered him whipped. "Frogface"—that's what Egoavil called him—twisted like a snake, but did not cry out.

When the whips finally finished with him, his lips were bitten through.

"If you want, come back tomorrow for the rest of what we owe you!"

He came back. He returned to Rancas looking just like Saint Sebastián in the church at Villa de Pasco. It took him three hours to travel the two and a half miles. He crawled into the village, leaving a trail of blood behind him.

"Don't go on with this, Don Fortunato," Alfonso Rivera pleaded with him that morning. "You can't do anything alone. One man can't fight against five hundred."

"They'll kill you, Papá," sobbed his daughters. "Alive, you can take care of us; dead, you can't even bring us water."

"You can't do it alone, Fortunato," repeated Rivera.

He did not answer. He kept on fighting. Day after day he went out to engage in useless battles. For the foremen it was not a fight, it was amusement. The ruffians argued over him. "Don't hit him too hard, we have to keep our little frog alive," joked Egoavil. The old man continued to keep his appointment. He fell and he got up again. He would not give in. He was like those tumbling toys that always stand up straight again no matter how hard you knock them down. Beating him was a routine that depended on Egoavil's moods. For example, the dawn following the night when "Electric Cunt" publicly turned him down after drinking up a whole bottle of Poblete anisette, Egoavil tried to get rid of his frustration. Eight men on horseback formed a closed circle around the white-faced old man. For an hour they passed him around, kicking and punching him from one man to the next. Fortunato lurched around the circle, barely able to keep his balance; his face was like a mask. When they let him go, his eyes were no longer visible. He collapsed like an empty sack.

He lay on the grass, gasping, his face to the sky, his mouth open. Some mule-drivers found him at noon: he was vomiting as they brought him into Rancas. He fell limply on to his straw mattress and stayed there for three days, his green-yellow-purple face covered with pieces of raw meat. He got up the fourth day. On the fifth morning he went out again to challenge the patrol. He found Egoavil a changed man. This time none of the riders dismounted.

"Get away, Fortunato, beat it!" they shouted as they rode away.

The old man tried to chase them, tried to throw stones, but he could not: he was too weak and the bastards were riding too fast.

Egoavil had begun to dream about him. Fortunato pursued him in his dreams. He appeared to him every night. In the dream he was wandering endlessly through a desert, beyond all fatigue, when he heard a voice; frightened, Egoavil quickened his pace, but it called to him again, jeeringly. Who could possibly know his name in that infinite solitude? He fled the implacable voice. Only leagues later did he realize in terror that the speaker was his horse; he dismounted, trembling, to find that the pony had the swollen, discolored face of Fortunato. He also dreamed that he found a likeness of the old man in his bedroom. Mad with fear, he tore the hateful face off the wall only to discover that it was a ghastly calendar and that under each face he tore off there were hundreds of other faces of the old man: Fortunato laughing at him, Fortunato sticking out his tongue, Fortunato crying, Fortunato winking at him, Fortunato with a blue face, Fortunato with his face full of holes, Fortunato covered with pockmarks. And he dreamed even worse things: he saw Fortunato crucified. He dreamed he was nailed to a cross like Jesus Christ. The faithful of Rancas, the devout from all over the world wept as they followed behind the platform on which his image was carried. The figure on the cross wore the same greasy pants and threadbare shirt the old man wore; instead of the crown of thorns, he wore his shabby hat. Egoavil could see the swollen face clearly. Apparently Our Crucified Lord of Rancas was not suffering; from time to time he freed one of his arms and raised a bottle of rum to his mouth. Egoavil followed him trembling, carrying a candle in his hand and trying to hide, but the man on the cross recognized him and shouted: "Don't run away from me, Egoavil! We have an appointment tomorrow!" and he winked with an eye closed by a hideous yellow swelling. Egoavil woke up screaming.

Calmly, sitting on a rock, the old man rolled up his shirt sleeves.

Egoavil's mouth was as dry as straw. "Don Fortunato!" he said hoarsely from the back of his pony. "I know too well that you're a real man." And his scornful hand gestured toward the silent patrol. "Not one of them's as good a man as you are. None of these pricks is even half the man you are. Why go on fighting? You can't do anything alone, Don Fortunato. The Cerro is powerful. All the villages have given up. You're the only one who keeps on fighting. Why go on, Don Fortunato?"

"Get down or I'll pull you down, you bastard!" shouted Fortunato.

"Please, I beg you, Don Fortunato, don't insult me."

"You mother-fucking son-of-a-bitch."

"We don't want to hurt you. If you stop coming here, the patrol won't come back either."

"Bastard! Son-of-a-bitch!"

Egoavil looked at the leathery faces of the men on patrol, remembered the face of Christ, felt the sweat he had felt in his dreams, and got down from his horse. The two men grappled. Fortunato attacked savagely, hitting out like a mule. Egoavil countered with blows as soft as wool.

CHAPTER NINETEEN: *Where the Reader Will Enjoy a Poker Game*

JUDGE Montenegro made the journey to El Estribo. Health Officer Canchucaja, Secretary Pasión, Arutingo, Sergeant Cabrera, and a squad of Civil Guards accompanied the Magistrate. Don Migdonio had prepared magnificent rest stops for him. Fresh horses and provisions were provided every six hours. Five days later they passed under the stone arch where the silver spur of Don Migdonio's grandfather had been hanging for fifty years. Dressed in jodhpurs, a leather jacket, English boots, and a very expensive silk scarf, Don Migdonio welcomed the "illustrious delegation," whose members were somewhat intimidated by the magnificent ranch house.

It was a huge house, a hundred yards long, dotted with discolored doors and windows. The builders' original plan was blurred by neglect. The stone patio had given way to grass. Ragged phantoms, farmhands without faces, emerged from behind the dung piles. The men crossed the patio and went into the dining room, which still boasted antique English furniture between walls covered with calendars. An enormous meal was waiting for them. Hours later they were still drinking rum and punch. This time they were official guests because normally—except for Dr. Montenegro, who was guest of honor at all banquets—the notaries and

Civil Guards invited themselves to every party. Finally, at six in the afternoon, Dr. Montenegro roused himself:

"I hope, Don Migdonio, that you can spare me a few moments."

They went into the office. No one knows what Don Migdonio de la Torre and Don Francisco Montenegro talked about for the next sixty minutes, just as no one has ever learned what San Martín and Bolívar discussed at Guayaquil.

"Would you come in, Sergeant?" Dr. Montenegro called from the door an hour later. The Sergeant put his glass of cognac down on the table and went into the room. What Don Migdonio, Dr. Montenegro, and Sergeant Cabrera discussed is also shrouded in mystery, just as the famous conversation between Napoleon and Alexander I is obscured by the mists of history.

"Do you mind, my good Canchucaja?" called Dr. Montenegro again, at home once and for all in the world of historical enigmas. And at this point there are conflicting theories. Certain historians maintain that the interviews did not last for hours but rather days, and that instead of having a meeting the authorities traveled out past the farthest boundary lines of the ranch. In answer to those witnesses who swear they saw the authorities come out of the office embracing and laughing, these historians introduce an irrefutable argument: that night—was it night or day?—the authorities agreed that Espíritu Félix and his fourteen companions had died of "collective thrombosis." Could such a fact have been established without a careful examination of the evidence? Such a thing is unthinkable. Or this at least is the reasoning of some historians, and they conclude that the authorities reached the distant boundaries of El Estribo only after days of arduous travel. Be that as it may, Dr. Montenegro's ruling was categorical: the farmhands had died of the first collective thrombosis in the history of medicine. Dr. Montenegro confirmed that the weak hearts of the herdsmen could not endure the giddy heights of power; hearts accustomed to galloping at an altitude of fifteen thousand feet were torn to pieces by the emotion the herdsmen felt when they sat down in the easy chairs of the El Estribo drawing room. The province was jubilant. The privilege of establishing this astonishing medical fact had been denied the cosmopolitan centers of the world; it had fallen instead to a humble though sincere Peruvian province. Genius does not choose to reveal itself only in great nations.

Because of a chestnut horse, because of Lopsided, Judge Montenegro became my enemy. Soon after Doña Pepita Barda, the owner of Huarautambo, had married Dr. Montenegro, the patrolmen captured Lopsided. I followed their trail and came to the ranch. Lopsided was neighing in the corral.

"Why did you bring in my horse?"

The guard was apologetic. "The Judge ordered us to capture any animal that was found grazing his pasture."

"He wasn't pastured on the ranch."

"I don't know anything about it, Don Héctor. Talk to the bosses."

I went to the ranch house and asked for the Judge. They took me to the patio. Dr. Montenegro was sitting in a chair reading a newspaper.

"How are you, Chacón?"

"I'm fine, Judge, but Lopsided isn't too well."

The Judge frowned. "Who is Lopsided?"

"One of my horses that's locked in your corral."

"It must have been doing damage."

"It's not your pasture, Judge. It's my own land."

The Judge looked at me with narrowed eyes. "I don't know anything about that. The only thing I know is that you are all ruining my pasturelands."

"But, Judge—"

The Judge stood up. "That's enough, I don't want to hear any more. Get out of here, you damned half-breed!"

I left with my heart on fire and went down to the town. That very morning I filed my complaint at the Sub-prefecture. They paid no attention to me. "The law," said Don Arquímedes Valerio, "cannot settle personal problems. This is a private dispute. I can't do anything about it."

I went back to Huarautambo and my heart sank: the patrolmen had captured my other horses: Sorrel, Chestnut, Cinnamon, Rosy, and my mare Cry Baby (I called her that because she cried when she was separated from the other horses), and they were all there suffering in the corral. The patrolmen never freed horses without collecting "damages": one hundred sols each. If the damages were not paid, the horses did not eat or drink. So many animals died!

I pleaded with the head patrolman, Palacín.

"Why are you doing this to me, Don Máximo? What am I going to do? I'm a poor man."

"You're very insolent, Chacón. The Judge wants to teach you a lesson."

"Where am I going to get three hundred sols?"

"The damages are eight hundred, Héctor."

I only had ten sols. I bought a bottle of rum and began to beg.

"Do something for me, Don Máximo."

"You're very arrogant, Chacón."

"Have a drink and let me off, Señor Palacín!"

"I can't let you off. We have strict orders."

I begged and begged while Palacín finished my bottle.

"I don't have eight hundred sols. I've never had eight hundred sols in my life. I'll never have eight hundred sols."

"I could accept one of your horses."

What could I do? Instead of losing five horses, I'd save four.

"Which one do you want?"

"I want that chestnut," and he pointed to Lopsided.

"Not that one, Señor Palacín. I really love that horse. Not that one."

It was no good; I couldn't save Lopsided.

The higher court upheld the Judge's ruling. Don Migdonio decided to travel down to the province to show his gratitude. When Dr. Montenegro learned from one of the hands on El Estribo that Don Migdonio, the only man who could impregnate seven women on the same day, was coming down to Yanahuanca, he immediately arranged for Doña Pepita to have an enormous quantity of pigs, goats, and chickens slaughtered. Except for the Senator, no other celebrity had ever favored the province with a visit. The wives of the leading citizens bought up all the cosmetics the stores had in stock. The leading citizens suffered. Whom would Dr. Montenegro, more involved than ever in his solitary musings, sunk deeper and deeper into the seriousness of his thoughts, invite? For once they were wrong: the Judge invited every one of his presentable neighbors.

They rode a league out of town to welcome the great man. Don Migdonio de la Torre y Covarrubias del Campo del Moral rode into Yanahuanca at dusk: his reddish sideburns in the style of Marshal Sucre and his sculpted copper-colored beard drove the people wild with enthusiasm. They applauded as the party rode through streets swept clean by the prisoners. By order of Sergeant Cabrera, the guards had lined up in military formation and were waiting in front of the police station. The red-bearded Don Migdonio de la Torre y Covarrubias del Campo del Moral spied the blushing Doña Pepita, doffed his hat with a princely gesture while still some distance away, and then dismounted and kissed her hand. Dr. Montenegro, who knew nothing of such refinements, hesitated over the handle of his pistol; his soul was shaken by the same stormy feelings that they say devastated the spirit of a general, the President of the Republic, on the day when shortly after his coup d'état an ambassador pressed his lips to the robust hand of the First Lady. Knowing how jealous the dictator was, the General's wife was so frightened that she could only call out "Apolinario, Apolinario."

That night the festivities began. Through the Judge's house (the patios were filled with mules laden with "little gifts" brought down by the farmhands from El Estribo) passed a procession of perfectly washed and groomed authorities and notable citizens (Glostora hair pomade was not to be had for love nor money).

Everyone had on a new shirt. The Sub-prefect, Don Arquímedes, wore the formal blue suit he kept for patriotic occasions, and a red tie. (Some years later this innocent luxury was to be his ruin. The fortunes of the service were to send him to another province, where the envious accused him of being an extremist; in the eyes of the Prefect, who could not bear the sight of him—the Sub-prefect failed to open a brothel in the province, a disappointment that prevented his superior from realizing his dream of having a whorehouse to depend on in every constituency—the red tie was proof of his fanatic communism: he lost his position and died in obscurity.)

Unable to foresee his turbulent future, the smug Sub-prefect came up to greet Don Migdonio de la Torre y Covarrubias del Campo del Moral.

The Judge had gone so far as to have the whole house swept, and had even ordered that the floor be scrubbed with oil, whose odor mixed with the vapors emitted from the armpits of matrons as they sweated with the effort of carrying their offspring. The little snot-noses—and they really did have nostrils stoppered with crusts of mucus—drowned out the grave musical efforts of the little RCA Victor dog with their squealing.

"They've seen you driving around
In a flashy car that must belong
To that whitish new boyfriend of yours."

Authorities and notable citizens tapped their heels and toes on the floor sprinkled with sawdust to keep the guests from slipping. It was the most stunning party that Yanahuanca had ever seen. Toward dawn, when the notable citizens' legs had grown too heavy for dancing, Don Arquímedes made a suggestion:

"Why don't we play a round of poker?"

"Delighted," said Don Migdonio, who was growing bored.

And since misfortunes never come singly, a few weeks later my friend Polonio Cruz entrusted his horses to me. My bad luck made me careless again, and again the patrolmen took the horses. Again I went to Huarautambo to protest. They paid no attention to me. This time they kept one of Polonio's horses. "It's your fault," Don Polonio told me sadly. And it was true: I was to blame. And I gave my friend a mare named Buzzard, an animal that Don Polonio learned to love.

And things got even worse: to try to improve my luck, I plowed an abandoned field named Yanaceniza; I planted ten sacks of seed. I chose the seed carefully. There are many kinds of potato: the brownish, mealy potato, the best for eating; the yellow potato, good for restaurants and the retail trade; the big shiri, best for making potato starch; the white potato that is used for everyday. I chose the seeds lovingly for their size and color. The land was grateful. The potatoes grew beautifully. It was wonderful to see them flower in April. And then misfortune struck: one night a herd of animals trampled my potato field. What bad luck! The next night the same sheep invaded my land again. Frantically, I tried to drive them away with stones. I couldn't. And then I caught one of the shepherds.

"Why are you doing this?" I asked him.

"The Judge ordered us to bring them in here." He lowered his head. "We're really sorry, Don Héctor."

In despair I went down to the province and went directly to the Judge's house. The Judge was just leaving.

"Judge, will you allow me to speak to you?"

The Judge kept on walking. "Is it about damages?"

"Yes, Judge."

He stopped for a second and then went on. "You're quite a troublemaker, Chacón. This is the third time you've pestered me. Don't you know yet that I don't bother with these things? Talk to Señora Pepita."

Doña Pepita, the owner, is a woman who hides behind her sex to insult people: her mouth is more offensive and more disgusting than a drunkard's. I asked to talk to her. It was impossible. She was in her attic counting her silver and her bales of wool. I waited the whole morning. Finally she appeared at noon. She came down to the patio.

"Cristina, Cristina!" she called.

Two worried-looking girls came running out.

"Come, comb me."

The girls ran and brought out two chairs. Señora Pepita sat down in one of them, and one of the girls sat in the other.

"Talk fast. I'm in a hurry," Señora Pepita said to me as her face was covered by a mane of hair.

"Doña Pepita, your animals are ruining my potato field!"

The girl who was combing her looked at me with beautiful eyes; I'd known her since she was a child; once I gave her a trout, once . . .

"Who told you it was your field, you damned half-breed?"

"Señora, I planted Yanaceniza."

She raised her head angrily. "Why did you plant there, you damned fool?"

"It's an abandoned field. The community gave me permission."

"And who is the community to give you permission? The hell with the community! There are no abandoned fields in this province. All the fields are my pastureland."

"What do you mean, they're your pastureland? Nobody has planted those fields since the days of our grandfathers."

Again she lifted up her black hair. "I'm glad!" she shouted. "I'm glad my animals are ruining your field. You're an insolent half-breed, a damned Indian. The worse you behave, the worse things will get for you. Words aren't enough for you. You're stubborn. Now you'll see what will happen to you."

They prepared the tables. Don Migdonio de la Torre y Covarrubias del Campo del Moral, Judge Francisco Montenegro, Subprefect Valerio, and the Mayor, Don Herón de los Ríos, sat down to play cards. By the second hand their weariness had disappeared. By the third, the Evil One advised Dr. Montenegro to call his opponent's bet. Don Migdonio de la Torre y Covarrubias del

Campo del Moral, who had a straight to the king, was indignant. Everyone grew excited and they raised the bets to five thousand sols: the Judge pocketed everything. They lost themselves in the frenzies of three of a kind. They did not stop playing until eight the next morning. They were interrupted and served some duck fricassee. It tasted like nettles to Don Migdonio de la Torre y Covarrubias del Campo del Moral: he was losing eleven thousand sols. The only thing greater than his fear of the Evil Eye was his greed. He was so stingy that in order not to lose ten sols he was capable of digging at night in a cemetery, purple with fear. Proclaiming how-pleasant-it-is-to-play-with-friends, he refused to allow the really enjoyable game to end. They caught a few winks in the bedrooms and went back to the game at eleven o'clock. They played the rest of the afternoon and evening, which is bad for the health of the sickly, but which improved the luck of Don Migdonio de la Torre y Covarrubias del Campo del Moral. When they were interrupted by a splendid chicken in hot pepper sauce, a real Sistine Chapel of creole cooking, Dr. Montenegro was losing fourteen thousand sols. Now the Magistrate was the one who expounded on the pleasures of entertaining his friends. He cursed Don Arquímedes' idea. They resumed the game, played through the night, and the Sub-perfect began to look a little better to him; at dawn he changed his opinion of him entirely: eighteen thousand sols were piled up before his straight with ace high. This time it was Don Migdonio de la Torre y Covarrubias del Campo del Moral's turn to proclaim the pleasures of friendship. They took a little nap and started the game again at twelve.

The game went on for ninety days.

I bit my hands to keep from crying.

I left. The sun beat down on the square. Some children ran by. An angry dog was following them. They turned and the dog ran away. That's how I was: a dog who ran whenever the ranch-owners turned around to look at me. My mouth was as dry as ashes. I went to Don Glicerio Cisneros' shop, and who was there but Salomón

Requis, the Municipal Agent for Yanacocha, having a drink with Abraham Carbajal. I attacked them as soon as I saw them.

"What kind of damned authorities are you?" I shouted, hitting out at Salomón with my fists.

"What's the matter with you, Chacón?"

"You can see they're ruining me and you don't do anything to stop them!" I was crying.

Requis wiped the blood from his mouth. "You're right, Chacón. We're no damn good."

"Have a drink, brother," said Don Glicerio. "It's on the house."

"Carbajal is right. We're no damn good. The Judge walks all over us."

"Why don't you round up Montenegro's cattle the next time they trample your field?"

No one had ever dared to round up the animals from Huarautambo Ranch.

"Round them up and put them in the corral. Then we'll take it from there."

I drank. "I'm sorry, Señor Requis."

"To your health, Chacón."

I talked with my neighbors Santos Chacón and Esteban Herrera, who were very worried about the land grabs the ranch was making. We were ready for the animals. The next night the cattle came into my potato field and I shouted for Santos Chacón and Esteban Herrera. "Help me put them in the corral," I asked them. With our slings we rounded up fifteen head of Montenegro's cattle.

We took them down to the Yanahuanca corral.

"Señor Municipal Agent," I said to Requis, "these animals have been damaging my potato field for a week."

"File a claim for your loss."

"Will you keep them?"

"We'll hold them as long as your damages are outstanding."

"Thank you, Señor Agent."

At that moment two Civil Guards appeared and pointed their guns at me. Requis turned pale.

"What are you up to?"

"Officers, I've brought in some cattle as proof of damages."

"There's a complaint filed against you. You stole those cows from Dr. Montenegro."

I turned around to call my witnesses. They were no longer there.

"These animals are doing damage. These animals—"

"You've stolen the cattle. Come with us. You too, Requis."

"I don't know anything," stammered Requis. "He brought in the animals. I don't know anything."

"All right. Turn the cows over to the men from the ranch and get out."

"Thank you, gentlemen," said Requis humbly. "You, Chacón, you come with us."

They held me for seven days. The following Tuesday they took me out of jail and brought me to Dr. Montenegro's house.

"All right," said the Judge, "you can go."

The guards saluted.

"Chacón," he said to me, "you think you're very smart. You won't put up with anything. Why did you round up my livestock?"

"Why did you damage my potato field, Judge?"

The Judge pointed at me with his finger. "This time I'll pardon you, but the next time you'll spend seven months in jail. Do you hear me, you shit?"

"Why did you damage my potato field? How am I going to live? What am I going to eat?"

"That's your affair. Look somewhere else. Yanaceniza belongs to me."

I went up to Yanacocha. Don Abraham Carbajal was surprised to see me free.

"How did you get out, Héctor?"

"On my feet, Don Abraham."

My father embraced me and looked at the authorities.

"What kind of damned authorities are you?" said the old man, and he spat.

"The Judge is the highest authority," said Carbajal sadly.

"You're worth less than horse dung," the old man repeated.

"The Judge," said Requis humbly, "is capable of putting us all in jail. There's nothing we can do. Power is power."

"Listen, Representative," I said to him. "Montenegro has warned me not to plant my crops in Yanaceniza. If I do, he'll send me to jail for life. Where am I going to live?"

"The community will give you another plot to live on, Héctor. We'll give you some high ground near Quinche."

"Let's go," said my father.

On the road I asked the old man: "Where did the ranch-owners come from, Papá?"

My old man kept on walking.

"Where did they come from?"

We stopped.

"Why are there any owners at all? Why is there an owner in Huarautambo, Papá?"

My old man sat down on a stone by the side of the road and answered my question.

Doña Pepita was scandalized as she followed the fierce competition of the game. Neither the Judge nor the ranch-owner would accept defeat. They lost themselves in labyrinths of royal flushes. They left the table only to wash or sleep; they ate right in the room with its generations-thick patina of cigarette smoke. Deprived of the talents of its highest officials, the province languished. Telegrams and official letters faded on their desks. Two weeks after the game began, somewhat cowed by the dimensions acquired by the cards, Dr. Montenegro's secretary, Santiago Pasión, dared to walk into the smoke-filled room.

"Santiago, what's the news, my friend?" asked Dr. Montenegro good-humoredly: he was winning twenty-four thousand sols.

"A thousand pardons, gentlemen, a thousand pardons," said the secretary in a daze.

"What's on your mind, Don Santiago?" the Judge encouraged him.

"The Senator is interested in the prisoner Egmidio Loro. He has sent a telegram, Judge."

"Which one is he?"

"The chicken thief."

"We won't have to interrupt the game, will we?" said Don Migdonio de la Torre y Covarrubias del Campo del Moral in a worried tone.

"Why don't you have the trial here?" suggested Arutingo.

Don Migdonio sighed. Five minutes later Egmidio Loro, accused of stealing four chickens, appeared in the patio. And it was his good fortune to have his case heard while the cards were smiling at the Judge.

"Are you guilty or innocent?" asked the Judge as he leafed through the file.

"Whatever you say, Judge."

The Judge laughed. "How long have you been in the lock-up?"

"Eight months, Judge."

"Dismissed," was the sentence of the court.

They grew accustomed to settling all their problems this way—in the patio when the players took a break. Encouraged by Loro's luck, other criminals asked to be tried. They were not all dismissed so easily. Many of them came up for trial when the cards had turned their backs on Dr. Montenegro: Marcos Torres, accused of stealing a sack of alfalfa, was hoping that the six months he had already spent in prison would make up for his crime: he received a three-month bonus. "As if I were pregnant," he muttered, and he earned another six. But not all provincial matters could be handled in the patio. They had to postpone the dance that the Eleven Friends of Yanahuanca Club was organizing to raise money for uniforms for the soccer team.

That same afternoon I told Sulpicia, Añada, Santos Chacón, and Esteban Herrera: "Montenegro has ordered us to leave Yanaceniza."

Sulpicia turned pale. "How can we abandon land that we plowed with our fingernails?"

"Why should we leave?" said Santos Chacón in despair.

"We'll die on our land," said Sulpicia bitterly.

"Don't leave, Héctor! If you abandon the land, there'll be nobody to help us," said Señora Añada.

"Do you want to fight back?"

"I'm ready to fight back until I die," said Don Esteban.

And we decided to fight. We watched by night and slept by day, taking turns. Sulpicia, Doña Añada, Santos Chacón, Don Esteban, and I were worn out with fatigue, but we did not abandon the potato field. And so, guarding it day and night, we were able to save the crop. The potatoes bloomed beautifully. The flowers swayed in the May breeze. One day we pulled up a few plants to see what they looked like. It was wonderful! We counted one hundred twenty potatoes on a single plant. One hundred twenty!

The foremen looked at the crop greedily. They rushed to tell Dr. Montenegro the news. "What beautiful potatoes Chacón has! That land really gives a beautiful potato crop.

He said: "We should be working that land ourselves. Try to throw Chacón out."

One afternoon, when Sulpicia was sleeping, exhausted, some foremen rode by on their big horses and told everyone: "Huarautambo Ranch will harvest every single one of these potatoes!"

"This potato field belongs to Héctor Chacón," Don Esteban Herrera managed to say before they hit him with their whips.

Señora Sulpicia woke up. "Don't expect Don Héctor to give up his potato crop. He'll die along with his potatoes. And he won't be the only one!"

"Chacón is a nobody, it makes no difference what he does," said the head foreman, Palacín.

That was too bitter for me to swallow.

"Everybody will laugh at us," complained Sulpicia. "If we pulled out one hair for every insult, would we have any hair left?"

That day we remembered again all his inroads into our land, his pride, his misdeeds.

"We'll see if Montenegro is the only man in this province," I said.

"Don't bring trouble down on your head, Don Héctor," said Sulpicia, staring at me.

I didn't answer. I got on my horse and rode to Huarautambo. The head foreman, Palacín, looked at me in surprise. He didn't even ask why I had crossed the bridge without permission.

"Excuse me for bothering you, Señor Palacín. I heard that you came to Yanaceniza with the news that the ranch would harvest my potato crop."

"Yes, that's right, Héctor. Dr. Montenegro ordered us to harvest it."

"I want everybody from Huarautambo to come and harvest my potato crop!" I shouted.

"Chacón, please don't shout, you'll get me in trouble." Señor Palacín, brave as he was with horses, was scared to death of Montenegro's shadow.

I lost control of myself. "I want every man on the ranch to come right now and pull up all my potatoes!"

Señor Palacín was terrified. "Please, my good Chacón, be careful, don't let the Señora hear you. She is counting her silverware!"

"I want you to come with all your animals to trample on the plants."

"Dear Chacón, I beg you, the Judge will hear you."

I pirouetted my horse around the patio, shouting. "I want you to come to Yanaceniza right now so you'll know what kind of man I am. Come on! You'll find out. You'll find out who Chacón is! You'll harvest over my dead body! I want you to come for the harvest right now!"

I left, crying like a baby. On the way down, near Yanahuanca, I met Don Procopio Chacón and Don Néstor Leandro. I went up to Procopio and said to him: "Nephew, in a couple of days now there'll be a battle to the death."

"What's wrong, Uncle?" answered Procopio.

"You'd better be ready to kill me when you come to harvest my potato crop, you bastards. You'll see. You're family, but I'm going ahead with it anyhow."

"Don't get angry, Héctor. The foremen are the ones who are breaking in. We're poor men too."

"Suddenly you're poor, you bastards!"

"We don't want to get involved," said Procopio. "We have mouths to feed too."

The month of June began with the rumor that "Huarautambo will harvest Chacón's potato crop." I couldn't sleep. Ignacia and I would lie there looking up at the ceiling.

"What's the matter? Why aren't you sleeping?"

"I'm thirsty."

"Ignacia, are you afraid?"

"I'm thirsty."

"Ignacia, what will happen to the children when they harvest our potatoes?"

"Why did you plant Yanaceniza?"

"It's the community's land, it's free land."

"Before, we didn't eat much, but we ate. They have their own justice," she sobbed. "They do what they want."

"We work for nothing: we won't harvest a crop, everyone will laugh at us."

"Señora Sulpicia is the one I feel sorriest for."

And I decided to get a shotgun. I had no money, so I went down to talk to Señor Rivas. One day I stopped him on the street.

"Señor Rivas, I want to talk to you about a shotgun."

"What do you want a shotgun for?"

"To hunt deer."

Señor Rivas looked at me with all his experience. "You're out of your mind, Chacón."

"You know that Huarautambo Ranch wants to harvest my potato field."

"They're taking advantage of you and it makes me angry. Why are they doing it? What right do they have to do it? We should all help each other."

"If you help me, the law will prosecute you too. Don't get involved. It's better for me to do it by myself. I need your gun. My rifle holds only one shot and can kill only one man at a time; a shotgun scatters death all around."

"All right, I'll rent you a shotgun."

"And cartridges, can you sell them to me?"

"They're expensive."

"I'll give you a stud ram. You'll like him. He'll give you lots of lambs."

"All right, twenty-five cartridges for a sheep."

"I'll give you a good animal, an animal you'll really love."

That same morning I went up to Yanaceniza with the shotgun. When the foremen rode up, I shot a bird right before their eyes. "That's how you'll die, you bastards!" and I stroked the beautiful shotgun. "This lady will suck out your blood."

And the result was they did no harvesting. I learned that cowards own no land. The potatoes bloomed, they were beautiful, enough potatoes for two years. And I hired forty men to dig them.

Until one afternoon I saw the head foreman, Palacín, ride up with thirty men on horseback. I saw the cloud of dust and knew that my luck had changed.

Head foreman Palacín looked me up and down, sizing me up. "Chacón, some horses have been stolen up here. You must know something about it. You come with us."

And they took me prisoner.

They did not dare celebrate without the authorities. Consequently, a tea that had been organized by Doña Josefina de los Ríos was postponed. That month three hamlets had made plans to celebrate the inauguration of a fountain, the opening of a cemetery, and the erection of a flagpole: they were left with plans but no celebration. But the prisoners were the ones who suffered most.

A little while before the game began, Sergeant Cabrera had ordered traffic signs painted on every corner. One morning Yanahuanca awoke to find itself covered with white arrows. It was a drunken whim of the Sergeant's. The citizens did not even know what the word "traffic" meant, but the Sergeant, who had decided on the change only because he was drunk, had to obey his own orders: twenty-three poor devils were taken to the barracks before the new law could be revoked. The Sub-prefect could not try them. "It's obviously impossible," said Arutingo, "to crowd the Judge's patios with flea-bitten slobs like these." They stayed in prison for the duration of the game. Ninety days later a black chingolo bird, a modest New World imitation of the dove that had announced the end of Divine Wrath to Noah, landed on the windowsill of the room where the players were growing older.

"It's December," said Don Migdonio. "Soon you won't be able to travel the roads."

"The rains are coming," conceded the Judge.

"We'd better stop now," sighed Don Migdonio, resigned to losing four hundred sols.

CHAPTER TWENTY: *Concerning the Pyramid of Sheep Which the People of Rancas Built Without Wishing to Emulate the Egyptians*

ONCE there was an old man as stubborn as a mule. An old man with a flat face and bulging eyes whose nickname was Frogface. He refused to understand that the Cerro de Pasco Corporation had a capital of five hundred million dollars at its disposal. He had about thirty sheep, anger, and two fists. And there was also a leader of a patrol named Egoavil, a giant almost two meters tall with the look of a brute and unfriendly eyes, who earned thousands of sols cutting the tails off cows and running down sheep with his horse. Despite these accomplishments, "Electric Cunt" drank up a bottle of his Poblete cognac and then refused to spread her legs for him. A snub the old man paid for with a beating that left him with more scars than the roosting pole in a chickenhouse. But then it happened that the brute began to dream about the old man. The bad dreams made him weak. The old man appeared to him with the face of Christ. Native craftiness. But one cannot strike Jesus Christ with impunity. One day the old man was resting —resting?—stretched out on his sleeping skin. Pieces of raw meat covered his wounds. The slit of sky that he could see through his swollen eyes was cloudy. But he lost sight of even that patch of sky. A thin man with bony cheeks and large, transparent ears cut off the light that came in through the door. The old man recognized one of the worst sons-of-bitches from the patrol. He stood up, ready for the fight. The man with the translucent ears walked toward him, gentle as a dove, with his hat in his hand.

The man with the transparent ears (not looking him in the eye): "Good morning, Don Fortunato. I'd like to talk to you for a moment. I've come to speak to you for Egoavil."

The stubborn old man: "Don't mention that son-of-a-bitch's name in my house."

The man with the transparent ears (sucking on his teeth, nervous): "Don't make me mad, Don Fortunato. Let me talk. Don Egoavil recognizes the fact that you're a real man. Because of you, he insults us and attacks us: 'I'd like to have men like Fortunato, not a bunch of imbeciles like you.' That's what Don Egoavil says when he's drunk."

The stubborn old man (spitting saliva green with coca): "What do you want?"

The man with the transparent ears: "Don Egoavil is tired of fighting. He wants to be your friend. If you want, you can pasture your livestock in our field."

The stubborn old man: "They're not your fields. You've abused us, fencing in land that doesn't belong to you."

The man with the transparent ears (defining the condition of the underprivileged): "I'm a poor man who takes orders, Don Fortunato."

The stubborn old man (frowning to hide his joy): "And how would you work it?"

The man with the transparent ears (hoping to avoid the violent insults of Egoavil): "You could bring in your animals at night. We'd pretend to be stupid assholes. Don Egoavil only asks that you bring in the livestock at night and don't get him in trouble."

The stubborn old man (displaying poor elocution): "Hmm!"

The man with the transparent ears: "Think it over, Don Fortunato. It's a crime to let the poor sheep die."

The stubborn old man (feeling real anger): "*Now* you think about that, you bastard!"

The man with the transparent ears: "Don't be angry with me, Don Fortunato. I'm a poor man. That's the truth. One does filthy things to feed a family."

"Watch out, Fortunato, it's a trick," warned the other shepherds. The old man answered: "What do I have to lose? Dying is the worst that can happen. How many sheep do I have left?" He rounded up the remains of his flock. That night he used a pair of pliers to untwist the wire fence around Querupata pasture. His sheep ate the whole night. The old man came back at dawn, frozen but happy. He came back. The shepherds stared at his revived lambs in fascination. "Take advantage of it. What do you have to lose?" repeated Fortunato. They did not dare. Who finally decided to do it was a woman, Doña Silveria Tufina, who asked him to combine the two herds. Fortunato rounded up the two flocks, convinced that the rest of them would stop being afraid that night. He untwisted the wire and led the animals inside. His eyes were closing. "Please, Doña Tufina. I'm worn out. I'm going to sleep for a while, I'll be back soon." The sun awoke him. He jumped up from his sleeping skin, alarmed, doused his head in a barrel of water, and ran for the prairie. The mist had not lifted. He ran and ran. From a distance he could make out Tufina, sitting on a rock. He calmed down.

"Are you all right?"

She did not answer.

"Is something wrong?"

"Bad luck," said Tufina, pointing vaguely at the rocks.

Fortunato climbed up the fog-damaged hill and looked out on a horizon of animals whose throats had been torn out. A raging fury boiled up inside him. He raised his eyes. The first, punctual vultures were circling around.

"Missy, go to sleep," sobbed the old woman as she caressed the head of a dying lamb.

Fortunato tore out a fistful of grass and threw it into the air. A cold wind scattered the weeds: three of them blew back in his face like whips.

"Who were they?"

"Missy, don't leave me, Missy!"

"It can't go on like this! It can't go on!" He pulled on the grass again, tearing his fingers on the thorns.

"It was those dogs, it was Egoavil!"

His jaws blended into the silhouettes of the sharp, pointed rocks. "Stay here," he ordered. "Watch over your poor dead sheep." And he ran toward Rancas, still hidden in the fog. Fortunato crossed the narrow street, ran to the bell tower, opened the door, ran up the fifteen steps, and rang the bell. His angry arm rang the bell unrhythmically, furiously. Instantly the square filled with serious faces. Fortunato came down. The men had surrounded the torn body of a sheep. He stopped in the door. Blood was spattered over his chest.

"Are you men or women?"

"What happened, Don Fortunato?"

"The foremen from La Cerro took Señora Tufina by surprise, trampled the sheep with their horses, and then turned the dogs loose on them. They killed them all. Men or women, I don't know what you are. What are you waiting for? Are you waiting for the Fence to come into our houses? Are you waiting for the time when woman can't lie with man?"

The faces contracted, turning a shade of blue different from that of the rising day. A long-forgotten courage flickered and was rekindled, born and reborn, in their eyes.

"We can't retreat any more now. Retreat means rubbing the sky with your ass. Men or women, I don't know what you are, but we have to fight."

The fog did not lift. The rocks exhaled whitish curls of fog. Incas, chieftains, viceroys, chief magistrates, presidents of the republic, prefects and sub-prefects were identical knots in a quipus, in the immemorial thread of terror.

"Fortunato is right," said an old-looking Rivera. You could hear old age in his raucous voice. "We have to file a complaint!" he shouted. "Let's go to Cerro! Against God, the Prefect, the Judge, the dogs, against whoever it may be, we'll file against all of them. Let them all see our suffering."

"The authorities all take bribes!" yelled Abdón Medrano. "There's nobody here to complain to!" He had a new face too, anointed with severity.

"It doesn't matter, we have to file a complaint."

Fortunato lifted the sheep and put it on his shoulders. Representative Rivera, who had the story of Christ in his house, remembered that one of the pictures in the book showed a prophet, another angry man, who had placed a sheep on his shoulders before preaching about perdition and hellfire, but he did not say anything: he did not speak easily.

"Let's get the sheep," said Fortunato, "and go to Cerro de Pasco."

They gathered up the animals. One hundred men, women, and children crowded together. The grim morning crouched on the prairie. Wild ducks flew by shrilly. The freezing wind cut into the anguished faces. They went down into the valley and gathered up the sheep. Other shepherds joined them on the road. They looked at the caravan and wordlessly they brought their sheep and marched with them: there were almost a thousand of them. They traveled the six miles in silence. They saw Cerro. An absent-minded sun was peeling the paint off the first houses. They entered Carrión Avenue and marched between the deep trails carved out by the hooves of mules.

The people made way for the procession. "What is it?" they asked, but then they looked at the line of men carrying dead sheep, and they were silent.

"Look at what the Cerro is doing to us!" shouted Fortunato. "They're not satisfied with fencing in our lands. They even kill our animals with their dogs. Soon they'll be killing us! Soon there won't be anybody left! Soon they'll fence in the whole world!"

His voice sounded as if the city were the clapper of an enormous, hollow bell. It was twelve o'clock. Poorly dressed clerks and laborers lined the sidewalks.

The old man summoned all the fury of his powerlessness. "They fenced in Rancas! They fenced in Villa de Pasco! They fenced in Yanacancha! They fenced in Yarusyacán! They'll cut off heaven and earth! There won't be any water to drink or sky to look at."

"They have no right!"

"They've gone too far!"

"These damned gringos have no right to throw us off our own land!"

"What are the authorities doing?"

The people were becoming indignant. A tall, thin miner took off his yellow helmet and held it to his chest as if he were at a funeral. A vendor of leather caps, a fat, toothless man, did the same. They marched along Carrión Avenue. Hundreds of them entered the square.

"To the Prefecture! To the Prefecture!"

The ragged crowd turned the corner and went toward the Prefecture of the Department, a dilapidated building with green windows and two bored Federal Guards standing in the door. The shabby guards looked at the crowd and raised their ancient 1909 Mausers, bought with money from a patriotic nationwide campaign to raise funds for the ransom of the captive provinces of Tacna and Arica.

A stocky corporal with a sour face came out of the Prefecture. His unbuttoned vest showed that his lunch had been interrupted. Six sullen guards backed up his evil mood. As always, the crowd stopped when they saw the weapons.

"What do you want?" shouted the Corporal.

"We want to talk to the Prefect," said Fortunato humbly.

The Corporal did not think it necessary to button up. "Who are you?"

"I am . . . we are from the Rancas community," choked Representative Alfonso Rivera. He wanted to speak, but he could not find the words. He was sweating.

Again the Corporal covered them with his contempt. "I'll go

and check," he growled, and he turned into the hallway. The silent crowd listened to the sound of his worn-out boots. Five minutes later he returned. To talk with his superior, he had buttoned his vest properly; but now, facing the crowd, he unbuttoned it again.

"Señor Prefect is not in," and he looked at them angrily. His steak with onions was growing cold and greasy.

"But we saw him at the window," complained Fortunato.

"If I said he's not in, he's not in!" snarled the Corporal.

The men's faces showed no disappointment. Inflamed by Fortunato's words, they had dreamed for a moment of filing the complaint. The Corporal was returning them to reality. The Prefect was not in. The authorities are never in. In Peru no one has been in for centuries.

"All right," said Fortunato in resignation. "We wanted him to see this," and he lifted his arms and placed his dead sheep in the doorway.

"Get out of here," growled the Corporal.

"Put down your animals," ordered Rivera.

The men hesitated. Sparks of fear burned in their eyes. They did not dare. For centuries they had lost every war, for centuries they had been in retreat.

"Do what I say," said Representative Rivera, laying down his bundle of suffering. Abdón Medrano did the same, then all of them. The shouts of the Corporal and the kicks of the guards could do nothing to stop the growing pyramid of bloodied heads. A dizzying mound of dead animals piled up in the doorway of the Prefecture, beneath the faded coat-of-arms that proclaimed that there, in that two-story building with eight green windows, was to be found the political representative of the Honorable President of the Republic, His Excellency Don Manuel Prado.

The Corporal's fear bubbled behind his shouts. He knew all about Indian obstinacy: twenty years of service in the mountain country had taught him that when the communities begin something, nothing can stop them. And wearily, sadly, unconsciously they continued to pile up their sheep, not knowing that if the

Prefecture should collapse they would be the first ones crushed. The Prefecture in Cerro de Pasco stands on a corner. On the right is the prestigious grocery store La Serranita, and on the left is Liberty Avenue (every city in Peru has streets called Liberty, Union, Justice, Progress). The Prefecture was leaning in that direction, weighed down by the dead ocean of wool. The dead sheep could no longer be distinguished from the dying ones. Sheep are noted for a peculiar trait: even when their throats are ripped out, they continue chewing their cud. And whether it was because the walk had comforted them or because they simply wanted to show off, the sheep chewed their cud. They continued their stupid, useless work.

Don Alfonso Rivera looked at the pyramid of bloody wool. "We'd better go! If the Prefecture falls down, they'll make us pay a fine."

"Yes, we can go now," said Fortunato, splattered with blood.

They went back to the highway. On the way up, when they had reached the church, they were overtaken by a van from Police Headquarters. An infuriated lieutenant shouted at them from the window.

"You're the ones who left all the sheep at the Prefecture?"

He spoke sharply. In the speed of his dry, definitive words one could recognize the coastal official whose contempt for the Indians is almost second nature.

"Yes, sir."

"Who's Fortunato?"

"I am, sir."

"Hurry up and get in! The Prefect wants to talk to you!"

Fortunato jumped into the pick-up, but before he landed on the floor of the truck, where three Federal Guards were cursing the cold, he forced a smile of triumph. The Prefect had sent for him. At last they could file their complaint. The van pulled away. Fortunato's smile was still floating over the excited crowd. Fortunato was right. The Ford sank into the mud of the narrow streets. It stopped in front of the Prefecture door. The Lieutenant jumped down from the running-board.

"Follow me!" he shouted without looking back, climbing the steps two at a time, holding on to the railing so as not to slip on the steep stairs. Fortunato respectfully climbed after him. The waiting room in the Prefecture was small and dilapidated, decorated with a pair of imitation Louis XVI sofas. Six straw chairs completed the shabby furnishings. The portrait of the President of the Republic, Manuel Prado, smiled from behind a triple row of decorations.

"Here he is," said the officer to a pale, fat man with slanted eyes.

"Are you Fortunato?" asked the secretary.

He took off his hat. "Yes, sir."

"Go in."

Fortunato went into the office of the leading political authority in the Department; it was as dirty as the rest of the building. A fat man with thick lips and an enormous double chin stood waiting before the modest desk covered with blue files. Señor Figuerola, Prefect of the Department of Cerro de Pasco, wore a threadbare four-button blue suit that he had bought in the bad old days before the President had favored him with a position.

"You're the man they call Fortunato?" he asked as if he were kicking someone.

"Yes, sir," the other man answered, his mouth dry as straw with emotion.

Prefect Figuerola began to pace the room. To control his anger, he cracked his knuckles.

"Do you think the Prefecture is a slaughterhouse, that you can leave your goddam sheep at my door?"

Fortunato's heart sank. "Señor Prefect, I only wanted you to see what they had done. Sir, I . . ."

The Prefect walked back and forth in front of the man, who made himself as small as possible.

"I'm going to throw you into jail for insolence. What were you thinking of, you poor bastard? Did you think you'd accomplish anything fucking around with your filthy sheep?" His voice was like a whip.

"All right. Now I know it's a crime to expose abuses," said the old man, ready to drink his thousand-year-old cup of humiliation.

The Prefect remembered his blood pressure and controlled himself to keep from slapping the fool. The Prefect, thank God, had not been born in this goddam town. The altitude had a deleterious effect on him.

"Listen, imbecile, exposing abuses is no crime. The crime is throwing filth in the door of authority."

"The Cerro de Pasco Corporation is forcing us to file a complaint, sir. You must have seen the Fence with your own eyes."

"I don't know anything. I've been an official for years. I've served in practically every Department in the country. I've never met an honest Indian. You only know how to complain: you lie, you cheat, you deceive. You're the cancer that is rotting Peru."

"Sir, your blood pressure," the secretary reminded him respectfully.

The Prefect sat down. "What are you going to do with all those filthy sheep?"

"I'll take them away, sir."

"How do you plan to take them away?"

"The same way we brought them."

"Are you crazy? Do you want to go through this same shit all over again? No, sir, you take them away in a truck!"

"We don't have a truck, sir," stammered Fortunato.

"Call the Council and have them lend you their garbage truck!"

"They won't pay any attention to me, sir."

"All right," said Prefect Figuerola, resignedly. "All right. Señor Gómez, call the District Council for me and tell them to lend a truck to these idiots."

CHAPTER TWENTY-ONE: *Where, Free of Charge, the Tireless Reader Will Watch Dr. Montenegro Grow Pale*

CONFIDENT that he still had thousands of hours at his disposal for choosing among thousands of peaches, Dr. Montenegro's plump hand decided on a fruit. His small hand with its short fingers rested on the rosy skin of the freestone. Three leagues away from the coolness of the sideboard where the Magistrate was hesitating, Inspector Galarza and the authorities from the Yanacocha community rode headlong down the Parnamachay Hill. Héctor Chacón reined in Triumphant. Twenty years earlier, on the same hill of reddish rock, another Triumphant had placed his thick lips in a pond. But this Triumphant did not drink. Chacón dug in his spurs. Triumphant charged down the hill in a clatter of stones. A mile below, the community was approaching behind its silent drums. Hawkeye waved a handkerchief. Sulpicia answered by waving a faded Peruvian flag. The penetrating sweetness of the peaches did not tempt the Judge, who was sated by his breakfast. Dr. Montenegro looked at the hands of the Longines. It was 11:42 on what was to be the last morning of his life. The noise of barking dogs broke out in the distance. He stood up and walked through the door of the bedroom.

Inspector Galarza marveled at the seven waterfalls on the Huarautambo River. "How marvelous! This country is really splendid," and he stopped, enthralled, on the white and black rocks where twenty years earlier the farting Arutingo had recounted the fearful things that happened on the day that "Electric Cunt" goosed "Ready Ass." Inspector Galarza admired the beauty of the seven waterfalls. He turned and his face clouded: a quarter of a mile below, he could see the dark mass of the community.

"You don't obey orders," he said bitterly.

The leaders of Yanacocha bowed their heads.

"Forgive us, Señor Inspector," said the Representative. "Those are the hamlets from the other side. A week ago we arranged to meet them here"—he took off his hat—"and there was no time to change our plans."

Señor Galarza did not want to confront the possibility of brazen disobedience. "Let's go on," he sighed.

A subservient Chuto Ildefonso pulled up the rocking chair. Dr. Montenegro sat down to take the sun. The servile foremen walked toward him. Sulpicia raised her foot to remove a thorn. A rider in a flaming red shirt appeared at the short cut.

"There's Kid Remigio!" and Sulpicia crossed herself.

"These flea-bitten punks," said Judge Montenegro, scarcely opening his lips stained by the juicy peach, "must learn their lesson once and for all. Beatings are the only thing these Yanacochans understand." His voice grew hard. "Today they'll have to deal with Montenegro. We've put up with cattle-rustling around here for too long. The authorities from Yanacocha are the thieves. They'll go to jail today or my name isn't Montenegro."

To get back to Inspector Galarza's good graces, the Representative obligingly moved a thorn bush out of the way. Huarautambo Ranch was visible beyond the rocks along the path. At that moment a sweating horse galloped up the other side of the ranch and dashed headlong to the stables. A yellow suit, its underarms dark with perspiration, leaped from the chestnut. Panting, Lala Cabieses ran along the galleries and into the stone patio where Dr. Montenegro sat resting.

"Judge, Judge!"

The black suit turned around. Lala Cabieses shouting, gasping for breath. The black suit recognized the signs of a serious matter on the contorted face of the yellow suit running toward him, waving a paper in its hand.

"Read it, Judge, read it!" said Lala Cabieses, handing him the piece of paper. That is when the Magistrate learned the power of literature. A few words scrawled by a writer who could not even boast of a good handwriting or correct spelling (the word "Judge" was barely recognizable without its "d"), a few smudged lines hurriedly scribbled by an artist who would perhaps never leave the obscurity of his province—these moved him to paleness. Back in his student days, when poverty had forced him to travel the hard road through libraries, Vargas Vila's novels had made the Judge weep with emotion. But not even *Mud Flower* or *Aura of the Violets* had moved him like this. He was ashen. Was it verse? Was it prose? No matter: the fruit of the unknown artist's inspiration had reduced the Magistrate to the color of the pale paper.

"What's the matter, Don Paco?" asked Arutingo in alarm.

By now the cavalcade could see the groves of trees on the ranch. The dogs snapped their welcome. The crowd passed among trees punished by the teeth of an early winter.

"Héctor!" shouted Fidel, and he handed a dirty little bag to Chacón. His eyes were two live coals. From a distance Kid Remigio's burning eyes stared at the hand of the man who was planning to kill him.

"Héctor!" repeated Fidel hoarsely. "Good luck!"

The riders milled around, the tired horses bumped against one another.

"Get hold of the Civil Guards' guns," said Chacón, the color drained from his face. "Don't let them fire."

Melecio de la Vega looked at Héctor Chacón's face lit by the double flames of midday and his fury, and his heart shuddered with him. "I'll never forget Chacón," he thought.

"What is it? Why aren't they moving?" asked the Inspector, pierced by foreboding. He sensed something wrong in the empty faces, in the stony silence with only neighs and barks to welcome him.

"The bridge is closed," said Rustler. Nine days earlier he had dreamed of the bridge weighted down with corpses. Twisted into strange postures, opened up by the bullets, the corpses stared at the sky with empty eyes. He reined in his horse, which sweated less than his hands.

"Who has the key?" insisted the Inspector.

"Dr. Montenegro has ordered the gate closed. You can't come in," Chuto informed him respectfully, but sternly.

"Get out of the way," yelled Chacón, and he forced Triumphant back and then rammed him forward against the gate that closed off the bridge. The gate trembled. Chacón compelled Triumphant to charge three times. The gate weakened. That was the moment when the green wasp of the huayno dance landed on Kid Remigio's head. The gate sagged. Rustler obligingly forced the rusty hinges with a bar. Triumphant cleared the barrier of violated wood and galloped off down the narrow street. The others followed. Here was where Juan the Deaf One had offended fate twenty years earlier. Clouds of dust swirled around the men of the community. Héctor Chacón rode into the Huarautambo square. On the bare earth, among anemic patches of weeds, he found only Julio Carbajal, the Huarautambo schoolteacher.

"Where's the Judge?" asked Chacón, filled with misgivings.

"He left for the high country."

"Didn't he know that the hearing was today?"

"They were waiting."

"And?"

"Lala Cabieses rode in half an hour ago."

"From which direction?"

"From the shortcut."

"And?"

"She was carrying a paper in her hand. The Judge read it and immediately gave orders to leave for the high country."

"And the guards?"

"They left with him."

"If he was notified, why did he run away?" asked Rustler. Three nights before, he had dreamed that Dr. Montenegro had turned pale at hearing Chacón's name. He could not believe it. His mind, expert in deciphering dreams, could not conceive of Dr. Montenegro being afraid of a mere human being.

"Go after him!" shouted the outwitted Inspector Galarza.

"Rivera, Reques, Mantilla!" ordered the Representative.

The riders' spurs flashed like lightning. They could not catch up to the Judge. An hour later the horses returned, covered with white lather.

Chapter Twenty-two: *Concerning the General Mobilization of Pigs Ordered by the Authorities of Rancas*

THEY continued fighting. Don Alfonso Rivera thought with envy and sadness, more sadness than envy, of Fortunato's talents. That man had the gift of speech. Words, on the other hand, made Rivera dizzy. He was an ass. But Fortunato was rotting in jail for contempt of authority.

Dressed in black, wearing a clean, unironed shirt and no tie, the Representative crossed the square. A storm hung like a tear on the wind that blew off the lake. Father Chasán was saying mass. Rivera dipped his fingers in the holy water and crossed himself. Father Chasán, a tall white man with bushy eyebrows, was in the pulpit promising that the lightning of Divine Wrath would strike down the unjust. Rivera sighed. Would the Lord Jesus Christ strike down the Company? Father Chasán wiped his forehead with a bandana. "The abusive and the violent will fall to the dust. The meek and humble, the poor without land, the trampled, the exiled, they will sit at the Right Hand of God the Father," thundered the dilapidated pulpit. The church reeked of dirt and poverty. A short while ago the authorities had met in the church. They had respectfully requested good Father Chasán to administer an oath to the directors.

"An oath for what?"

"To fight against the Cerro de Pasco Corporation, Father."

Father Chasán's bushy eyebrows flew around like crows. "Are you prepared to fight the Cerro seriously?"

"Yes, Father."

The crows looked around the pitiful walls. "This isn't a game. Fighting the Cerro is no joke. I can administer the oath to you only if you are prepared to fight to the end."

The Representative and the authorities knelt down, with great lumps in their throats. Now the pulpit was promising Divine Wrath. "Those who proclaim themselves masters of the earth, the princes who dare to fence in the earth, they shall all perish. And who will dare to appear before God when He commands the bones to rise? The Pharisees? The publicans? Those who dare to fence in the world? Those who cut off the rivers? Those who block the roads?"

Father Chasán blessed the faithful with a hand more full of anger than compassion. The people dipped their black-rimmed fingernails in the holy water. On Sunday the square in Rancas, deserted during the week, had teemed with long, heavy skirts and ponchos, but there had been no market for many Sundays. Nevertheless, on that Sunday the square groaned under the weight of the crowd. The Peace Officer from Rancas had ridden through the countryside around Rancas for a week to announce the meeting. Representative Alfonso Rivera had ordered all Rancasans to attend or be fined.

The authorities left the church with piously clasped hands. The Representative walked through the church door. It was going to snow. Soon the angry eye of Lake Junín was going to shed a snowstorm. The Peace Officer rang the bell. There was no need for the warning: all of Rancas stood waiting in the first big snowflakes. The Representative was again saddened by his lack of talent: he would have liked to speak of his breaking heart, to tell them that a blue angel had come to him in his dreams, that he, Rivera, was prepared to sacrifice his life for them, but he could not find the words. He sighed, and wiped his perspiring brow.

"Let the deeds be read!" he ordered.

The crowd was stunned. A community's property deeds are guarded by the Representative. Only one other person (in case the Representative dies) knows the hiding place of those documents, which are only read aloud at times of crisis. A son of Rancas, a student at the Daniel A. Carrión National Secondary School, began to read. The skinny boy with bony cheeks and timid eyes stood on a table and read in a monotone. The reading began at 12:12. It lasted for two hours. The people stood quietly, almost perfectly still, as they heard the listing of boundary lines, waterholes, pastures, and ponds that proved that the land, the snowstorm that whitened their hearts, belonged to Rancas. The reader finished at two o'clock and coughed.

The Representative stood up. The wind flattened his faded black hat. "Brothers, great evil has fallen on us." He twisted his fingers. "Great suffering has been born of our sins. The land is sick. A great enemy, a very powerful company, has decided that we should die!"

He leaned on the table. His shoulders were bent, rounded as if from the weight of distant snows.

"Rancas is small, but Rancas will fight. A louse can harm an animal. A pebble in his shoe can hurt a man's foot."

"There is no such thing as an unimportant enemy!" shouted a pair of eyes where fear and courage were fighting like dogs.

Despair fluttered across Rivera's face. "The authorities are the henchmen of the Cerro de Pasco Corporation. Our sufferings don't concern them. All right: we'll fight by ourselves. Brothers, next Sunday each of you will bring a pig. Every man, every head of a family is obliged to bring a little pig. I don't care what you do to get them. Maybe you'll steal them, or buy them, or borrow them. I don't know. All I know is that next Sunday we will meet here in the square with the pigs. That is what every member of the community must do: bring a pig to this square next Sunday."

The people were bewildered. Was the Representative crazy? Some of them laughed. Why pigs? But they had to do what the Representative said.

It is difficult to find pigs in the uplands. The shepherds avoid them. They don't like the pig, that destructive colony of parasites. The pasture rooted by swine is contaminated pasture. Three hundred pigs? The farsighted members of the community bought up Rancas' supply of pigs that same afternoon. On Monday there was a shortage; then the collectivists went to the neighboring villages. People laughed at them.

"Señora, sell me your pig."

"I can't, I'm fattening it."

"Rent it to me, please, Señora."

"Are you crazy?"

"Just for a week, Mamá."

"What do you want it for?"

"To keep a vow I made to the dead."

"When have you ever seen pigs in church, you half-breed fool?"

"I'll pay you ten sols."

"What will you give me as security?"

"I'll give you my poncho."

Where money failed they offered their labor. The Gallos built a fence; Señora Tufina traded a blanket for a pig; the Atencios roofed over a corral. Everybody managed somehow. The following Sunday Father Chasán came out of the church with his eyebrows raised in annoyance: the squeals were drowning out his sermon. Sitting on the last clumps of grass left in the windy square, the Rancasans waited impatiently. Representative Rivera heard all of the mass, dipped his fingers in the holy water, crossed himself, and knelt down; only after he had traced three small crosses on his forehead did he slowly walk out of the church.

The Peace Officers were with him.

"Close off the square!"

The constables fenced in the square with planks and earth. In a little while the square had been turned into a corral. When the carpenters had finished hammering the corners, Rivera spoke.

"Mark your pigs!" he shouted. "Brothers, leave your animals

here. The Peace Officers will take care of them. Come back next Sunday."

A murmur greeted his words. But by now they were accustomed to the miserly speech of the Representative, and the authorities' faces permitted no joking. They marked their animals and turned the pigs loose. The decent people left; the simpletons and the curious stayed near the pen. By late afternoon the pigs had eaten all the grass.

"What will the animals eat tomorrow?" asked the worried owners.

"Nothing," answered the Peace Officers. "We have orders not to feed them anything."

"Nothing at all?"

"They'll only get water."

"It must be some kind of joke."

It wasn't. The Representative had ordered an absolute fast for the pigs. On Monday the pigs began their unforgettable squealing. On Tuesday they dug down under the roots with their snouts: the earth in the square looked like a sieve filled with spittle. On Wednesday the people got out of bed with enormous circles under their eyes: no one could sleep. On Thursday the Director of the School complained to the Representative. It would be impossible to continue classes if the pigs were not silenced. On Friday the shopkeepers complained en masse. On Saturday the old women began a solemn rogatory: Had the Representative lost his mind? On Sunday Father Chasán categorically refused to say mass. "Father, don't deprive us of God's help," pleaded Rivera. Father Chasán moved his angry lips, but to no avail: the squealing drowned out everything.

Sinners chosen to expiate monstrous sins, the pigs fasted for a week.

Nothing could move Don Alfonso Rivera. On Sunday he put on his black suit again and crossed the village with a dark look. The people had crowded into the school. Representative Rivera ordered the doors closed. Nobody could hear him even then. Realizing how useless words would be at the meeting, he picked up a piece of chalk and wrote on the slick surface of the blackboard: "Each of you will tie up your pig." The pigs shattered the fragile Sunday walls. He erased and wrote: "Now we will let them loose in the Company's pastures." He erased and wrote: "We will turn the pigs loose in the Company's best pastures." He erased and wrote: "I want to see the gringos' faces when they find out their sheep are going to eat infected grass."

He was grinning from ear to ear. The crowd burst into uncontrolled laughter. It would be wonderful to see their faces turn red. Rancas had not laughed for months. Unfortunately, the squealing drowned out the spluttering guffaws and giggles. But they knew that everyone else was laughing too by their gestures, their tears, the way they held their stomachs. Infect the Company's pastures with the starving pigs! It was fantastic. Rivera wrote the instructions in his large, childish hand: each man would take his pig, tie its feet and snout, and carry it to the boundaries of the Cerro's lands. The finest sheep fed in those fields. An army of veterinarians cared for the legendary sheep. Just one of those expensive Australians was worth more than a whole flock of the Rancasans' skinny animals. But how much would the Australians be worth after they had eaten the grass contaminated by the pigs from Rancas?

Clouds passed over the sun. They ran to the square, where the pigs were going mad. It took two or three men to tie each one of them. The strange procession left Rancas praying: women, children, and dirty, emaciated dogs marched to the Cerro with three hundred and four pigs. They came within sight of the Cerro's boundaries at three o'clock. Grim-looking guards came toward them, waving their Winchesters. The bullets were waiting for the community to cross the boundary lines. But they did not trespass. Rivera stopped at the edge of the property. Three hundred and four men did the same.

"What's going on?" shouted Clazo, the foreman on duty, a rawboned laborer. "Where are you taking those pigs?"

"We're taking them for a walk," answered Rivera.

"Just watch yourselves! Don't cross the line because we'll let you have it."

Rivera knelt to untie his pig. The animal went wild at the sight of the grass.

"We'll shoot the man or the animal that crosses the line!" shouted the bony cheeks.

The pigs ran and the bullets flew. A thunder of teeth martyrized the field. The farmhands shot too late: a millennium of hunger rooted through the pasture. The world turned into a grunt. A storm of squeals fell on the delicious grass like hailstones. The guards kept firing. Eight, ten, fifteen pigs fell just as they were about to taste the grass that the Company's splendid herds would never feed on again.

The next day the Cerro de Pasco Corporation abandoned fourteen hundred hectares.

CHAPTER TWENTY-THREE: *The Life and Miracles of an Ear Collector*

ONE should not confuse Wind-cutter with Ear-cutter. Wind-cutter was a horse that died during Colonel Marruecos' trip to Chinche to found a new cemetery. Amador, the Ear-cutter, was a man. Ask Carmen Minaya, his brother-in-law; his was one of Amador's first ears. He cut it off on the seventh day of Egmidio Loro's drunken celebration of the first communion of his daughter, the Mute. The heavenly event drove Loro wild with joy, and he locked the guests in with a padlock and threw the key into the dark shadows of a bottomless jug of rum. Their sense of honor obliged them to respond to the challenge, and the guests gave up all thought of leaving. It took them a week to recover the key. The discovery caused so much happiness that Amador contributed with his raucous, rum-soaked voice:

> *"Give me back my mother's rosary—*
> *you can have all the rest."*

"Don't crack the mirror," protested a tall, rough, pockmarked man from Michivilca who was dozing in the corner.

"If you don't want to hear me, take off your ears," answered Amador resentfully.

"Midnight Virgin,
Cover your nakedness."

"You take them off for me!" was the retort of the Michivilcan, and he stood up and walked forward, rolling back his shirt sleeves. He scarcely felt the flash that sliced off his ear.

"Anybody else have too many ears?" asked Amador with a gleam of madness in his eyes. "Keep on playing, you faggots!" he shouted at the orchestra.

The guests and musicians threw themselves into the foaming waters of a furious cachaspari. The widespread joy was contagious, and Amador danced until seven in the morning; then he took off for the high country.

Such expressive signs of harmonic predilection did not convince the Yanacochans that Amador's ears were shriveling for lack of music. Not even his brother-in-law, the musician Carmen Minaya, who by profession and kinship was obliged to nurture his melomania—not even he understood him. He not only abandoned him, he went so far as to stand in his way on the day when Amador, drunk as a Babylonian, asked the orchestra to accompany him while he defecated in a neighboring cornfield.

"Pretty please," begged Amador.

Minaya told Amador to go to the place where he was planning to deposit his evil-smelling pearls.

"Don't make me hit you, my dear brother-in-law."

"Get out of here, you drunkard!"

"Don't call me a drunkard."

Carmen Minaya made the mistake of grabbing him by the lapels. He would have made better use of his hands if he had held on to his ear. The one who held on to it was Amador.

"Are you coming or not?" he shouted at the orchestra.

The clarinets and the trumpets meekly accompanied him to his defecation. On the way Amador cut a thorn from a cactus and pinned the ear to the lapel of his grimy jacket. He danced until seven in the morning. Sporting the barbaric boutonniere, he ran through the village shouting: "There's not another man like me in Yanacocha!"

And there wasn't.

And so, even in the bosom of his own family, a place where talent is so often unappreciated, his genius was recognized. He fled to the backlands again. Now there was no dearth of clients. Calixto Ampudia, the blacksmith, was the first to purchase his talents. On New Year's Eve he discovered that a newly arrived schoolteacher was getting into his wife. He scarred his wife's face. But he would not lay hands on the little schoolteacher: if he touched him, it would mean a life sentence. He preferred to bend his six-foot body and walk through Amador's door. Without saying a word, he put three orange-colored bills on the table.

Ear-cutter unsheathed an ill-tempered smile. "What are you looking for, Calixto?"

"The ears of a man from Jauja," answered Ampudia, taking a bottle of rum out from under his poncho.

Ear-cutter gulped a fast, redeeming drink and coughed. To be polite, he pretended that the rum burned his throat. "What do you want them for?"

"I want to know what kind of ears are listening to my wife's moans."

"That pleasure will cost you five hundred sols."

"I work for my pleasure."

A week later Calixto Ampudia held the velvety-smooth ear that had listened to his wife's panting for months.

This time Ear-cutter appeared in court. Just by reading the records of the case, Dr. Montenegro realized that Amador Leandro's talents were being wasted up in the pastureland. He not only walked away a free man: the Judge also gave him a fifty-sol bill. The crafty Judge ordered him to join the village carpentry shop immediately.

That same afternoon Chuto Ildefonso hired him. It was not a demanding job. In five years—the time of Héctor Chacón's imprisonment—they needed him only thirteen times. His reputation spread far beyond the modest boundaries of the province. Ranch-owners, who loved the ears of those people who refused to remove their hats, asked the Judge for his services. Dr. Montenegro, who was the soul of generosity, always agreed to expand the modest lend-lease program which Yanahuanca was administering at almost the same time as a great nation to the north.

Amador's knife, the province's only export, established peace and tranquillity on the cattle ranches.

On the day Dr. Montenegro learned from Lala Cabieses' own mouth that Héctor Chacón's hand thirsted for his throat and he palely fled up to the mountains accompanied by foremen and Civil Guards, his first thought was of how much pleasure he would derive from stroking Hawkeye's ears. They fled, covering their tracks. No one dared say a word to the Judge. Even Arutingo and ex-Sergeant Atala were somber, not speaking of the excesses which unfortunately occurred on the day when "Ready Ass" asked "Iron Drawers" to lend her a needle, an incident which provoked the smashing of six hundred glasses. They rode six hours without daring even to drink their rum. When it was dark they returned to Huarautambo. The first stars were twinkling when Ear-cutter walked into the Judge's office.

Three days later seven horsemen with their faces muffled rode into Yanacocha, trampling stray dogs underfoot. They stopped at Hawkeye's door. Ear-cutter kicked open the door, but it was Hawkeye's good luck to have traveled to Pillao that day to close a livestock deal. The infuriated Ear-cutter made his way to the tavern, put down his money, and ordered the first dozen beers. Between bottles his thugs went out to spy. Hawkeye was late. After they had agreed on a price, the buyer had asked him "to stay and have a little bite with him." Héctor Chacón accepted the chili stew. Delighted at having paid one hundred sols for a young bull that was worth at least twice that much, the master of the house had some beers brought in.

"They say that in this village there's a real tough guy named Chacón," said Ear-cutter, throwing out his chest and digging his hands into his hips. "What a shame all the tough guys disappear when I come to visit them."

It was seven o'clock. An hour later Ear-cutter realized that some kind soul had delayed Chacón's trip.

"What the hell are you doing here?" he shouted at his gang of bullies.

"We're waiting for orders, Don Amador," his toughs answered, not wanting to be weaned from the bottle.

"Orders! What orders? I can handle Chacón all by myself."

He belched up Cartavio rum and withered the flowers on a brightly colored calendar. He kicked them out. Hawkeye slowly rode down the steep hill from Pillao. Three hundred meters away he saw a woman sitting on a rock at the side of the road: Sulpicia. Hawkeye sensed danger. Who was Sulpicia waiting for? He dismounted, tied the horse, and cautiously approached on foot. Sulpicia, who lacked his powers of vision, did not see him until Chacón was three paces from her.

"Héctor, you scared me! You'd better get moving, Héctor!"

Hawkeye smelled the woman's fear.

"Huarautambians with guns have been looking for you since this morning, Héctor! Amador wants your ears!"

"Where?"

"At Santillán's."

"Find Rustler and Horse Thief, Sulpicia. Tell them to meet me there."

"Be careful, Héctor, be careful."

Sulpicia went off into the darkness. Hawkeye disappeared among the rocks. His forebodings ripened in the foggy night. Leading his horse by the reins, he went into his corral, unsaddled him, and gave him water and feed. He washed his hands and face slowly. Without combing his hair, he left for the place where the toughest man in the province sat drinking. Amador was toasting his own shadow cast by the flickering kerosene lamp when Chacón came out of the darkness and through the door. Santillán's face turned white.

Without saying excuse me, Chacón picked up the glass and made a great show of spilling it.

"So you've been looking for me?"

Only half of his mouth was smiling. At that moment the transitory nature of human desire was amply demonstrated. Feverish in his longing to find him, Ear-cutter had searched all of Yanacocha for the face that swam behind the yellowish foam, but now that the frantically looked-for face was in front of him, his desire withered and died.

"Good evening, Don Héctor," said Ear-cutter with a greeting so suddenly polite that Santillán's hand trembled. "Good evening, Señores," he said to Rustler and Horse Thief. Only Horse Thief's burning, catlike eyes were visible between his knit cap and raised scarf. Rustler dusted off his hands, which were sprinkled with flour.

The silence swelled under the foaming glasses.

"So you like my ears?" and Hawkeye slowly rubbed the lobe of his left ear. Showing no respect for the private property of the man who had paid for the beer with his own money, he poured himself another glass.

"Who told you that, Don Héctor?"

"A little bird."

Rustler, who lacked Hawkeye's sense of humor, smashed the bottle.

"What are you doing here? What do you want, you motherfucker?"

"I had an argument with Señora Pepita," said Ear-cutter. Embers of uncertainty smoldered in his eyes.

"What kind of argument?"

Ear-cutter let a minute ooze by.

"Señora Pepita told me to kill the Yanacochans."

As if begging pardon for his hand's bad manners, Rustler's foot pushed the scattered pieces of glass to one side.

"And what did you say?"

Vaguely bored, Horse Thief put his hand in a sack of wheat; to pass the time, he began to sift the fistful of grain from one hand to the other.

"I told her that I didn't want any more fights with my brothers. I've had enough fights. I want to be friends with my in-laws. That's what I told her, but Señora Pepita got angry and threw me off the ranch."

"When did she throw you out?"

"Three days ago."

Horse Thief threw the handful of wheat in his face. "Why are you lying, you son-of-a-bitch? Yesterday you ran into my brother at Huajoruyuo Point. You were with the hands from Huarautambo and you ordered him whipped. You came to spy on us."

"Search this prick's pockets." Chacón was as hard as bronze.

Santillán flattened himself against the wall. Like swift-moving snakes, Rustler's hands went through Leandro's pockets. He emptied the contents and put them on the table: three keys (one of them rusty), a bottle-opener distributed free by English Kola, a blunt pencil, a letter, and a .38 revolver.

"Why are you carrying a revolver?"

"To shoot deer."

Rustler's hands were surprised. A bill of an unfamiliar pink color bewildered the investigator.

"What's this?"

It was the first time they had seen a five-hundred-sols bill.

"My savings," stammered Ear-cutter.

"So you carry your savings with you when you get drunk?" Rustler was leaning across the bar. "The game's over, Amador! You'd better tell the truth!"

Now Chacón was as cold as ice.

"All right," said Chacón, "let's take our time and think it over." And he turned to Santillán. "Do you have any rum?"

"Yes, Don Héctor."

"Sell me three bottles."

His nervous hands put out three dark bottles, unlabeled and

sealed with corncobs. His eyes almost missed the fifteen wrinkled sols on the bar.

"Let's go down to the province."

Chacón's eyes were hurting. The night crouched like a cat among the sparse growth. In the mountains, flashes of lightning battled one another. Without Hawkeye's warnings about stones and precipices, they would have fallen over the cliffs. A few scattered lights burned in Yanacocha. They rode for a mile and made the descent to Urumina. Covered in silence, they rode down to Antac. Only Ear-cutter's breathing trembled in the starless night. They passed Yurajirca. Neither Ear-cutter nor his guards opened their mouths. They saw Curayacu.

"Stop," ordered Hawkeye.

In the valley they could see the ragged lights of the province. Leandro grew brave as he looked at the glow of the city, where the Guardia Civil was on duty. His fear longed for the province just beyond the rocks.

"What are you muttering about?"

"Who do you think you are, dragging people through the back country? You won't get away with it! You'll see when we get to the province!"

Chacón's hands forced the coward down on the rocks. "Sit down, you bastard!" he lashed him with his voice. "You're not going to the province!" and as if realizing that he was a friend and the joke was over, he grabbed him by the hand and whispered: "Escape!"

Ear-cutter felt as if a band of hatred and disgust had been soldered between him and that bony hand.

"Try, run, escape!"

Leandro's ears rang with the contempt that was vaster than the night. Words alone would never convince them to let him go.

"Don't kill me, Uncle." He fell on his knees, trembling.

His fear had refreshed his memory. Suddenly he remembered that the man he had been hunting since morning, a morning that now seemed months away, was the same man who had taught him to fish for trout twenty years ago, when he had been his uncle.

"Don't stain your hands with the blood of your own nephew, Uncle." He shivered.

"Are you dancing the huayno?" Rustler made fun of him.

"Don't scare me, Uncle! My heart is pounding."

"Stop playing games!" shouted Chacón. "Tell us the truth."

"Señora Pepita will find out."

"We're all friends here. How can she find out? Do you want a drink?"

Ear-cutter cauterized his terror with a fiery drink.

"Is it good?"

"It's good liquor, Uncle."

"Drink some more."

"I'm half drunk now, Uncle."

"Drink some more, bastard!" and he placed the pistol next to his ear. "Tell the truth, you son-of-a-bitch!"

In the darkness the special eyes of Hawkeye counted the drops of sweat beading the forehead of the faint voice.

"Señora Pepita knows everything you do, Don Héctor. When you have a meeting, when you sleep, when you walk, the ranch knows everything."

"If you tell who the traitor is, I'll let you stay in the community." Chacón was as soft as velvet.

"They'll take it out on my parents, Uncle."

"I'll give you a house and land. I'll make it up between you and the Minayas."

Ear-cutter sighed. "Widow Carlos is the one who informs the most."

"She doesn't go to the meetings. How does she know?"

"She's a witch. She has animals who tell her. She sends trained dogs, animals who hear what you say and then tell her about it."

"And what else?"

"Birds too, she has tame birds."

"And what else?"

"Señora Pepita wants you killed."

"By your hand?"

"I agreed as a joke, Uncle."

"This prick will turn us in," said Rustler in a rage.

"I swear to you, Boss . . ."

"This faggot will ruin us."

"By the Blessed Virgin, I—"

"Drink," ordered Chacón, giving him the second bottle.

The rum did not burn any more.

"Drink it all up."

"My head's spinning."

"Did you tell Montenegro that we were planning to kill him?"

"Yes, Uncle."

"How did you warn him?"

"I sent a paper with Lala."

"What did the paper say?"

" 'Judge, run, Héctor Chacón has a gun and will kill you at the hearing.' "

"That's enough."

"Don't hurt me, Uncle."

"It's time for this bastard to show how brave he is."

The storm was passing. Ear-cutter saw that the voice had a face with hard cheeks, narrow forehead, and straight hair.

"Amador, you've always made your own law with your hand. You used your knife whenever you wanted. I don't give a damn about that, but for a few pounds of butter, for a couple of damned favors you betrayed your own community. You sold us out. Hold him!"

Rustler's trunklike arms and Horse Thief's strength held Ear-cutter in a vise.

"Pick him up!"

They lifted him as if he were a child. In the unexpected milky light of the moon, Hawkeye saw again for a moment the eyes of the child with whom he had jumped over streams or stolen fruit long ago. But he wiped out memory's face and replaced it with the face of the traitor. He took out a handkerchief and jammed it brutally into Ear-cutter's mouth. Amador's eyes opened wide as he suffocated. He twisted like a snake, but, little by little, his body filled with panic, with silence, with stale air.

CHAPTER TWENTY-FOUR: *Oil Portrait of a Magistrate*

THE pigs devoured fourteen hundred hectares, but they could not digest their ration of lead from the Winchesters. The brave animals died. The Fence continued to advance. After wolfing down forty-two hills, eighty ridges, nine ponds, and nineteen waterways, the Eastern Fence crawled to its rendezvous with the Western Fence. The prairie was not infinite, but the Fence was.

Rumors come and go like the wind on the prairie. Whose idea was it to file a complaint? It was not the child of Rivera's brain, or of Abdón Medrano's mind, or of Fortunato's head. One day Rancas awoke with the startling idea of filing a complaint. To whom? There was so much gossip that the leading citizens met in the school, spontaneously, with no official summons. Representative Rivera himself and the authorities went to the meeting without knowing why: perhaps with the notion that after Father Chasán's blessing, some kind of resistance was possible. Who knows? They met. Complain to whom? The Prefect? The Military Chief of the region? The Cerro itself? Not many words were wasted in proving how senseless those appeals would be.

"And if we went directly to the Judge?" suggested Abdón Medrano. "After all, the Fence is committing a crime. Nobody has the right to close off the roads."

"That's it!" The Representative jumped to his feet. "The Judge will defend us. It's the Judge's job to protect the needy."

Where did the Representative get the idea that the Judge's work is to administer justice? What a thought! The leading citizens of Rancas decided to file a complaint. It was a sunny day, and perhaps the extravagant golden light festooned their spirits with hope. Nothing debilitates a man more than the false promises of hope. The leading citizens searched through their trunks for their suits and dressed themselves up. Carefully washed—face, neck, hands (some, like Abdón Medrano, even put on a necktie)—they left the next day for Cerro de Pasco.

The Cerro de Pasco Courthouse has no sidewalks. Deep holes surround its two stories of peeling paint. Day and night a crowd of petitioners sits and waits to talk to the Judge, Dr. Parrales. The courtroom is a chamber with cracked plaster, a wobbling, shabby desk, a few armchairs, and some hard-backed chairs. On His Honor's desk, almost buried under a mountain of legal documents, a silver-framed photograph reveals the purity of His Honor's family feeling. In an inspired moment the artist captured His Honor solemnly sitting in his armchair; behind the Magistrate, standing in front of charming lakes and graceful swans painted on cardboard, their hands resting timidly on the shoulder of justice, are the shaded figures of his wife and six children, who could not hide from view even half of His Honor's fat body.

Respectfully, almost invisibly, the members of the committee from Rancas entered the office. Dr. Parrales did not raise his eyes from a sheet of paper that bore an official stamp: he continued his slow reading of the document. The men from the community were not surprised. The poor and humble of Peru are perfectly aware of the absolute unimportance of their business, and are always prepared to wait hours, days, weeks, months. This time they waited only thirty minutes. His Honor finished reading the appeal.

"What do you want?"

His coppery face was an unapproachable blank wall.

"Judge," stammered Rivera, "we are from Rancas . . . we have come . . ."

"Hurry up, I don't have much time."

"I don't know if you know about the existence of a Fence on the prairie, Judge." The embarrassed Representative of Rancas spoke in a fearful, anemic whisper.

"I don't know anything. I don't leave my office."

"The Cerro de Pasco Corporation has built a Fence. The prairie has been fenced in. Roads, villages, rivers, the Fence closes in everything, Judge."

"We have almost no sheep left, Judge," said Abdón Medrano. "Half of our animals have died. There's no grass. The Fence's teeth have chewed up all the pastures. Even the roads are cut off, Judge. Travelers don't come to Rancas any more."

"We don't even have a market any more." The Representative had recovered.

"Thirty thousand of our sheep have died," explained Medrano.

"It must be the plague," said the Judge.

"It's hunger, Judge," said Rivera.

"I'm no veterinarian." The Judge was annoyed. "What do you want?"

"We want you to confirm this abuse, Judge."

"That costs money."

"How much will the validation cost, Judge?" asked Rivera in better spirits.

"Ten thousand sols . . . perhaps fifteen," answered the slightly defrosted voice.

"We could never raise that much, Judge. Perhaps you could give it to us a little cheaper. . . ."

Dr. Parrales' eyes flashed and his hand slammed the desk violently. The sudden loud noise left the authorities speechless.

"What are you thinking of? This is no market. I try to do you a favor and still you argue. It's all up to you."

"Thank you, Judge."

"When can we come back?" Fortunato was half smiling from the door.

"Whenever you want," said a sullen Dr. Parrales.

They went out full of optimism.

"Didn't I tell you?" Fortunato rubbed his hands together. He could barely contain himself.

"We're fools. Why didn't we come sooner?"

"Ten thousand sols is a lot of money. We'll never be able to raise that much," said Rivera skeptically.

"We can take up a collection," said Medrano.

"Five thousand, six thousand would be the most we could get our hands on."

"You're right. We'll never raise that much."

"What if we organized a fiesta, a bazaar?" suggested Medrano.

They threw their arms around him. Instead of trying to raise the money with an uncertain collection, it was better to organize a raffle. People from the other villages would come when they learned the reason for it. It was a brilliant idea. In Rancas, Don Teodoro Santiago put on the finishing touches: why not invite the Mayor of Cerro de Pasco?

"He won't pay any attention to us!"

"What do we lose by trying?"

"Maybe he'll buy some raffle tickets."

"That'll be the day!"

"Nothing ventured, nothing gained."

"What do we have to lose?"

A storm threatened. The sky was putting on its livid plate armor. They ignored the snowstorm and went to the City Hall, a two-story building with green doors and windows that is another of Cerro's architectural horrors. Fortunato went in alone. He came back beaming.

"Come in, come in! The Mayor will see us!"

They scraped the mud off their shoes with stones. God forbid they should dirty the floor of the City Hall.

Genaro Ledesma, the Mayor, a man about thirty years old, stood waiting for them in front of a table covered with green cloth.

"All right, what can I do for you?" It was a warm, slow voice.

"We're from Rancas, Your Honor," explained Fortunato. "I

don't know if you're familiar with our problem. The Cerro de Pasco Corporation . . ."

"The Fence?" he asked.

They were dumbfounded. An authority had finally admitted the existence of that invisible serpent.

"You've seen the Fence, you've seen it?" asked Rivera in disbelief.

"Yes, like everybody else."

"But you've seen it?"

"Yes, yes. How could I not see it when it's right outside Cerro?"

"What do you think of it, Your Honor?" asked Fortunato prudently.

"It's an intolerable abuse. The Cerro has absolutely no right." He spoke unhurriedly.

Rivera felt encouraged. "We've come to ask a little favor of the Municipality, Your Honor."

"What do you have in mind?"

"We'd like the Municipality to help us and buy some of our raffle tickets."

"What do you have in mind?"

"We're organizing a raffle to raise Dr. Parrales' fee."

"The Judge?"

"Yes, Your Honor."

"Fee for what?"

"The Judge is asking us to pay ten thousand sols for a validation of the existence of the Fence. We can raise five thousand. If the Council helps us, we'll have the full amount," Fortunato said quickly.

"Are you crazy?"

They bowed their heads in dismay.

"Dr. Parrales has no right to ask you to pay him. He is *obliged* to execute that validation. The Judge has no right to charge anything. He received his salary from the State. It is his obligation to verify abuses."

"Then you can't help us?" asked Rivera, withdrawing into his discouragement.

"It would be unethical to give you money so that you can bribe the Judge. The Municipality can help you in another way, but not like this."

"How, Your Honor?"

The Mayor thought.

"This question of the Cerro is very serious. It's the most serious problem this Department has ever faced. And it's only the beginning—how will it end? Friends, we have to expose them. It is the only way to solve the problem. Today I'm going to speak on the radio, and I'll expose what they're doing. And before I do anything else, I am going to expose Dr. Parrales."

CHAPTER TWENTY-FIVE: *Concerning the Will Executed by Héctor Chacón While He Was Still Alive*

"I WAS a witness! I signed!" boasted Kid Remigio, thrusting out his hump.

Kid Remigio was talking just to hear himself talk. The night when Hawkeye gathered his children together to tell them his last will and testament, the hunchback was snoring in the barracks prison. Sergeant Cabrera, a firm supporter of the unopposed candidacy of the general who in time would compete with the man with the twisted legs, had learned that Remigio had spread the story around the city that the ballot boxes were magic containers where a vote against the general was automatically changed into a vote in favor of the general. The joke cost Kid Remigio fifteen days in jail. How could he have been present at the reading of the will? He was not there, he did not sign, he could not have signed. The document never existed. The only ones present were Ignacia, Chacón's wife, and their children Rigoberto, Fidel, and Juana. Hipólito was not there.

Chacón woke them at three in the morning. He lit a candle end. The light sputtered. Chacón wet his fingers with saliva, steadied the flame, and then he said:

"I've killed a man!"

"Holy Virgin!" Ignacia knelt down. Fidel looked at his father's face, tired and old before its time; this would be the last time he saw it. Rigoberto blinked his eyes in silence. Juana sobbed.

"Children, I've killed an abusive man. As soon as it gets light, the police will come looking for me. I've got to leave tonight."

"When will you come back, Papá?" asked Rigoberto.

"I'm not sure I will come back. If they catch me alive, the sentence will be a long one, but they'll have a hard time capturing me."

"Papá," whimpered Juana, "you never talked like this before."

Hawkeye sat down on a sack of barley. "Children, it's because of the pastures we have all this violence. If Montenegro had left us a little piece of pastureland, things would be different, but now it's too late. I'm in trouble. I could die any time now. If the police get their hands on me, they'll kill me."

"Kill the landowners, Papá," said Rigoberto, swallowing his tears. "Even if you must die, kill them. Break their backs."

"Don't talk like that to your father," Ignacia scolded him.

The candle turned Chacón's eyes yellow. This was the face that Rigoberto would remember. Years later, when he was lost in the labyrinths of obscure jobs, he would not remember the smiles of the good days, but only that face lacquered with anger.

"Whatever happens, Montenegro is finished. I'm determined to organize a band of men who will free us from the oppressors. I have friends ready to drink their blood."

"That's good, Papá," said Rigoberto. "Kill the bosses."

"I won't be the only one to die. I'll kill too. If I live, I'll come back. If I die, I'll die."

"What is it? What's going on, Papá?" complained the women again.

"I'm not sad, I'm angry. I'm not suffering, I'm happy."

He stood up.

That would be the face that Juana would remember. Years later, when remorse gnawed at her heart, the mist floating in those eyes would haunt her.

He sat down on the sack again. "Children, I own three cornfields: Ruruc, Chacrapapal, and Yancaragra. That land is mine. Those fields will be divided equally among my sons. My grandfather built this house. He left it to me. It will be divided equally among my sons."

"And the women?" asked Ignacia.

"The land at Lechuzapampa will be for the women. Nothing for you, Juana. You'll live with your husband. Obey him in everything. Don't abandon your mother."

"Why don't you let me go with you, Papá? I'm a man now, I know how to shoot," said Fidel.

"Don't cry. I have to avenge the poor people. Even if he has a thousand bodyguards, I'll kill Montenegro. He won't always be protected by his bootlickers. May will soon be here. He'll have to go out to supervise the harvest, and then he will die."

"I can go wherever you go, Papá. I can carry your bags of ammunition for you. That way you could sleep," insisted Fidel.

"Break the backs of the ranch-owners, Papá," repeated Rigoberto angrily.

"Rigoberto, you have to help the younger ones. They'll be after you here. You'd better go to work at the Atacocha mine. Stay out of trouble. This is the month I take care of everything once and for all."

"That's good, Papá, do it. The people say that you'll die. All right, die, but don't die without doing something. You have guns, don't let them kill you."

"They can't even shoot deer at a distance, let alone us. You heard what I said: I'm dividing everything I own among you. I have only two things left: a calendar they gave me in Yanahuanca and a package of confetti I was going to use at Carnival. The calendar is for you, Rigoberto; the confetti is for you, Fidel. Now get my horse ready. I'm going."

CHAPTER TWENTY-SIX: *Concerning the Mole-men and the Children Who Were Almost Named Harry*

ONE stormy Friday, Mayor Ledesma contributed to the bad weather with the thunder and lightning of a speech against Dr. Parrales. Radio Corporation was broadcasting his weekly lecture. The Mayor, a history teacher at the Daniel A. Carrión University, took advantage of the emotion caused by the singing of Jorge Negrete to attack the Judge. When the microphone was turned off, the electromagnetic rays discovered by Hertz carried the news to the four corners of the earth: Judge Parrales was trying to increase his private collection of circulating currency. The city hummed with rumors. Hundreds of Cerronians knew about the parade of sheep. The centennial of Daniel A. Carrión, the medical martyr, was approaching. The Prefect was not resigned to the ridicule of the authorities from Lima. But no sooner had the sparks of the denunciation died down than the very same radio station broadcast the news that Dr. Parrales would sue the Mayor for defamation and slander. The city was concerned. What would the lawsuit lead to? No one ever learned why an epidemic attacked Cerro de Pasco. An unknown virus infected the eyes of its citizens. Apparently the victims enjoyed perfect vision except for a mysterious partial blindness that made certain objects invisible to them. A patient affected by the disease, who was able to describe, for example, the spots on a sheep half a mile away, could not see a fence at a distance of one hundred yards. Even the orderlies at the Health Unit realized that something was happening that was without precedent in the history of medicine. Unfortunately, Cerro de Pasco has no ophthalmologist. No eye doctor would accept the position that was perpetually open at the Workers' Hospital. The impossible altitude, the cold, the damned isolation kept them away. The government took advantage of the situation to proclaim the existence of "full employment" in the Department. But, political controversies aside, one could appreciate the invaluable loss to the science of opthalmology occasioned by the disconcerting and unstudied virus. Perhaps the Medical Unit could have filled the vacuum in some way; but, unfortunately, the epidemic coincided with a monumental canasta tournament. For two weeks the Medical Unit practically never opened its doors. People said that the virus came from the jungle. Very possibly. Cerro de Pasco is a necessary stop for the trucks that transport fruit from Tingo María to Lima. Was it the fruit? The poor people, the children of the miners, never tasted papayas and apples. The leading citizens enjoyed the coolness of peaches and the sweetness of bananas from Tingo María. Perhaps for this reason they were the ones affected by the virus. Prefect Figuerola, Judge Parrales, Commandant Canchucaja, District Attorney Moreyna, and even the officers of the Guardia Civil barracks stopped seeing certain things. Happily, the disease was mild, and normal business was not interrupted. The authorities, especially Prefect Figuerola, were models of civic-mindedness. They did their duty. The Mayor's efforts failed: because of the epidemic, no one could see the Fence. Don Teodoro Santiago said that the sick ones were color-blind also, but one morning Prefect Figuerola, ordered his car to stop at the door of the Hotel France so that he could buy a beautiful Ayacuchan blanket. There it was learned that he could see colors. But, nonetheless, he could not see the Fence. On the two roads out of Cerro, on the Huánuco Highway as well as on the road to La Oroya, the work crews built two wooden gates, six meters high and as wide as each road. The city was alarmed. But the authorities could not see the gates either. Only the Mayor was free of the disease; perhaps because he was from Trujillo, perhaps because he was in the habit of drinking large quantities of tea, he did not succumb to the epidemic disease. Protected by his immunity, he called an extraordinary Council meeting only to discover that half of the Councilmen—who possessed an Aprista blood composition —were also victims of the epidemic. The other half hesitated. Officious friends informed the worthy Councilmen, especially the businessmen, that they were a hairbreadth from earning a place on the Company's blacklist; another disease attacked them: a malaria of the teeth. The meeting was in an uproar. Certain Councilmen accused the Mayor of being premature in his denunciations. There were other ways. After six hours of debate the Municipality approved a peace-making resolution: to use the good offices of the Municipality to negotiate differences between the communities and the Cerro de Pasco Corporation. The Mayor requested an interview. The office of the Superintendent of the Cerro, Mr. Harry Troeller, granted him one in two weeks. The Mayor persisted and they changed the appointment to four days later. The news spread. On the appointed Friday a crowd of petitioners accompanied the Mayor and the Councilmen. The municipal officials entered the imposing Stone House at six o'clock and came out at six fourteen. The Cerro did not know anything about the Fence either. The legal counsel for the Cerro, Dr. Iscariote Carranza—a fat mestizo whose face housed two little rat eyes and a turnip nose—took five minutes to inform the Mayor of this fact. The other nine minutes and forty-four seconds of the interview were used by the Superintendent himself, Mr. Harry Troeller, for since he now had the pleasure of meeting with the leading official of the proud city of Cerro de Pasco, he would take advantage of the opportunity to mention a much more serious problem than that of a presumptive fence: as the Señor Mayor knew, the Cerro de Pasco Corporation owned the electrical plants at Llaupi and Malpaso (a real disaster area for the imprudent workers shot there in the year

1931). The electric power enjoyed by proud Cerro de Pasco originated in those plants, but at what price? Ten centavos per kilowatt. Was it a fair price? No, no, it was not. Then what was it? It was a subsidy made in deference to the splendid city of Cerro de Pasco. Out of kindness, the Company had absorbed the deficit for decades; but the Señor Mayor was also not ignorant of the fact that the price of minerals was falling in the international market. What a shame that the Señor Mayor did not speak English. Consequently, the Cerro could no longer withstand the economic pressure and was extremely sorry to inform him that, starting at that very moment, the Cerro found itself obliged to sell light at thirty centavos per kilowatt. The Señor Mayor answered that it was true that the Cerro de Pasco Corporation sold them electric light at ten centavos per kilowatt. The Municipality resold it at thirty centavos; the small price difference was a traditional municipal income thanks to which they had been able, to cite only one example, to provide uniforms for the Department soccer team; black pants, yellow shirts, "Cerro" written in blue letters, and new shoes. Only last Sunday the valiant yellow shirts had defeated (five to one) the arrogant team from El Callao. And that was no small feat: another team would have a hard time stopping the Cerro de Pasco team. The soccer championship was coming up. Soon the yellow shirts— Mr. Troeller interrupted: he had not even known that they could play soccer at this altitude. The Mayor laughed and said that— Mr. Troeller regretted having to insist: the price would treble or they would cut off the electricity. The Mayor was shocked. Did the Fence have something to do with the sudden rise in prices? Dr. Iscariote Carranza laughed good-naturedly. Please, we live in a democracy, don't we? The one who did not laugh was Mr. Troeller. He was very sorry to insist there was another small bill to be settled. If he was not mistaken, the Honorable City Council of Cerro de Pasco owed the Cerro de Pasco Corporation a little account of 44,820 sols and 40 centavos for back light bills. He regretted saying that if the Honorable City Council did not pay within the next forty-eight hours, the Cerro would suspend service. Slightly irritated by now, the Mayor said that it seemed as if the Company were treating the Municipality like an unruly child. The native Peruvian, Dr. Carranza, laughed again. "I really am surprised," said Ledesma, "Mr. Troeller, that a company as powerful as the Cerro de Pasco Corporation, which, incidentally, showed a net profit of five hundred million sols on its last statement, is in such dire need of a miserable forty thousand. Money does not bring happiness. On the contrary, it corrupts the soul. Gauguin himself—" Mr. Troeller retorted with a little smile: it was obvious that the Señor Mayor—a teacher, after all—was a humanist. Dr. Iscariote Carranza noted that, if he were not mistaken, the Mayor wrote poetry. The poet agreed modestly. "But we," continued Iscariote, "are simple, ordinary men—working people, Señor Mayor. Businessmen see the world differently: five hundred million sols are made up of fifty billion centavos." No, no, it was impossible, he was really sorry; either the bill would be paid or they would cut off the electricity.

"That gringo Troeller is a damned son-of-a-bitch!" said the irate Mayor when he left.

Such an obvious characterization did not keep Cerro de Pasco from waking up on Sunday in darkness. Cerro is a dark city: the shortness of the day, the continual snowfall, the fog make it necessary to burn lights day and night; even then people lose their way in the narrow, winding streets. Deprived of the dim comfort of electric streetlamps, Cerro turned into a tunnel. It was not the first time. Long before the arrival of the unforgettable redbeard, Cerro de Pasco had lived in darkness. There had been no electric light. The ruinous work in the mines had decimated the Indian population. Let us not speak of the charnel house of the mines during the colonial period. Even after the republic was established, the shrinking veins of ore languished for lack of workers. Despite all the security measures, the Indians ran away. There was nothing else to do but confine them for life in the mines. Golden-mouthed recruiters traveled the provinces with dazzling promises of enormous salaries. They paid them money in advance. Tempted by good liquor, convinced by lengths of cloth, shirts, and even shoes, the farmhands signed up. They went down into the tunnels in Cerro de Pasco: they never came out again. Armed guards kept them inside the damp mine entrances. They lived and died in the mine galleries. From time to time the overseers would take a mole-man into the sunlight: he would plead with them to take him back to the shadows. That's how much the light of day wounded them! The only thing the mole-men won was permission to bring down their relatives. Whole families, including dogs, went down to live in the mine tunnels. Thousands of mole-men worked, ate, made love in a subterranean city as large as Cerro de Pasco itself. A race with unusual eyes, the mole-children, was raised in the galleries, not believing in fairy tales about a sun different from the mining lamps. No one will ever know how many people lived there. They are not buried in the cemetery of Cerro de Pasco, but in an underground graveyard. The situation was not as bad in the year 1960. The darkness into which Mr. Troeller plunged the city only upset everyone's routine. The mundane task of buying bread became wildly fanciful. A haircut turned into an adventure. Nobody could find his way around the streets. People stumbled in the darkness. The rancorous benefited from Mr. Troeller's uncivil behavior: they took advantage of it to attack their enemies. For the pure pleasure of watching respectable people fall, hooligans stretched ropes from corner to corner. Everything was in a state of chaos; for the friends of other people's possessions, it was the advent of a longed-for golden age. Pickpockets ruled the shadows. Beggars grew fat and even the poor would only eat chicken. The enraged city was divided between those who said what-the-hell-are-we-getting-involved-with-the-gringos-for and those who maintained it's-about-time-we-started-to-fight-back. In the second faction were those who had been pierced by Cupid's arrows. The darkness crackled with kisses. The girls went out to buy bread: they came back pregnant. Lovers blessed the Cerro de Pasco Corporation. Adulterous wives learned to leave a sack of potatoes in their beds to calm the angry suspicions of cuckolds. Thanks to

Mr. Troeller's stormy nature, severe fathers, abusive husbands, and unbearable mothers learned their lesson. Deceived husbands and disillusioned fathers searched the streets and squares in vain: the wind in Cerro permits no torches. In his well-lit office Mr. Troeller never learned how many hearts were grateful to him. Nine months later the dispute with the Cerro was translated into a rise in the demographic curve. Couples filled with gratitude dreamed of baptizing the new citizens with the name of Harry. But the Cerro de Pasco Corporation did not know how to take advantage of the situation. The distribution of baby clothes or even simple congratulation cards would have been enough. But so elementary a piece of public relations did not occur to the Stone House. And so the Cerro missed a golden opportunity.

CHAPTER TWENTY-SEVEN: *Where, Still Free of Charge, the Amused Reader Will Again Meet the Carefree Pisser*

THE gossips, the province's only archives, disagree. Doña Josefina de la Torre, dean of viperish tongues, openly proclaims the falsity of this chapter. Eduvigis Dolor, the Health Officer's mistress, swears that she heard it all from the sawbones' own lips. But who witnessed it? Certain historians affirm that as soon as he learned of Ear-cutter's unfortunate end, Dr. Montenegro shed a tear. For pity, according to some; for pure joy, according to others. The chroniclers who brand the Judge's sobs as crocodile tears maintain that he was wearing a smile identical to Lucifer's in the celebrated Final Judgment at the Yanahuanca church. At last he had the Yanacocha authorities where he wanted them! Accompanied by notaries and Civil Guards, the Judge identified the corpse of the ill-fated Ear-cutter. Disproving the historians who claim that the judges in Peru are incapable of weeping, the black suit wiped away another fat tear and ordered Ear-cutter's body moved to Yanahuanca. And so Amador entered the province like certain politicians: on the backs of the people. At this point the scholars again disagree. But sympathy prevailed. Instead of sending the body to the Health Department, the black suit had it taken to his own house. And so Ear-cutter shared the same destiny as other great artists: doors were opened to him in death that had been closed in life. The black suit ordered the curious onlookers to be dispersed. Only Procopio, the dead man's brother, remained with the corpse, feeling more apprehension at sitting on the green plastic chairs than worry for Ear-cutter's demise. Then, while Ear-cutter swelled, Dr. Montenegro explained to Procopio that the Yanacocha community had deprived the art of the knife of one of its most outstanding practitioners. Unfortunately, there was no proof, but justice existed to right wrongs. "If we scratch Amador's face a little," sobbed the Judge, "the guilty will not be able to mock your family." "It would be a sin, Judge," said an embarrassed Procopio. The Judge objected to this theological definition: "It would be a sin if criminals could make a laughingstock of justice. And you would be the one responsible for it," said the Judge, and he fixed his eyes, which were unfortunately very small for such a great scene, on the ratlike eyes of Procopio, whose only clear idea after all the discussion was that he might be guilty. "Whatever you say, Judge," muumured Procopio. Chuto was called. Ildefonso entered the room visibly moved. Aflame with a righteous fury, he led the corpse to the inner patios. Perhaps they did more than scratch him there, because when Ear-cutter returned he was covered with multicolored bruises caused by a storm of clubs and stones. Procopio almost fainted when he saw the impressionistic display, but he was comforted by three hundred sols charitably donated for "funeral expenses." And the fact is that essence of money is a better tonic than fruit juice or even liver extract.

That afternoon the Health Officer declared that Ear-cutter had obviously been stoned to death by a mob. Attentive to the interests of the famous blindfolded lady, the court of Yanahuanca executed an immediate order for the capture of the allegedly guilty parties: the officials of the Yanacocha community. Graciously summoned by Sergeant Cabrera, they all went to jail: Agapito Robles, Blas Valle, Alejandro Gui, Sinforiano Liberato, Felicio de la Vega, Jorge Castro, José Reques, and the three Minayas—Carmen, Amador, and Anacleto.

A week later they received a written invitation from the

Huánuco Prison: they lodged there a year.

Only Héctor Chacón, the Denied, did not heed the thundering call of justice: he crossed the provincial limits under the protection of a hailstorm. The snow that made roads disappear did not stop him: seven days later he came down to Huamalíes, home of the bravest man he had met during his five-year imprisonment: Pisser, with the golden smile. It was not the foul breath of dental decay or the kick of a mule that had deprived Pisser of his teeth: it was women. To dazzle them, he had had his magnificent enamel set extracted and replaced with a brilliant smile of gold. He could afford it: he raised poppies and relieved the ranches of their excess cattle. But he did not enjoy it for long. On one of his excursions he made the mistake of laughing: a farmhand recognized his golden joy. When he was in prison he tried to exchange his gold smile for a more discreet set of silver teeth. His companions dissuaded him from committing such an outrage. But it was not only his lavish mouth that caused the Federal Guards to esteem him: they feared his skill with poisons. On the day his mother, driven to despair by the effort of feeding seven mouths, had abandoned him in the Huánuco square, Pisser had the good fortune to fall into the hands of Don Angel de los Angeles. The master of poisons took him to the forest. There he learned the power of plants. Pisser was the mysterious assistant who attended Don Angel de los Angeles during the famous duel. Don Angel did not provoke it, but rather a mindless government which insisted on finding a position for some unemployed medical-school graduate. It is common knowledge that when the people learned that the government was sending them a doctor, the Governor rode for three days on horseback to send the following telegram:

PRESIDENT OF THE REPUBLIC
PALACE OF THE PRESIDENT
LIMA PERU SOUTH AMERICA

HAVE HONOR INFORM YOU PEOPLE DON'T NEED DOCTOR STOP HEALTH PERFECT THANKS INVALUABLE SERVICES DON ANGEL DE LOS

ANGELES STOP THIRD OF POPULATION OVER HUNDRED YEARS OLD STOP
YOUR EXCELLENCY'S HUMBLE SERVANT

GOVERNOR PADILLA.

But even this salutary text did not stop the arrival of a fat and sweaty personage: the new doctor. The people tolerated him, accustomed to the visits of white men who soon wearied of the climate and left cursing the unhealthy atmosphere around the ponds. Any sensible man would have understood that the only thing to do was to concentrate on the straights in poker games, but the fat man would have none of it and he began to harass Don Angel. The herbalist, who had grown old surrounded by gratitude, put up with him, but one Sunday when he was crossing the square the quack doctor insulted him outright:

"Listen, you witch," he shouted before an open-mouthed, disbelieving crowd, "if you're a man, I'll be waiting for you next Sunday in this square! Then we'll see if you can heal yourself!"

Don Angel sighed and showed up the following Sunday on a black horse. The square was filled with people who had traveled in from ten leagues around.

They agreed on three doses. Don Angel asked to take the doctor's three poisons all at once. He drank the toxins and then he chewed three plants. He perspired purple, yellow, and blue. Pisser, who was then thirteen years old, wiped the perspiration away with a handkerchief covered with crosses drawn inside a waning moon. The so-called doctor drank Don Angel's potion with a little smile; five minutes later he began to bleed. Vainly he injected himself. He plugged himself with cotton and tried to control the speed with which his blood flowed out. He had sprung leaks in his nose, his mouth, his ears, his anus. The disciple of such a master put fear in the hearts of even the Federal Guards, who were, moreover, anxious to obtain love potions which would make them irresistible to disdainful girls or triple the potency of their tools.

Héctor Chacón fled Yanahuanca with his thoughts fixed on Pisser. He understood that by himself he could never successfully confront the swaggering contempt of the Civil Guards. On the road to Huánuco he dreamed of creating an armed band capable of expelling the ranch-owners by the brute force of guns. Humans were not the only ones who were suffering: Rustler had told him of the bitter misery of the animals. And he dreamed of organizing desperate men and coming back to kill Montenegro. Pisser would help him. The man with the costly smile had a score to settle with the exploiters. Chacón himself had heard him in prison unraveling a long history of abuses. Pisser was no ordinary man: and Chacón dreamed of Pisser's hands sprinkling powder in the Civil Guards' water, withering the outposts with poison, making the bosses urinate blood.

He could see Huamalíes. He stopped and tied his horse and washed his face in a watering hole. He crossed the village and came to Pisser's house by the side of the road. Even from a distance you could hear the loud laughter. A fleshy woman, a magnificent female, came to the door.

"Is this Pisser's house?"

The woman's suspicious eyes looked him up and down.

"Doña, Pisser and I lived together for five years in jail."

A pair of roguish eyes peered through the half-open door, then a pair of rough shoes kicked it wide open: a fat man with a red face offered his arms and a smile. He laughed and slapped his thighs.

"Chacón, Chacón, how I've missed you! What a long time it's been, Chacón! I thought about you so often, brother! But you're not the man for visiting poor people. Brothers, come and meet my compadre Chacón."

They embraced. Two other men came out. The first, the thinnest man Chacón had ever seen, was wearing ragged pants and a leather jacket in shreds. The other, huge and muscular, flashed a friendly smile.

"This is my compadre, Héctor Chacón." Pisser slapped him on the shoulder.

"We've heard a lot about you, Don Chacón!" said the Thin Man.

Pisser smacked his wife on the buttocks.

"Listen, honey, kill a chicken right now and fix a good stew for my compadre."

The room was a confusion of chairs, sacks of potatoes, harnesses, and ropes. Six empty beer bottles and six full ones showed they had been celebrating even before the reunion.

Pisser opened another bottle. "To what do I owe the pleasure, compadre?"

"I came to see you like we promised."

"Can I come in?" asked a solid, muscular man from the door, a villager from Choras.

"This is Chacón," said Pisser.

The newcomer's eyes grew less suspicious.

"I am Héctor Chacón, from the province of Daniel A. Carrión."

"I've heard a lot about you, Señor Chacón," said the man from Choras.

"Salud!" said Pisser. "I like to drink with men, not with pricks. What's on your mind, compadre? I can see it on your face. You can talk. You can trust these men."

"I'm in trouble, brothers. I killed a man."

"I've heard a lot about that Judge Montenegro," Pisser spat when Chacón finished his story.

Another twelve beers were waiting for the throats of the angry men.

"That Judge has taken advantage of his power and walked all over everybody for twenty years. Whoever defies him goes to jail. That man has two jails: one on his ranch and another in the province."

"I heard that the jail in Huarautambo has no windows," said the Thin Man.

"It's true. It has a hole as big as your fist, just big enough for them to pass one potato a day to the prisoner."

"And what do you want to do, compadre?" asked Pisser, opening another bottle.

"I want to fight and get back my land. There's no use talking to ranch-owners. I want to start a war."

"And what does your Representative think?"

"He's in prison."

"And the President of the Community?"

"He's in prison."

The Thin Man stood up. "We can't put up with so many abuses."

"Héctor is right," said Pisser. "It's a lie when we say we're free. We're slaves. Killing is the only way we'll ever change anything."

"Señores, we should start in Daniel A. Carrión Province," said Chacón. "We should begin the killing of the rich in Yanahuanca. I'm ready to stake my life. Will you help me, compadre?" He looked at Pisser timidly.

Pisser rolled his playful eyes. I'll help you, compadre. What do you need?"

"Rifles and advice, compadre."

"We must answer injustice with blood," said the Thin Man excitedly. "We must make a revolution."

"They'll bring in men with guns," said Pisser.

"Then we'll answer with guns," continued the Thin Man. "I'm a veteran. There are lots of ways to stop an army."

"We'll begin with Montenegro," said Chacón.

"I'm ready, compadre."

Pisser's small hands caressed and then deflowered another bottle of beer.

CHAPTER TWENTY-EIGHT: *Which Will Demonstrate That There Is Some Difference Between Hummingbirds and Sheep*

IN almost all the villages of Cerro de Pasco—and in most of the Peruvian Republic—the best lands in the village are plots that suffer under the ill-smelling rains of public necessity. They are monuments to hope. The Municipality reserves them for promised, imaginary public buildings. Every time the Prefect or the Deputy promises a school or a health department, the optimistic Municipality sets aside a piece of land. The City Council and the people attend the solemn laying of the "first stone" of the public building. The second stone never follows it. The humblest town has dozens of "cornerstones": markets, schools, medical centers, farming offices, imaginary avenues display a single stone in all its untouched purity. All of Peru is a cornerstone. Cerro de Pasco, since it is a departmental capital, obviously has many more "cornerstones" than an ordinary province. But, as the saying goes, who knows what tomorrow will bring? The Municipality of Cerro has at its disposal many plots of land overgrown with weeds. Such negligence warranted the community's request that the Council permit them to bring their emaciated flocks into the chimerical public buildings. The Council, moved by the necklace of spittle that lay dying on the Huánuco Highway, granted them the use of its lands. The grass maintained the Rancasan flocks for two weeks.

When the weeds had all been eaten, the community asked permission to graze the animals in the Municipal Stadium. The soccer field, where the agile yellow shirts of Cerro had just defeated (four to one) the proud team from Huancayo, fed them for nine more days. It was the end of October.

The first of November, All Souls' Day, is an important holiday in Cerro de Pasco. From every corner of Peru, from the dusty cities of the coast, from the hot villages of the jungle, from the Huancayan countryside, the Pascans come up to visit their dead. It is the only time of the year when it is difficult to find a room. No flowers grow in Cerro de Pasco; precisely for that reason the families go out of their way to present their dead with the unheard-of luxury of wreaths. Calla lilies, roses, geraniums, Madonna lilies, spikenard come by the truckload from the warm lowlands. A throng invades the cemetery on November 1. For one morning the graveyard regains the former grandeur of the time when Cerro boasted twelve vice-consuls. The crowd prays and sobs before the tombs; at noon it leaves to find consolation in the food stalls scattered for a half a mile around. They eat, they drink, and they dance until nightfall to the health of those who are gone but not forgotten. Enchanted by the magic wand of memory, the cemetery is changed, for a day, into a city. On the other three hundred sixty-four days the wind is the only guest who comes to visit.

On that first of November of 1959 the dead received more flowers than ever.

The communities from Rancas, from Villa de Pasco, from Yarusyacán, from Yanacancha, from Huayllay visited the cemetery too. They brought no flowers; they came to weep, longing to talk with their dead. Without money to buy the steaming marvels of the food stalls—mutton-head broth, duck and rice, roast pig, kid Northern style—they contented themselves with a meal of toasted corn as they sat among the gravestones.

Then Don Alfonso Rivera looked at a chingolo. The black bird flew in confident circles and then landed on a gravestone, shook its head, and hopped up to peck at some spikenard.

"Look at the little chingolo!" whispered Rivera. "Blessed creature of God!"

They continued chewing with their eyes on Jirishanca, an inaccessible, indifferent needle of snow buried in the forehead of the sky.

"Look at it, look at it!"

"What's wrong, Don Alfonso?" asked Medrano.

His eyes were blazing. "How it eats the flowers!" and he took in the cemetery with his arms. "Look at all the flowers! Good flowers, delicious flowers to chew and eat!"

"The cemetery really looks beautiful, Don Alfonso," agreed Medrano.

"Lots of flowers, delicious flowers to feed on and chew," continued Don Alfonso.

"What are you thinking of, Representative Rivera?"

"Flowers that can feed little lambs."

"Don Alfonso!"

"Let's steal them," said Rivera excitedly.

"Shh . . . shh . . ."

"Why steal them?" asked Medrano. "Maybe they'll give them to us. Why not? The Mayor can give away flowers. They only die here."

"They won't want to," said Gora.

"It would show a lack of respect."

"You can't lose anything by trying," said Rivera.

"They'll never give them away! They'd rather let them die," said Gora.

"If they give us the flowers, the sheep could last another week," said Fortunato.

"They'll say it's sacrilege," insisted Gora.

"We have to get more time."

"For what?"

"I don't know," said the old man, "I don't know. Wouldn't you be happy to bring your animals here?"

The sexton's bell meant they had to leave, but they did not go away. They stayed at the gate, talking. When it was dark, they went down to Cerro de Pasco. All the way back to Rancas they did not stop talking. Early the next day they visited the Mayor of Cerro.

"The flowers in the cemetery?" The Mayor was perplexed for a moment, then he burst out laughing.

"Could you do it, Your Honor?"

"Why not?" asked the Mayor. "But I can't make the decision alone. I'll have to consult the Council."

The flowers in the cemetery? The honorable Provincial Council raised a storm of protest. Councilman Malpartida was indignant. What would the people say? Was the undeniable problem of the collectives to become the city's problem as well? Cerro de Pasco was suffering too. The rise in the cost of electricity was only a warning. Watch out! The flowers of the dead were sacred. If not even the grave was respected, where would it all end?

The Mayor insisted. The way things stood, the community would soon be the guests and owners of the cemetery.

"No one knows if they're alive or dead. As future residents of the cemetery, perhaps the flowers already belong to them. It's only a question of time."

And he argued from a legal point of view. The Constitution of the Republic of Peru is explicit: no one is obliged to do what the law does not command, nor *impeded*—do you hear that, gentlemen?—*impeded* from doing what the law does not prohibit. Was there a law against giving away the flowers in the cemetery? Peruvian jurisprudence in its wisdom had codified no law stipulating: "In the event a foreign company fences in all free land, the collectives of Pasco are prohibited from bringing their livestock into the cemetery."

"Bring them in?" Señor Malpartida was overwrought. "Wouldn't it be better to take the flowers out?"

"And how would you take the flowers out?"

"Wouldn't it be better to bring the livestock in?"

"It would be blasphemy."

"Blasphemy exists only when there is intent. What sacrilegious intent is harbored by the sheep? Aren't there animals in the cemetery right now?"

"What did you say?"

Mayor Ledesma smiled. "The birds eat the flowers."

Can sheep commit sacrilege? What is the difference between a lamb and a chingolo bird? Is it blasphemy to remove the flowers? How should the flowers be removed? Should they be thrown over the wall? The delicate theological problem was debated for six hours. Why not? At the beginning of the Conquest the Spanish philosophers debated, not for six hours but for sixty years, the question of whether or not the Indians belonged to the human race. Didn't the problem even come to the papal throne, so that, waving the keys of the kingdom, a bishop of Rome would announce ex cathedra that those creatures discovered in the Indies with body, face, and gesture frighteningly similar to those of man were, in effect, men?

The debate in the Municipality of Cerro de Pasco took less time. At four in the morning the following motion was approved: "The Provincial Council of Cerro de Pasco authorizes the communities of Cerro de Pasco to bring their grazing animals into the city cemetery so that said livestock, which are in a state of hunger, may feed on the flowers left by the relatives of the dead on the first day of November of the present year."

Let it be known, to Señor Malpartida's honor, that the motion was approved unanimously.

CHAPTER TWENTY-NINE: *Concerning the Universal Insurrection of the Horses Planned by Rustler and Horse Thief*

DR. Montenegro was living under the protection of the Guardia Civil guns and the suspicions of four hundred compadres. Could five men defeat them? That is what the gossips ask. They talk for the sake of talking. It is true they were five men against seven hundred armed defenders, but they were five extraordinary men.

To begin with, Héctor Chacón, Hawkeye, could see as well at night as during the day; his eyes penetrated the darkness as easily as the light. How could the Guardia Civil ambush him? Then Horse Thief and Rustler skillfully organized an insurrection of the Yanahuanca horses. Rustler patiently explained the broader implications of the conspiracy to the horses of the province. With tear-filled eyes the wretched horses learned that the dawn of an open prairie was approaching. Solemnly they agreed to revolt; all they were waiting for was the signal to kick in the heads of the Civil Guards who dared to undertake the persecution that would follow the inevitable death of Dr. Montenegro. Distinguished horses directed the plot and, aided by mares with maddening rumps, even involved the animals of the Guardia Civil. Dumb Bird and Morning Star, winners of the July 28 race, headed the conspiracy and recruited colts as shockingly rebellious as Crooked Shoes,

Seven Winds, and Rosemary to the cause. The horses would trample the Civil Guards on the day a two-year-old with yellow eyes galloped past the ranches with the news that Montenegro was hanging from a tree. And that mighty insurrection would be only the beginning, because then Pisser, dread ambassador of abelmosk, poisons, and poppies, would come out of the Huánuco jungle. Just sprinkling the water of the Civil Guards with iron-bearing powders would make them bleed from every orifice: nose, mouth, ears, and anus. And there were the dream powers that let Rustler know about raids in advance. Besides, they weren't five, but six, although the man from Choras never opened his mouth. In the course of a mysterious journey he had lost his voice. During the months they rode together he made only three statements: "The rains are coming," "It's better to wait for the harvest," and "Watch out for bad luck."

The Thin Man spoke with the nickel-plated voice of his deadly marksmanship. "Why didn't you tell us that the horses would rebel, compadre?" he asked.

"I wanted to be sure of them, compadre," answered Héctor Chacón.

"And what will be the signal for the animals to rebel?"

"As soon as Montenegro is dead, a black colt will carry the word to all the cattle ranches."

"We'll hang the Judge and start a real revolution," said Pisser enthusiastically as he uncorked a bottle of rum.

"If you want your land, you have to kill the landowners," Chacón said with a cruel smile.

The man from Choras smiled indifferently.

"After we kill the Judge they'll send troops. We'll fight back. I can get two hundred riders from this Department," said Pisser.

"It's the only true way, compadre," said the Thin Man. "The law's a joke. My community in Ambo has been trying to get the law to do something about its lands for fifty years."

"That's nothing," said Pisser. "In the south the Ongoy community has been trying to get the law to do something for four hundred years. Seven dead Representatives is all they've gotten."

"There's a hut." The Thin Man was pointing, overjoyed.

"No," said Chacón. "Let's go on. It's better if we travel by night. We'll be in Tuctuhuachanga by dawn. From there we'll go on foot. They'll know us if we ride: six men on horseback are suspicious."

They rode the whole night, and at dawn, white with frost, they reached Tuctuhuachanga. The wind tore at them like a pack of dogs. On the way down, the Thin Man found another abandoned hut. They awoke when the sun was high, ate their cold food, and waited for dusk. It was still raining. At twilight they made the descent to Yanahuanca. After they had traveled a league, they saw two riders: a woman and a boy. Chacón moved away too late.

"Héctor!" they called to him. "Héctor! Come here!"

It was the voice of Cirila Yanayaco.

"Where are you heading, Héctor?"

"I'm going to Yanacocha to buy animals."

"Don't go, Héctor," said Doña Cirila Yanayaco, making a face. "The guards are looking all over the province for you. This morning they were at your house, and they were so angry at not finding you they seized your brother's horses."

"And what is Teodoro doing about it?"

"They took away eight of his horses. He's walking around crying."

"We'd better go to your house to find out what's going on," said Pisser.

The Yanayaco woman went off into the Tuctuhuachanga night.

CHAPTER THIRTY: *Where One Can Learn of the Not Insignificant Usefulness of Paw-breakers*

REPRESENTATIVE Rivera was wrong: the flowers in the cemetery lasted for eight days. On the ninth day even the sheep realized how fruitless their browsing was, and they lay down, here and there, among the graves. On the seventh day Rivera called a meeting. Before three hundred mourning faces he admitted his error: if on the day of the fatal birth he had been less trusting, perhaps the night, mother of the Fence, would have aborted, but he had not suspected. The prairie had always belonged to those who traveled across it. Now the land, all the land, was growing old as a spinster behind a fence that no man's feet could follow. The closest villages were days away. Fortunato, poor man, rotting in the Huánuco Prison, had been right: there was no going back. They had to fight.

The silence drizzled down. They knew that to prepare himself to say those words Don Alfonso had wandered the back alleys of insomnia for weeks, endlessly pounding the cobblestones of Rancas in the bitter cold.

They decided to attack.

Twenty miles away from their grief, lying on a leather sofa with a letter in his hands, a blond man with blue eyes was dreaming. That beauty which radiates from the faces of dreamers lit his

shots. The bloodied work crews ran away. The Republicans recovered from their surprise and charged, riding over the troublemakers and knocking them into the frozen river. But they did not retreat. The light faded. In an instant the afternoon turned gray and the pebbles of a terrifying hailstorm clattered down.

"Guards, retreat!" shouted the corporal. "Bastards!" he shouted again as his squad pulled back. "You'll learn what it means to attack the Armed Forces!"

Ignorant of the fact that the Military Code prescribes that "the individual or individuals who dare to attack the Armed Forces are subject to a summary court-martial and . . . ," the villagers danced for joy. The storm did not let up. The road washed out under the fury of the hail. The Representative spat out a tooth and ordered them to bring pickaxes and crowbars. They pulled out the paw-breakers. In the hailstorm they hurried to knock down the posts. Three hundred meters of barbed wire suffered from vertigo. They shouted and danced as if possessed. When the Fence was broken, they brought in the last exhausted sheep. Marcelino Muñoz—third in his class at the District School—had the idea of building a scarecrow. In the purple twilight he nailed the scarecrow to the mountain of vanquished paw-breakers. During the battle the guards had abandoned an overcoat and a helmet. Marcelino asked permission to dress the scarecrow as a Republican Guard. Rivera agreed. What happens when man is obliged to retrace his steps back down the path toward bestiality? What happens when man reaches the upper limits of misfortune, regresses to the primal fear of the hunted carnivore, and must choose between becoming an animal again or finding the spark of greatness?

Fortunato was right: retreat meant bumping into the clouds with your ass.

CHAPTER THIRTY-ONE: *Concerning the Prophecies Made by the Corn*

"HECTOR," shouted Ignacia, dropping the knife she was using to peel potatoes. "Why have you come? You madman! Don't you know that squads of armed men are looking for you? The Civil Guard knows you're riding with strangers." The woman clutched at her head. "Oh, my Jesus, what sin did I commit to suffer so!"

"Be quiet, girl, be quiet, and give me something to eat."

Ignacia stood up, but immediately sat down again ashen with terror: footsteps sounded on the stone patio. Chacón's revolver flashed in the shadows. He raised his index finger to his lips and hid behind a pile of barley sacks that took up half of the windowless room.

The head of a slender man with an Asiatic face and straight hair peered into the room.

"Teodoro, what do you want?" asked Ignacia, relieved at seeing Hawkeye's brother.

Mud-spattered trousers and a filthy sweater collapsed on the bench.

"What is it, Teodoro?"

The man held his head and raised the frightened pools of his small eyes. "It's your husband's fault I have no horses! I don't get involved in anything. My only trouble is that I'm Héctor's brother. What am I going to do? Eight horses and a mare they've taken from me. How am I going to get them back? How will I pay the fine? How will I work?"

But he grew silent as he looked at the face that came out of the darkness.

"Listen, Teodoro," said Hawkeye angrily, "don't be a coward, don't fight with women. Fight with men. If you talk this way to the Judge, you'll get your horses back. You're not in trouble. Why don't you file a claim for them? Or were your horses stolen?"

"They're not stolen. Everybody knows them."

"Why don't you file a claim, then?"

"And what if they arrest me?"

"Why should they arrest you?"

Teodoro hung his head. "I know you're working for the good of the community, but they're taking it out on me. The Judge's hand is heavy. Where will it end?"

"Wherever our feet carry us, that's where it will end."

"I'm afraid to file a claim. I'm not brave enough to go to the barracks."

He stopped short and left suddenly. His sobs could be heard from the door.

"Everybody's afraid," sighed Ignacia.

"Why?"

"They think the police will burn and kill because of you. That's what they're afraid of."

"They're talking just to talk."

"You've changed. You weren't like this before. You're a different man now. I'm your wife and I hardly know you."

Resentment lit the dark room like bad kerosene.

"We'll get Teodoro's horses back, Ignacia."

"The Guardia Civil has those animals."

"Don't be afraid, Ignacia. Pay attention to what I'm saying. I don't have much time. You go to Montenegro's house. Knock at the door and tell him: 'My husband came to Yanacocha with four strangers with guns.' "

"Oh, my God!"

" 'My husband came with men ready to do anything, and I was afraid.' This is what you'll tell him: 'Chacón is planning to attack the ranch to avenge the horses taken from Teodoro. Let them go so that nothing happens.' That's what you'll say to the Judge."

"And if he asks me anything else?"

"Just answer with tears. Go down to Yanahuanca early tomorrow," Chacón said to Ignacia as he disappeared.

Ignacia spent the night tossing on her sleeping skin, but at seven the next morning, with reddened eyes, she made the descent to Yanahuanca. She crossed the square with her head lowered. The shadow of a Guardia Civil blocked the street. Ignacia took off her hat, trembling. The guard, with his rum-filled eyes, did not see the fear under the hat. Ignacia kept walking, but when she saw the big three-story house half a block away, dominating the horizon with its pink walls, blue doors, and green roof, she hesitated and turned away. Like a drunken woman, she stumbled through the town until noon. At twelve o'clock she went up to the guarded door.

"Come in, my girl, come in," said Dr. Montenegro, adjusting his hat. "What's this that Chuto was telling me?"

"It's true, Judge. My husband is in the province with strangers. To kill you, that's what they've come for."

Dr. Montenegro had just had a cup of chocolate for breakfast. At that moment one could observe the pernicious effect of chocolate on people with liver ailments: the Judge turned green.

"I knew that your husband was riding with armed men," said the liverish Judge. "I didn't need your warning, but it doesn't matter. Now I know that you're a law-abiding woman. You did well to warn me. If you always act like this, you'll stay out of trouble."

"I want my children to have a father, Judge."

"And what does your husband plan to do?"

"Kill and steal on your ranch if you don't let Teodoro's horses go. It's better to free the animals, Judge. I'm afraid."

"What are you afraid of, girl? You're innocent. As an authority, I'll protect you."

"I'm afraid for my children, Judge."

"That's why you have to be law-abiding, Ignacia. If only all the hypocrites were like you. And to show you that things go well when you do the right thing, I'll free the horses."

"They're ready to murder. Let them go, Judge."

"I'll let them go for your sake. Not for fear of your husband. I'm not going to change my ways or abandon justice just because of a couple of bandits," and he raised his voice: "Pepita, Pepita!"

Doña Pepita, who had been listening through the half-open door, came into the room, similarly affected by the famous chocolate of Cuzco.

"Pepita, my dear, go down and talk to the secretary and tell him to go to the barracks for me so they'll let Teodoro's horses go. It's not that poor man's fault if he's related to a bandit. How many horses are there, Ignacia?"

"There are nine, Judge."

"That Teodoro is a rich man. Nine horses! All right, my dear girl, we'll be seeing you."

"Thank you, Judge."

"Where did you say your husband was?"

"How should I know, Judge? That man has forgotten where he lives."

The black suit showed the tartar on his teeth. "He must be with his girlfriends. They say your husband is really something."

"What do you mean, Judge?"

"That's all right. Anything you hear, you let me know. Nothing will happen to you. You're on authority's side now."

Then a sudden affection for Hawkeye's children blossomed in Dr. Montenegro's heart. Here the scholars disagree. Certain chroniclers maintain that the Judge asked Ignacia how many children she had and what their names were. Other historians state that the Judge simply took out a ten-sol bill and gave it to the astonished Ignacia.

"Buy something nice for your children, Ignacia."

The father of the children so affectionately referred to got off his horse in a rocky pass with steep walls.

"This is Yerbabuenaragrac," said Chacón, his eyes shining. "There are mountains on both sides. Montenegro has to pass through here on Saturday on his way to Huarautambo."

"Has to?"

"There's no other way up to Huarautambo."

The Thin Man caressed the barrel of the Winchester. "He'll leave his blood here."

"We'll hide our horses and wait. There's enough to eat and drink. I'll go up ahead and throw pebbles as a signal. We don't want to shoot innocent people."

"Soon everyone who says 'The land belongs to me' will be dead," said the Thin Man.

"The trouble is we don't know Montenegro," said Pisser, annoyed. "We might attack someone else."

"Don't worry, I'll keep watch. You go to sleep."

They waited Thursday, Friday and Saturday, the twenty-four hours of Saturday and the nine hundred sixty hours of the next forty Saturdays. Dr. Montenegro never came. The members of the Committee for Shooting the Biggest Bastard in Yanahuanca (Pisser's words) waited at Yerbabuenaragrac in vain. Neither cards nor memories comforted them. Dr. Montenegro locked himself inside his big house. Overcome by a sudden attack of melancholy, the Judge did not even go out to the courtroom. The Guardia Civil brought the criminals to his patio. And the rumor spread that as long as the members of the Committee for the Execution Free of Charge of the Fattest Son-of-a-Bitch in the World (Pisser's lyrics) were at large, the Judge would not leave his rooms. The unhappy directors of the Committee for the Public Execution of the Biggest Mother-fucker in the Province of Yanahuanca (Pisser's lyrics and music) had no other recourse but to consult with Rustler.

"What do you see in your dreams, Rustler?"

Rustler did not see anything. "I can only see prairie. I only see an empty prairie."

"As long as he doesn't know where you are," said Horse Thief, "Montenegro won't leave his office."

"How do you know?"

"Sergeant Cabrera was talking in his house. His cook overheard."

"What shall we do?" asked the Thin Man, discouraged.

"Wait," said Pisser. "These sons-of-bitches are more greedy than scared. He won't miss the harvest."

"Wait until harvest?" Chacón grew solemn. "No, brothers, that's a very long time. You'd better go back home. You're taking a risk. Go home. I'll come for you when the harvest is over."

Pisser bit his nails. "You're right, compadre."

"You let us know when and we'll come right away," said the Thin Man, caressing the barrel of his rifle. "This gentleman will be ready too."

"What do you think?" asked Horse Thief.

"I'm going to see what the corn says," answered Pisser.

Pisser spread out his brown poncho and threw a handful of corn on it.

"You be Montenegro," he named a black kernel. He exhaled cigarette smoke.

"You be Chacón," he baptized a white kernel.

He scattered the kernels and exhaled smoke three times. Three times he threw the corn, his face perspiring.

"I don't know what's wrong," he said. "Treacherous relatives always show up."

"Relatives?"

He threw the corn again. "Yes, relatives do us harm. We'd better check," and he took out other kernels. He named them quickly.

"You be Chacón."

He exhaled the cigarette smoke three times.

"And?"

"There is a relative who betrays you."

"I don't believe it."

"You'll die in your house, Héctor."

"They're afraid of me. They never come to my house," said Chacón, adjusting his chin strap.

"Be careful, Héctor, be careful."

CHAPTER THIRTY-TWO: *Introduction of Guillermo the Butcher or Guillermo the Reliable, Whichever the Client Prefers*

LIEUTENANT Colonel of the Guardia Civil Guillermo Bodenaco is called either Guillermo the Butcher or Guillermo the Reliable. Where does truth reside? The disciplinarians insist that "duty is duty" and they add that "an official is an official," anaphoristic statements which have the advantage of leaving us as the Cerro de Pasco Corporation left Cerro de Pasco: in the dark. The enemies of Guillermo the Butcher maintain that the Commander loved nothing better than a little blood. We Latins eat our blood fried, with onions and good-smelling herbs. "We are not referring to that kind of blood," argue his enemies, "we are talking about human blood." His partisans retort: Do you mean that good old Guillermo was a cannibal? And they respond: "No, he was not a cannibal, but he did love his little bit of blood." And they take out papers and documents and recall that during the second term of President-Engineer-Doctor-Lieutenant Manuel Prado, Commander Bodenaco took part in dozens of "evacuations." Thanks to his valiant efforts during that six-year period, more corpses grew cold than in our epic battles (half the number killed in the Battle of Junín and twice the number of heroes in the Battle of the Second of May, including Spanish casualties, two of them caused by colic). That's how life was during the second Presidency of that charming humorist who, in a rapture of inspiration, distilled this drop of philosophical elixir: "In Peru," specified President Prado, "there are two kinds of problems: those that are never solved and those that solve themselves." The ignorance of the peasantry interfered with the propagation of this most interesting philosophical axiom. Rural problems were resolved with bullets. In that six-year period the government shot one hundred and six farmers. Guillermo the Butcher or Guillermo the Reliable took part in almost all the "evacuations." To circumvent the difficulty once and for all, this chronicler has decided to call Commander Bodenaco alternately by his two names. This method should avoid hard feelings. Guillermo the Reliable knew his trade. In the field, before doing anything else, he would invite the farmers to withdraw from the disputed land. The obstinate farmers would insist on remaining on their land, mouthing incomprehensible words, showing grimy documents and waving little Peruvian flags. First mistake: the use of the national bicolor, denied civilians without permission, wounded the patriotic sensibilities of Guillermo the Butcher. The law is categorical: the national banner is to be flown only by institutions and authorities.

This being the state of affairs, Guillermo the Reliable stopped at the fork in the road between Cerro de Pasco and Rancas. Guillermo the Butcher got down from the jeep. A column of heavy trucks, filled with assault guards, immediately froze in place. On that spot, approximately fifty thousand days before, another leader had halted his army: General Bolívar, on the eve of the Battle of Junín, fought on that same prairie. At almost the same time of day, give or take a few minutes, Bolívar had contemplated the greenish roofs of Rancas.

A horseman galloped up.

"The enemy is crossing Reyes, my General," said an aide-de-camp gray with dust.

Bolívar grew somber. Canterac was escaping! The dust of one thousand kilometers of fruitless marching covered his face.

"What do you think, my General?" Sucre looked small, exhausted.

"We must start the battle any way we can," muttered Bolívar.

"How far away is the infantry?"

"Two leagues, my General." General Lara's uniform was hidden under the dark poncho.

"Attack with the Hussars!" ordered Bolívar.

Lara gave the orders. The aides-de-camp galloped off. From the clearing at Chacamarca, Bolívar watched the cavalry spread out. The squads slowly reached the prairie. At three kilometers the cloud of dust from Reyes stopped. Canterac wheeled around. The horizon bristled with galloping horsemen. Fifteen hundred Hussars opened into a fan like the feathers of a huge, deadly peacock. The Hussars delighted in the beauty of their line and cantered three hundred meters forward, then spurred their horses: the prairie flashed with lightning hooves and lowered lances.

Bolívar grew pale. "What's the matter? Why doesn't our cavalry deploy?"

But Guillermo the Reliable did not grow pale. He looked with annoyance at the plain where the Federal Guard advanced at a turtle's pace. It was irritating. But he accepted it philosophically, leaned on the jeep, took out a cigarette, lit it, and exhaled the smoke.

"We drink and make merry,
we only laugh at death,
and if you want to fight,
we're ready for that too."

Guillermo the Butcher hummed, remembering with affection the author of the famous waltz: Commander Karamanduka. On another march, forty years before, the king of merrymakers had composed the immortal lyrics: it was the day when the Republican Guard, on Commander Karamanduka's orders, massacred the Huacho workers who were demanding an eight-hour day.

The Republicans, those devilish troops, crept at an ant's pace.

"Pass me the bottle,
Pass me the bottle,"

hummed Commander Bodenaco. The fighting man enjoys music. Peru has fought eleven wars. Fortunato emerged from the rocks. He was wearing trousers splattered with grease and a dirty checked shirt. We won the war with Bolivia in 1827. The losers paid for their excursion to Titicaca.

"I won't pass it to you,
Not even by chance,"

hummed Guillermo the Reliable. Fortunato had gotten down from the truck named *Your-Sister-Loves-Me-No-Matter-What* more than two hours ago. We lost the war in 1828 with Gran Colombia: a general who became President betrayed another general. Nieto raised his lance against Camacaro in vain. Fortunato had finished his term in the Huánuco Prison: contempt for authority. We lost the war of 1838, again with Bolivia. To avoid feeding him an extra meal, they had let Fortunato out of prison the night before. We won the war of 1837 against the Chileans, but Peru allowed the encircled Chilean army to retreat intact, playing triumphant marches. Fortunato asked permission to sleep under *Your-Sister-Loves-Me-No-Matter-What,* which was to leave for Cerro de Pasco at three in the morning. We lost the war of 1839, again with Chile: but of course two future presidents of Peru, Castilla and Vivanco, were counted among the victors. Fortunato reached Cerro at eight, anxious to return to his house, but he could not resist the smell of mutton broth cooking in one of the stalls on the square. He had three sols left.

"We drink and make merry,
We only laugh at death,"

sang Commander Karamanduka, cutting down the line of white shirts with the first volley.

"Some broth, please," asked Fortunato.

The owner, a woman with enormous buttocks, stared at the highway.

"What's the matter, compadre?" asked Fortunato, very interested in being friendly so there would be no delay in getting the broth. The curve vomited up the first truck. Again we lost in the war of 1841, again with Bolivia: someone shot President Gamarra in the back in the middle of the Battle of Ingavi. The trucks filled with assault guards slowly moved forward. Conversations withered. The buzzing of the crowd died down.

"They're evacuating Rancas today," whispered one of the customers. With a lump in his throat Fortunato recognized a villager from Junín.

"The evacuation's today," he repeated.

Fortunato tried to drink all he could of the hot broth. We won the war of 1859 without firing a shot. Ecuador had to pay: it was agreed that the loser would pay for the excursion to Guayaquil, but inexplicably Peru provided money, provisions, and equipment. His throat rejected the burning broth. His trembling hand held out his last three sols, and he walked to the truck crossing. Five minutes later he climbed into a truck that had reduced its speed for the ascent; but the asthmatic *I-Was-Once-a-Latest-Model* traveled only a few kilometers. In Colquijirca a line of guards was stopping traffic, rifles in their hands. We lost the war of 1879, lit by the solitary torch of the ship *Huascar. I-Was-Once-a-Latest-Model* took its place in line. Fortunato jumped off before the driver could see him. The Guardia Civil was checking papers. Of course we lost it: General Iglesias, the new President, went out to fight the Morochucans uniformed and armed by the Chileans. Fortunato recognized a villager from Ondores among a group of miners wearing yellow helmets.

"Pst," he whispered.

"How are you, Froggy, what's new?"

The old man raised his eyebrows and put his index finger to his lips.

"Shhh . . . shhh . . ."

"What's wrong?"

"Listen, they're evacuating Rancas today. I have to get there. Lend me your helmet!"

"And how will *I* get through?"

"With your identity card. Lend me your helmet!"

"Okay, Froggy."

They passed through the roadblock lost in the crowd of miners. The Civil Guards were excited, and they stamped everything in sight. In the chaotic terror of the retreat, when the war was lost, the desperate colonels wrote: "Send more ropes so we can drag in more volunteers." Fortunato passed through the roadblock, calmly walked three hundred yards, then broke into a run. The prairie was magnificent. We lost the war of 1930 with Colombia. Bitter forebodings ran along with him, their tongues hanging out. But between 1900 and 1911 four thousand tons of rubber were taken out of Putumayo at a cost of thirty thousand Huitoto Indians. A good price: seven lives per ton. Each bush, every stone on the plain was different, unforgettable for him. We won the war of 1941 with Ecuador: three paratroopers captured Puerto Bolívar. The old man ran and ran. Eight wars lost to foreigners; but, on the other hand, we've won so many wars against Peruvians. We won the undeclared war against the Indian Atusparia: one thousand dead. They do not appear in the textbooks. We do record, however, the sixty killed in the conflict of 1866 with Spain. In 1924 the Third Infantry, without any help, won the war against the Indians of Huancané: four thousand dead. Those skeletons established the prosperity of Huancané: Taquile Island and Sol Island sank half a meter beneath the weight of the corpses. Fortunato had grown up, loved, worked, lived on that prairie where man enjoys so few hours of sunlight. He ran and ran. In 1924 Captain Salazar surrounded and burned alive the three hundred inhabitants of Chaulán. The roofs of Rancas shone in the distance. In 1932, the Year of Savagery, five officers were murdered in Trujillo: one thousand men were shot in retaliation. During the six-year term of Manuel Prado we were also victorious: 1956, the Battle of Yanacoto, three dead; 1957, the Battles of Chin-Chin and Toquepala, twelve dead; 1958, the Battles of Chepén, Atacocha, and Cuzco, nine dead; 1959, the Battles of Casagrande, Calipuy, and Chimbote, seven dead. And in the first few months of 1960, the Battles of Paramonga, Pillao, and Tingo María, sixteen dead.

"We are the most pampered children
of this beautiful, noble town
because we are clever and wise."

Forty years before Guillermo the Bloody sentimentally hummed this tune in his honor, Commander Karamanduka composed the song on the day his regiment reduced the strikers of Huacho to a clotted pool of blood. Fortunato remembered the names of his sheep: Cotton, Little Feather, Amadeus, Wild Flower, Streamer, Blacky, Toughy, Flirty, Joker, Clover, Lazy, Fortunato. His eyes filled with tears.

Guillermo the Reliable had a clear view of Rancas, the objective, in his gunsight.

"And if you want to fight,
We're ready for that too."

Chapter Thirty-three: *Valid Reasons Why Héctor Chacón, the Brave, Was Obliged to Disguise Himself as a Woman*

When Arutingo, with his erupting backside, wants to humiliate Yanacocha, he asks: "Was Chacón the bravest man in this province?" The people, who can see what's coming, try to ignore the question, but the compadre slams the bar and says in his insulting voice: "Was he or wasn't he?"

"Yes, he was, Don Ermigio."

The drunkard slams the bar again and laughs out loud. "Then why did he dress up like a woman?"

There is no use denying it. One rainy night Chacón put on woman's clothes. Sulpicia got him the clothing. And since Sulpicia had only one set of clothes, she borrowed the shawl and the hat from a widow. That night Chacón put on a skirt, a shawl, and a hat. It is true, but it is also true that Judge Montenegro had been hiding in his house for months. That man who had been so fond of strolling through squares and meditating on balconies changed his habits; suddenly disenchanted with the pleasures of the landscape, he buried himself in the solitude of remote rooms. He renounced his walks. The notable citizens grew whiskers as they waited on street corners for the leading citizen to stroll by. The Magistrate had lost his taste for wandering about. Dr. Montenegro deprived the province of his black suit. The court swelled with documents. It was

Señor César's golden age. The peace-loving secretary came to the Judge's house every morning with a mountain of legal papers and walked through the door that was grimly guarded by swarms of mean-looking men; an hour later he reappeared in the large blue doorway with the sentences under his arm. On the street, the relatives of those who had been judged pestered him with questions.

"What's happened to my husband, Don César?"

"Free."

"Do you have any news about Don Policarpo?"

"He'll get out at the end of the month."

The Judge was filled with compassion for human suffering. He paced his corridors in silence, his face clouded, pulling his hat now to the left, now to the right. His iron fist softened, it understood need, it pardoned errors, it reduced sentences; it was as if he, who had never asked favors of his friends, were turning now to listen to the pleadings born of love. The Judge did not go out. Even so, months passed before the people grew brave enough to appear on the square at the hour when the black suit used to come out to contemplate the dying day. One late afternoon a pair of lovers, intoxicated with happiness, presumed to walk through the square at six o'clock; they took the walk again the next day. The Civil Guards and the shopkeepers did not dare to interfere. "Why doesn't the Judge go out?" asked the traveling salesmen in surprise. "He is studying," their companions answered unwillingly. What was he studying? Was he pondering the mysteries of the cosmos? Was he wandering through the labyrinths of the occult sciences? Was he traveling the paths of magic? Every day the foremen were seen coming out his blue door, and they were seen returning with purchases or messages from the ranch; there were kids, chickens, preserves, liquors, but no books were ever seen. Where could he have bought them? No one sells books in the province. The Picot almanac is the only reading matter available. "The Judge is practicing black magic. The foremen buy owls and bring them to him. I've seen them," said Kid Remigio slyly.

One night when the sky was filled with thunder, Hawkeye jumped Sulpicia's corral fence and crept through the darkness to the hut where the old woman was preparing her sleeping skins.

"Who's there?" Sulpicia grabbed the handle of a rusty machete in alarm.

"It's Chacón, Mamá."

"Praise be to Jesus. Where have you been, Héctor?"

"Don't put on a light, Mamá."

"Come to the fire, Héctor, you must be cold. Have you eaten?"

He shivered, but did not answer.

"What can you be eating up there in the high country, Héctor?"

"Lots of times I don't eat."

"Where do you sleep?"

"I sleep wherever night falls. But everything's all right. It's all worth it if I can kill that man."

Sulpicia shook her head. "You'll never kill him, Héctor. Dr. Montenegro doesn't leave his house any more. Three hundred farmhands guard him day and night. He won't go out until you're captured. Squads of Civil Guards look for you everywhere; they have orders to kill you."

"I know, Mamá."

"The Civil Guard has sentries all over the square. You'd have to be a spider to get past them."

"Say that again, Mamá."

"You'd have to be a little spider!"

In the rich warmth of the fire his eyes were flashing. "What if I disguise myself?"

Sulpicia stifled a laugh. "What disguise would you use, Héctor?"

Maybe I'll disguise myself as a woman. . . ."

Sulpicia laughed out loud. "What would people say if they saw Chacón dressed as a woman?"

"What if I get all the way into Montenegro's bedroom disguised as a cook?"

"They would laugh. How they would laugh!"

"And what if I came back with Montenegro's head under my skirt?"

The candlelight etched the old woman's features. "Let's ask the coca leaf, Héctor."

He was no longer shivering. They sat down and took out handfuls of coca. Coca tells the future for the one who asks with a pure heart. If the coca burns your mouth, it is a warning of danger; if it softens into a sweet ball, there is no risk. They knelt down.

"Mamá Coca, you know everything. You know all roads. Good and evil, danger and risk, you know them all. Mamá Coca, Chacón wants to dress as a woman to kill an abusive man. Is there danger? Green leaf, green Mamá, Mamá Leaf, tell us. I believe in you. I don't trust animals, I don't trust water, I don't trust metal, I only believe in you, Mamá Leaf."

Their entire being was concentrated in the chewing of their jaws.

"Dear Mamá Leaf, green Señora, Mamá Leaf. Sulpicia is talking to you, Mamá. Sulpicia wants to know the truth: What will happen if Chacón changes his clothes? What will happen if we go down to kill the man with the black heart? Will they capture us? Will we live or die? Leaf, dear little leaf, answer me."

"My coca is sweet." Chacon was beaming. "They won't catch me. What does your coca say, Sulpicia?"

"The coca says all right," answered the woman, relieved. "I don't have any clothes besides the ones I'm wearing. I'll lend you an underskirt, but I don't have clothes. There's a widow who lives close by. I gave her half a bushel of potatoes, she'll let me have a few clothes. Wait, Héctor, wait."

Sulpicia returned half an hour later with a threadbare blue shawl and a weatherbeaten felt hat. Then Héctor Chacón the Brave dressed up like a woman.

"Go to the square, Sulpicia, and buy something."

When Sulpicia came back, her face was distorted with sorrow. "Things are bad, Chacón. Sergeant Cabrera checked up on me."

"What do you mean?"

"He stopped me and asked: 'What are you doing here? Why are you out walking at this time of night?' "

"What did you say?"

" 'I come from Cerro de Pasco, my Sergeant, and I'm looking for a place to sleep.' He took off my hat and said, 'You're not Héctor Chacón by any chance?' "

"What do you think?"

"If you go out, they'll capture you. You'd better escape."

"I'll go to my house."

"To your house?"

"The guards are searching for me in the high country. They'll never dream that I'm hiding in my own house."

The thin man with sharp cheekbones, with a full-grown beard, looked at her. His face, consumed by deprivation, trembled in the old woman's tear-filled eyes for the last time.

Midnight exploded into another tantrum of lightning flashes. Chacón slipped through his door. In the shadows Héctor saw Ignacia's face darkened by fear. "It's Héctor," he whispered, but he saw clearly that the fear grew no lighter. Without lighting a candle, he crept to Ignacia's sleeping skin while he lowered his trousers. Before she could say a word, Ignacia felt his gentle thrusts between her legs. They made love until dawn.

Héctor sat in the growing light and lit a cigarette. "What's the matter, Ignacia?"

"Are you going to keep on being your own law?"

"I'll keep on until the end, Ignacia."

"The community is afraid. Even the Guardia Civil is troubled."

"You'll have to get used to it."

"What can you do by yourself, Chacón? When something happens to you, who'll watch out for your children?"

"If I die, I'll die. If I live, I'll live. That's up to fate."

The cigarette stared at her as it burned.

"I can't give up this struggle, Ignacia. We have to fight them head on, with blood and bullets."

"You've changed a lot, Chacón. I hardly recognize you."

"I'll never get along with the rich. They're abusive. Am I going to die in prison? It's better to die fighting."

The woman was suffering from weariness, nights without a man, hardship.

"Listen, Chacón, the potatoes are ready for storing. Your children go out to play, they don't help me."

"I'll help you. I'll stay."

"They never look for you here. The guards go to your girlfriends' houses."

"Poor things, they oblige me because their men are in prison or on the run. That's all."

"It's getting light, Héctor. You must be tired. I'll fix your breakfast. Lie down, rest. Poor man, what kind of sleep can you get in strange houses?"

"Sometimes I travel all night."

"Here you can rest."

"First I'll sleep, then I'll store the potatoes."

"I'm going to buy some things. I'll be right back."

But it was the Guardia Civil who came back. And here the historians disagree. Those who wish to put Hawkeye down whisper that Ignacia turned him in, and they go so far as to state that her poverty stretched out its hand that rainy morning to receive a fistful of orange bills. Kid Remigio disagrees, and when he recovers from his attacks (he gets worse and worse—not a day goes by that he does not fall to the ground, his mouth foaming) he says: "It was his daughter. It was Juana. I've denounced her in my huayno." Was it Juana? "They drafted her husband for military service. Ampudia was twenty-eight years old, but they pretended he was younger. Juana's womb was on fire. She traded him for Héctor," says the hunchback. "I saw them cross his name off the list of conscripts." Impossible! They only let Kid Remigio into the Patrol Officer's headquarters to take out the trash.

Chacón plunged into a jet-black sleep. He had not slept under a decent roof for months. He dreamed that a thorn was piercing him. He lifted his foot and saw that there were pebbles imbedded in his sole, that it was covered with rows of little stones, like corn kernels. He pulled them out, only to feel his skin collapse into a boneless void. But he was so tired that he awoke only when the dogs and the bullets began to whine. He opened his eyes. The bullets fell like hailstones on the little window of the storeroom. The Civil Guards surrounded the house. They fired for an hour to frighten him. Crouched behind some sacks, Hawkeye heard the shots crackling against the wood. At noon they stopped firing. A silence bitten only by the dogs crashed down on Yanacocha's terror. He crawled to a crack and peered through.

"Chacón," shouted the voices of the Civil Guards. "Don't shoot! There are schoolchildren!"

The eyes that could follow a lizard on a moonless night saw nine guards and a dozen sharpshooters hiding behind the skirts of the schoolchildren. Hawkeye recognized some of them, looked at his revolver, tested the weight of the little ammunition bag heavy with cartridges.

"Shit!"

"Chacón," shouted Sergeant Cabrera, "I'll spare your life if you don't fire."

He half-opened the window and blinked in the gold of midday. His eyes took in Yanacocha, the horse corrals, the road to Huarautambo, Lopsided's face, Pisser's warnings, the failed rebellion of the horses, his thirty years of prison, and the rifles pointed at his chest. He came down the ladder.

Sergeant Cabrera looked at him with joy, with envy, with anger.

"Now you slipped up, we've got you now!" he shouted.

CHAPTER THIRTY-FOUR: *Concerning Conversations Between Fortunato and the Representative from Rancas*

THE old man could see the roofs of Rancas. He stopped and sat on a rock. Fifty thousand days before, General Bolívar had stopped there too: the morning of his entry into Rancas. Bolívar wanted Liberty, Equality, Fraternity. How amusing! They gave us Infantry, Cavalry, Artillery. Fortunato could barely breathe as he came down the narrow street. In his chalky face they could see disaster.

"They're coming! The Assault Guard is coming!" He panted, his mouth open.

"Which direction?"

"From Paria!"

He sat down, exhausted. Approximately fifty thousand days before, on that same spot, Commander Rázuri—five afternoons later he would lead the charge of the Peruvian Hussars—had avoided the kick of an animal maddened by the orange swirl of a butterfly.

"Help, Virgin Mary, help us!"

"Our time has come!"

"We have to do something!"

"They'll kill us like dogs!"

"What do you mean, kill us! The uniform is supposed to defend Peruvians, not attack them!"

"Where's the Representative?" asked Fortunato.

Men and women, their faces destroyed by fear, ran around the square. Against his will, the old man thought of insects flying like fools around the lamplight.

"We're not bugs," he said aloud.

"What did you say, Fortunato?"

Teodoro Santiago resumed his shouting. "Sin, it's sin! Why wasn't the altar finished? There was always enough money for good times and corruption, but for the Good God? Who cared about Him? You're sinners, you're corrupt, you're shameless!"

"Shut up, damn it!"

"You're shameless, you don't fear God! Down on your knees!"

"Quiet, damn it!" shouted Fortunato, grabbing Santiago by lapels that still were mourning, still wept for Társila Santiago. "Be quiet! It's not the time for shouting, it's the time to fight. Today we'll fight to the death. Arm yourselves with clubs, stones, anything! To the death! Do you hear me?"

Eighty work-soiled hands picked up stones. As they bent down, they saw Representative Rivera.

"Where are they coming from?" yelled Rivera as he ran.

"Three different directions," answered young Mateo Gallo, out of breath, "from Paria, from Pacoyán, and from the highway!"

Three hundred horsemen cantered down from the ranches, led by Dr. Manuel Iscariote Carranza. About fifty thousand days before, at almost the same speed, General Necochea, leader of the loyal cavalry, had advanced along the same road.

"Now they'll kill us all," sobbed a woman.

"Don't be alarmed, neighbors," said Rivera. "Nothing will happen. In Villa de Pasco, Adán Ponce fought an army. Is he dead? Doesn't he work in his café? Just yesterday I saw him eating some delicious broth. Nothing will happen. Everything will work out fine!"

He stopped abruptly. The arrogant faces of the Assault Guards were coming through the Gate of St. Andrew. Approximately fifty thousand days before, General Córdova's advance party had also passed that way, five days before his regiment had founded the

Republic of Peru on that prairie. The Assault Guard advanced. At about thirty meters they raised their submachine guns. The Rancasans watched the awful rhythmic beauty of their marching as if they were hypnotized. It seemed to Don Mateo Gallo—they'd soon be wrapping him up like a mummy!—that the mouths of the guns looked bigger than the mouths of the cannon he had once seen on parade at the celebration of the anniversary of the Battle of Junín. A thin lieutenant with a spotted face, suffering from the altitude, stepped forward. Rivera was waiting for him.

"Gentlemen, what's the reason for this?" he asked in a voice made thin by fear.

"Who are you?"

"I am the Representative of Rancas, my Lieutenant. I would like to know . . ."

His voice disappeared. The Lieutenant looked at him phlegmatically. Three years in the service had taught him that the uniform makes even the bravest voices hoarse. Rivera sweated with the effort to recover the words hidden in his guts. He wanted to talk, to tell the Lieutenant that they, the villagers, were walking on their own land, that if they had the time they would show him title deeds issued by the Audience of Tarma, parchments issued before the Lieutenant, before the Lieutenant's great-grandfather was born, that just living on that plain whose bitter enemy was the sun is an accomplishment, that those pasturelands grow nothing, that on the prairie where the sun shines one hour a day a sack of seed produces barely five sacks of potatoes, that they almost never had bread, that only in good years could they buy crackers for their children, that they . . .

Fortunato was the one who spoke. "Why have you come here, my Lieutenant?"

"We have an evacuation order. You have trespassed on property that does not belong to you. We have orders to evacuate you. And you are leaving. You're leaving right now!"

"We can't evacuate this land, Lieutenant. We were born here. We haven't trespassed anywhere. Others have trespassed on our—"

"You have ten minutes to evacuate." The uniform turned toward the grayish line.

"It's Cerro de Pasco who's trespassing, my Lieutenant. The gringos are fencing us in and chasing us like rats. The land doesn't belong to them. The land belongs to God. I know all about the Cerro. Did they bring the land with them on their backs?"

"You have nine minutes."

The squadron of Republican soldiers converged on the Gate of St. Andrew.

"There have never been fences up here, my Lieutenant. We never knew what a fence was. Since the time of our grandfathers, and even before, the land belonged to everybody. No wire, no fences, no locks until the goddam gringos came. They brought the locks. Not only locks. They—"

"You have five minutes," murmured the braided uniform.

The old man saw the sudden flames. The soldiers were setting fire to the houses.

"Why are you burning? Why are you attacking? You have no respect for anything!" he said angrily. "You don't know what it means to earn a living. You never held a hoe, you never plowed a field—"

"You have four minutes."

"The government pays you to protect us, not to abuse us. We're not disrespectful to anybody. We're not even disrespectful to the uniform." He pointed at the khaki. "That's not the uniform of our country." He pulled on his jacket: "These rags are the real uniform, these rags—"

"You have two minutes."

The people ran away, shrieking. The fire was spreading. A tear furrowed down the copper-colored cheek.

"You think we're animals. You won't even talk to us. If we complain, you ignore us; if we protest . . . I complained to the Prefect. I carried the sheep, my Lieutenant. And what did he say?"

The Lieutenant slowly took out his revolver. "Time's up," he said, and he fired.

His anger drained away into absolute weakness. Fortunato felt as if the sky were caving in. To protect himself from the clouds, he raised his arms. The ground opened up. He tried to hold on to the grass, to the edge of the dizzying darkness, but his fingers would not obey, and he fell, he toppled down to the center of the earth.

Weeks later, in their graves, no longer sobbing, accustomed to the humid darkness, Don Alfonso Rivera told him the rest. For they had been buried so close together that Fortunato could hear Don Alfonso sighing, and he managed to make a small opening in the mud with a twig. "Don Alfonso, Don Alfonso!" he called. The Representative, who had thought himself condemned to eternal darkness, began to weep. He cried for a week, then he grew quiet, and when he was calm he told him that with the first bullet he, Fortunato, had fallen face down in his own blood.

"And what happened then?"

" 'Now you know we mean it,' shouted the Lieutenant. The people scattered like chicken feathers. I couldn't stop them. 'You have five more minutes,' he warned."

"And what happened?" asked Fortunato as he patiently widened the opening.

"It occurred to me to get the flag. Everyone respects the national flag. That's what I thought."

"It was a wonderful idea, Don Alfonso!"

"I asked them to bring the flag from the school. Don Mateo Gallo said he would."

"That's right! You couldn't leave your post."

"They returned with the flag. The guards surrounded Rancas. A ring of soldiers closed in from three sides. Dr. Iscariote Carranza rode in from Paria with three hundred men."

"Bastards!"

"Egoavil led two hundred riders from Pacoyán and Commander Bodenaco himself was on the highway."

"And?"

" 'Let's sing the national anthem.' My voice wouldn't come out, Don Fortunato. Finally we began: 'We are free, may we always be so.' I thought, 'They're going to come to attention and salute.' But the Lieutenant got angry. 'Why are you singing the anthem, you idiots? Drop the flag,' he ordered. But I didn't drop the flag. You don't drop the flag."

"That flag has an embroidered emblem and cost six hundred sols, and I remember."

"That's what I thought, Don Fortunato, but the guards let loose and started kicking me. I fell, but I kept on singing, 'And the sun will stop shining before we forget our solemn vow. . . .' They were furious and they wouldn't stop kicking me. They split open my mouth. 'Drop it.' 'I won't drop it.' 'Drop it, you mother-fucker.' 'I won't drop it.' They went at me with their bayonets and they cut off my hand. 'Drop it.' Another cut and they chopped off my wrist."

"And the others?"

"They ran away. I was left alone."

"And then?"

"I saw the open stump of my hand and I thought, 'They really screwed me. Now how am I going to work?' I don't remember any more except for the gunfire."

"And then?"

"I don't know. I woke up here, happy to hear your voice, Fortunato."

"I know what happened then," said a faint voice.

"Who is it? Who's speaking?"

"It's me, Tufina."

"They killed you too, old woman! Sons-of-bitches!"

"Don't blaspheme, Fortunato. Remember where you are. Think of God."

"We can't hear you very well, Doña Tufina," said Fortunato. "Can't you make a little opening?"

"I can't, my fingers are broken. They pounded them."

"Sons-of-bitches!"

"Just tell us now, Mamá," said Rivera. "What happened? What happened to my children?"

"I saw your children alive, crying over your body. Your wife was shouting, 'The flag's a lie, the anthem's a lie!' "

"Are you sure you saw them?"

"Bloody but alive, Don Alfonso."

"Tell what happened next, Doña Tufina," said Fortunato, trying to change the subject for Rivera's sake.

"You fell, Don Alfonso. The guards advanced, spraying death. The bullets sound like roasting corn. That's how they sound. They advanced. Sometimes they stopped to wet the roofs with gasoline. The houses were burning. I saw Vicentina Suárez fall. The people were furious. They threw stones. Don Mateo Gallo fell."

"Was that the only resistance?"

"No, there was more. The little schoolboys climbed up the hill and tried to roll down a boulder."

"But that land doesn't have enough slope!"

"That's right, they couldn't do it: the stones wouldn't move. The guards chased them with bullets. The boy Marcelino fell there."

"The one who made the scarecrow?"

"That's the one, Señor Representative. I saw the boy fall and I felt a burning in my blood. I took out my sling and shot a stone into the face of one of the guards. He fired his machine gun at me. I fell backward with my belly ripped open."

"Did you die immediately?"

"No, I didn't die until the afternoon."

"And nobody helped you?"

"Who could help me? Rancas was in flames. It was all fire, shouting and bullets, smoke and crying."

"Poor Doña Tufinita!"

"I vomited out my life at five o'clock. The last thing I saw was the smoke of the tear gas."

"Shsst," whispered Rivera, "shsst. Don't you hear? They're lowering some more of the dead."

"Who can they be?" said Tufina.

"If they're from Rancas, they'll know something," said Rivera.

They were quiet so as not to frighten the gravediggers. They did not open their mouths until the muted pattering of the spades shut out the noise of the morning. Softly, delicately, they tried to communicate with the newcomer.

"Who is it? Who are you?"

Their only answer was the quiet sound of a sweet song.

"It's a child," said Tufina.

"What's your name, son?"

The child kept on singing. They got no answer, but three days later they heard the clanging noise of another burial. They were silent, afraid that the gravediggers would bury the body far from their voices.

"Who are you?" asked Fortunato.

The murmur of Our Fathers grew louder.

"Forgive me, Lord Jesus, for not kneeling! Pardon me for not kissing your hand!" pleaded the new arrival.

"It's Don Teodoro!"

"I have sinned. It was my fault and my fault only that you were crucified!"

"Calm down, Don Teodoro. The worst is over."

"Who are you?"

"I'm Fortunato."

"Don't frighten me, Froggy."

"What happened to you, Don Teodoro?"

"I've been very sick, Don Alfonso! The day of the massacre the guards kicked me in the side. I spat blood. I didn't take care of myself. That was my mistake: I caught a chill. I suffered for two weeks. I died only yesterday."

"What's the news up there?" Rivera asked simply.

"Things are very bad, Representative. The police are hunting down all the talkers. They've taken many prisoners. Even the Mayor of Cerro is in the Huánuco Prison. You were right, Froggy. It's not Christ Who is punishing us, it's the Americans."

"You changed your mind, Don Santiago?"

"You convinced me, Fortunato!"

"But what's going on?" Rivera grew impatient.

"The ranch-owners want to wipe out the communities. They've seen that the Cerro could massacre us when they felt like it. They are going even further. Do you remember School 49357?"

"The Uchumarca school?"

"The day after the massacre the Londoño family ordered the school closed. They took out the children, emptied the rooms, took down the roof, and padlocked it. It's not a school any more: it's a pigsty."

"But that school had an emblem sent from Lima!" Rivera was astonished.

"There are no children, only pigs! The same thing's happening all over the prairie. There are too many of us in the world, brothers."

"Shhst," warned Tufina. "Here come some more."

"Who are they?"

"Are they from Rancas?"

"God knows," sighed Fortunato.